·SLAY·

THE GEORGIA SMOKE SERIES

NEW YORK TIMES BESTSELLING AUTHOR
ABBI GLINES

Slay
The Georgia Smoke Series
Copyright © 2024 by Abbi Glines
All rights reserved.
Visit my website at https://abbiglinesbooks.com

Cover Designer: Sarah Sentz, Enchanting Romance Designs
Editor: Jovana Shirley, Unforeseen Editing
www.unforeseenediting.com
Formatting: Melissa Stevens, The Illustrated Author
www.theillustratedauthor.com

No part of this book may be reproduced or transmitted in any form or by any means, electronic or mechanical, including photocopying, recording, or by any information storage and retrieval system without the written permission of the author, except for the use of brief quotations in a book review.

This book is a work of fiction. Names, characters, places, and incidents either are products of the author's imagination or are used fictitiously. Any resemblance to actual persons, living or dead, events, or locales is entirely coincidental.

• THE FAMILY •

started by Jediah Hughes. It began with horse racing, moonshine, and illegal arms in the early 1900s

Jediah Hughes

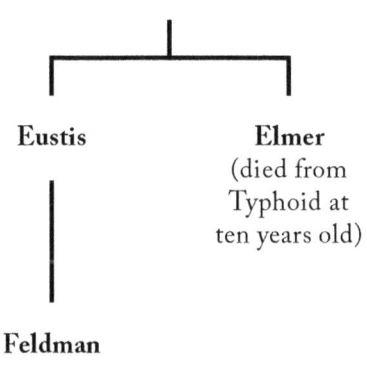

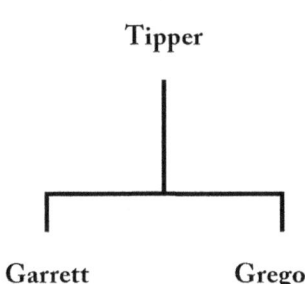

Eustis

Elmer
(died from Typhoid at ten years old)

Feldman

Tipper

Garrett

Gregory
(died at three years old in a house fire)

• THE HUGHES •
Hughes Farm

Garrett Hughes (BOSS in books 1-9)
Wife: **Fawn Parker Hughes** → *SCORCH*

Blaise Hughes (Current BOSS/oldest son)
Wife: **Madeline Walsh Hughes** (parents Etta Marks/dead and Liam Walsh/President of Judgment MC)

Cree Elias Hughes →
SMOKESHOW and *FIREBALL*

Trev Hughes
Fiancée: **Gypsi Parker** (also stepsister) → *FIRECRACKER*

• THE SHEPHERDS •
Oldest family inside the southern mafia other than the Hughes

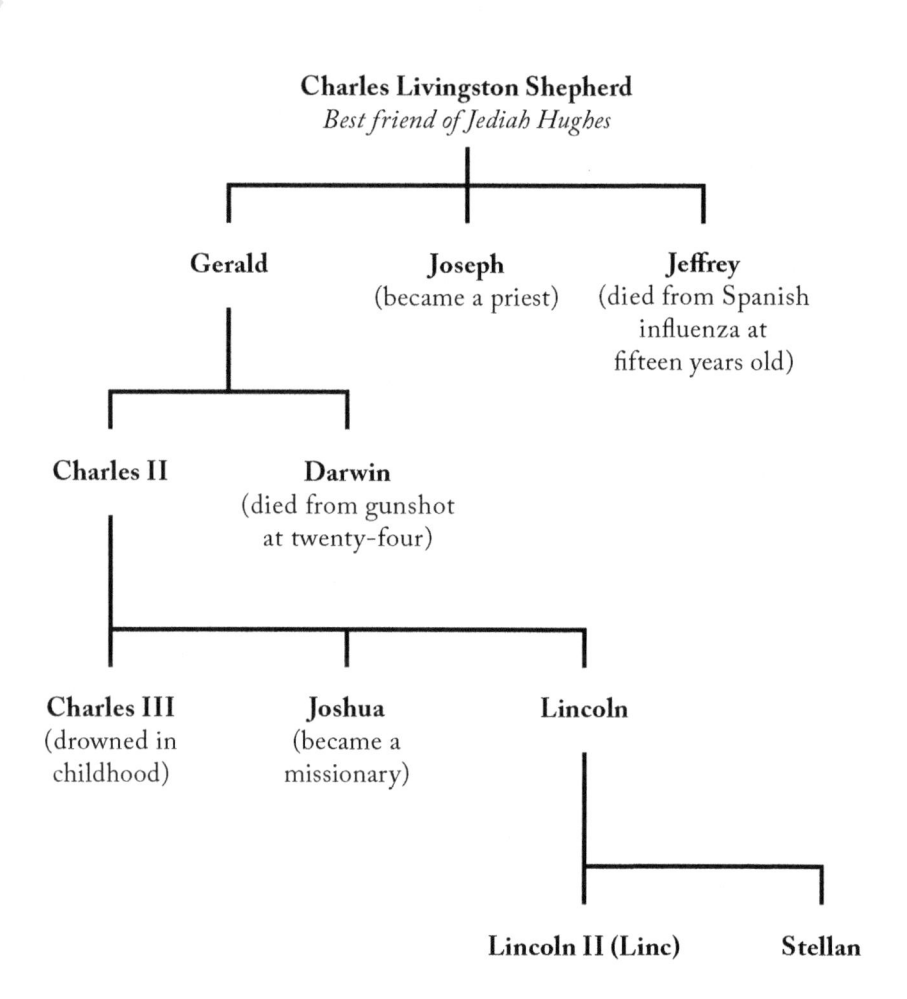

Charles Livingston Shepherd
Best friend of Jediah Hughes

- **Gerald**
- **Joseph**
  (became a priest)
- **Jeffrey**
  (died from Spanish influenza at fifteen years old)

Gerald's children:
- **Charles II**
- **Darwin**
  (died from gunshot at twenty-four)

Charles II's children:
- **Charles III**
  (drowned in childhood)
- **Joshua**
  (became a missionary)
- **Lincoln**

Lincoln's children:
- **Lincoln II (Linc)**
- **Stellan**

Mississippi Branch

Linc Shepherd
(left Florida to run Mississippi Branch when **Levi** was twenty-two)

Florida Branch

Levi Shepherd
Wife: **Aspen Chance Shepherd** → *WHISKEY SMOKE*

Georgia Branch
Shepherd Ranch

Stellan Shepherd
Wife: **Mandilyn Shepherd**

Thatcher
→ *DEMONS July 2024* and
THATCHER'S DEMONS
August 2024

Sebastian
2 books coming
Fall 2024

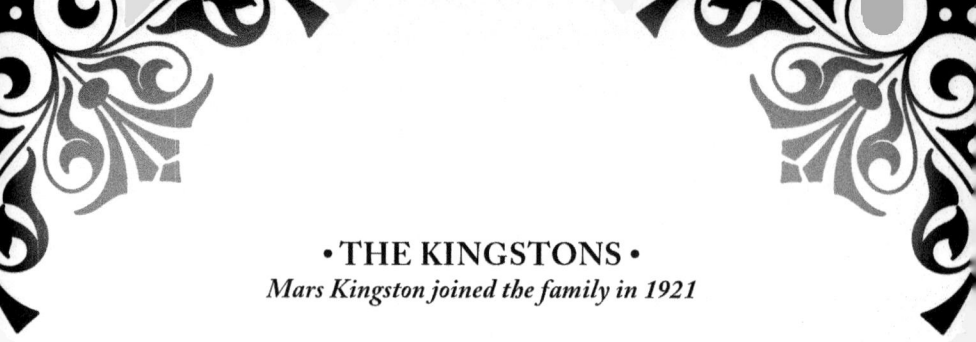

· THE KINGSTONS ·
Mars Kingston joined the family in 1921

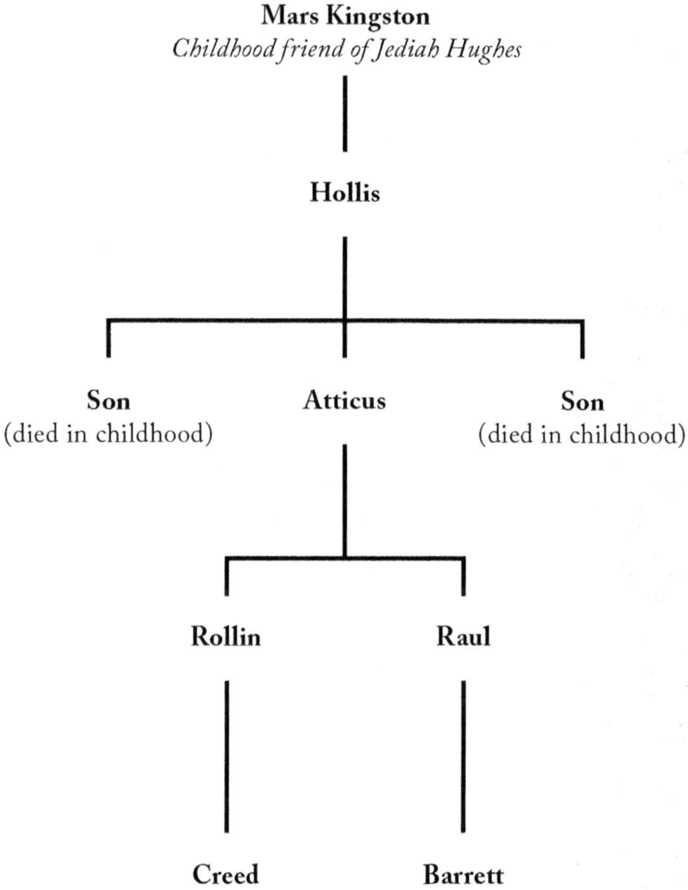

Mars Kingston
Childhood friend of Jediah Hughes

Hollis

Son
(died in childhood)

Atticus

Son
(died in childhood)

Rollin   **Raul**

Creed   **Barrett**

Florida Branch

Creed Kingston (dead)
Wife: **Abigail Kingston** (dead)

Huck
Wife: **Trinity Bennett Kingston**
→ *SMOKE BOMB*

Hayes (dead)
engaged to **Trinity** at his death

Georgia Branch

Barrett Kingston
Wife: **Annette Kingston**

Storm
→ *SIZZLING May 2024* and *STORM June 2024*

Lela
Book coming in 2025

Nailyah
Book coming in 2025

• THE HOUSTONS •
Joined the family through horse racing in 1938

Kenneth Houston Wife: **Melanie Houston**
Moses Mile Ranch

Saxon Houston
Wife: **Haisley Slate Houston** →
SMOKIN' HOT

Winter Noel Houston

• THE LEVINES •
Joined the family in 1977

Alister Levine

|

Mississippi Branch

Luther Levine
Ex-Wife: **Chloe Wall**
(Moved from Florida when **Kye** was nineteen)

|

Florida Branch

Kye Levine
Wife: **Genesis Stoll Levine** → *BURN*

|

Jagger Henley Levine

• THE PRESLEYS •
Joined the family after graduation

Gage Presley
Best friend of Blaise Hughes in high school
Wife: **Shiloh Carmichael Presley** → *STRAIGHT FIRE*

• THE SALAZARS •
Joined the family through horse racing in 1958

Georgia Branch only

Efrain Salazar

|

Gabriel Salazar (dead)
Wife: **Maeme Salazar**

|

Ex-Wife: **Estela Salazar** — **Ronan Salazar** — Wife: **Jupiter Salazar**

King Salazar
→ *SLAY March 27, 2024* and
SLAY KING April 14, 2024

Birdie

· THE JONES ·
Joined the family through joined real-estate in 1966

Georgia Branch only

Hoyt Jones

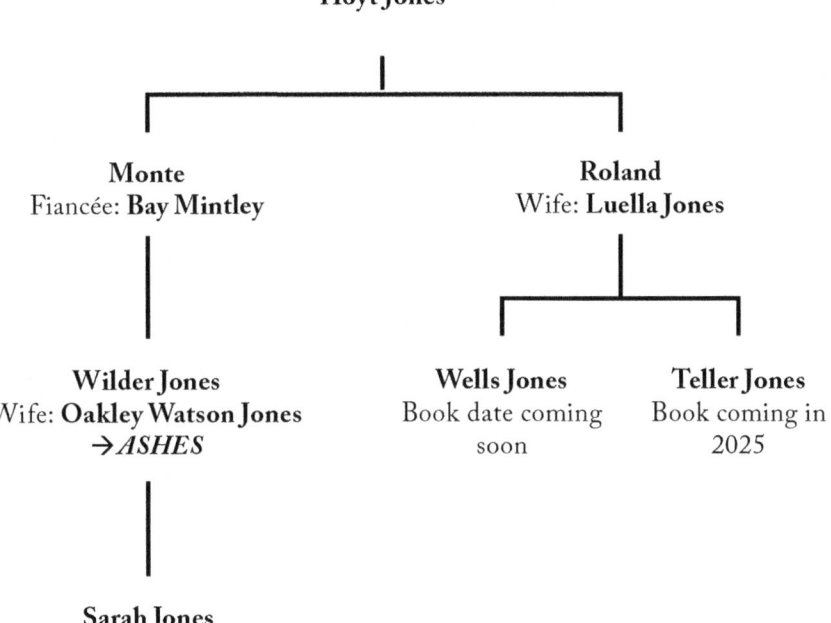

Monte
Fiancée: **Bay Mintley**

Roland
Wife: **Luella Jones**

Wilder Jones
Wife: **Oakley Watson Jones**
→*ASHES*

Wells Jones
Book date coming soon

Teller Jones
Book coming in 2025

Sarah Jones

• PLAYLIST •

Church Bells
·*Carrie Underwood*·

Wait in the Truck
·*Hardy*·

Fight Song
·*Rachel Platten*·

Trustfall
·*Pink*·

The Fireman
·*George Strait*·

You Shouldn't Kiss Me Like This
·*Toby Keith*·

Climax
·*USHER*·

Addicted
·*Saving Abel*·

Let Me Go
·*3 Doors Down*·

I Wanna Make You Close Your Eyes
·*Dierks Bentley*·

I'm Only Me When I'm With You
· *Taylor Swift* ·

Back To Me
· *The All-American Rejects* ·

https://open.spotify.com/playlist/5Wbe5AToh3gNVGjJ3rQVSI?si=34d5980f19324c5f

• ACKNOWLEDGMENTS •

As much as I loved writing *The Smoke Series* and my boys from Ocala, I'm gonna admit that writing the Georgia branch of the family has made me insanely giddy. Adding the deep south to the characters (because unless it's Northwest Florida it's not really the south) was a blast. Little things like Maeme asking for a "bite of sugar"- that was what my Granny Campbell used to always say when we went to visit her. It meant she wanted a kiss on the cheek. Speaking of Maeme there is nothing more amusing as writing a badass grandmother who cooks for her family, doesn't allow cursing in her house, has everyone say the blessing before they eat but will shoot a man between the eyes and not even flinch.

I hope you loved reading about the Georgia side as much as I enjoyed writing it. I can't wait to dig deeper…and get to Thatcher's book. That one is already simmering in my head. It's gonna be epic.

To all the people I couldn't do this without-

Britt is always the first I mention because without him, I wouldn't get any sleep, and I doubt I could finish a book.

Emerson, for dealing with the fact that I must write some days and she can't have my full attention. I'll admit, there were several times she did not understand, and I might have told my seven-year-old "You're not making it in my acknowledgments this time!" to which she did not care. Although she does believe she is famous after attending some signings with me. But that is not my fault. I blame the readers ;)

My older children, who live in other states, were great about me not being able to answer their calls most of the time and waiting until I could get back to them. They still love me and understand this part of Mom's world. I will admit, I answer Austin's calls more now because he happens to have my first grandbaby on FaceTime when he calls.

My editor, Jovana Shirley at Unforeseen Editing, for always working with my crazy schedules and making my stories the best they can be. This summer she has gone above and beyond with this crazy schedule of mine and this fall it doesn't slow down. She's a rock star.

My formatter, Melissa Stevens at The Illustrated Author. She makes my books beautiful inside. Her work is hands down the best formatting I've ever had in my books. I am always excited to see what she does with each one. Each book seems to be better than the last! It's amazing.

Autumn Gantz, at Wordsmith Publicity, for saving me from losing my mind and taking over all the things that I can't keep up with anymore. Her help allows me to write more. Send her cookies.

Beta readers, who come through every time: Jerilyn Martinez, and Vicci Kaighan. I love y'all!

Sarah Sentz, Enchanting Romance Designs, for my book cover. I am in love with the way it looks.

Abbi's Army, for being my support and cheering me on. I love y'all!

My readers, for allowing me to write books. Without you, this wouldn't be possible.

*To everyone who has survived a narcissist.
To those who are in the battle, be strong.
Choose you. You are worth more.*

PROLOGUE

The silence. It wasn't comforting. It didn't bring me peace. When it came, I knew it was the calm before the storm. My entire body was drawn up tight, preparing for the next moment. The one when the rage would explode from him and I would be the recipient. But it hadn't always been that way. If it had, I'd not be here today. The six-carat diamond ring that weighed down my left hand would never have been placed there.

How easy it had been for him to charm a girl like me. Looking back, I knew I'd been an easy mark. Not hard to impress, desperate for affection, to belong, to be wanted.

Now, as I stood in the three-million-dollar home in Buckhead, Georgia, all I wanted was to be alone. A small house in the country with no one. Perhaps a dog as my companion. He'd be golden and big. We would sit on the worn, faded sofa and watch television at night together. He would sleep at the foot of my bed. There would be no moments of fear. My constant state of anxiety would no longer control my every move. I wouldn't have to please anyone. Except my dog. I'd call him Bear. Because he would be as fluffy as one.

"Where the fuck is my striped Brunello Cucinelli blazer!" Hill shouted from the staircase.

I tensed. I'd known from the look in his eyes this morning when I served him breakfast that this was coming. The unsettled, agitated glower had been simmering in his gaze. I'd made his favorite breakfast, asked about his day, done my best to pretend that I cared what he had to say. It was a chore that I'd perfected. Pretending this was perfect. Trying my best to give him his idea of how it should look, how I should be, what he wanted the world to believe we were.

"Hanging to the left of your shoes, two blazers over on the top row," I replied, knowing exactly where I had put it once I picked it up from the cleaners yesterday.

He had an important meeting today with a company who wanted to buy one of the buildings from a company he represented.

His heavy footsteps as he stomped down the stairs sent a shudder through me. I fought the instinct to run. Scanning the living room, I tried to decide the best place to be when he approached. Somewhere that there were no sharp edges I could fall on, free of any objects that could be used to cause more damage than just his fists. As I hurried over to the far corner, my mind raced with things I could say to defuse him. I knew his blazer was there. He'd probably found it before asking me. He had been looking for an excuse. Any reason to hurt me.

The moment he entered the room—his blond hair styled perfectly; his lean, toned body dressed in the white linen pants I had also picked up from the cleaners yesterday and a light-blue shirt that was perfectly pressed—he swung his gaze to me. The rage boiling in those eyes I had once trusted knotted up my stomach. This was a very bad day. It was rare there was ever a good day anymore, but the bad days had different levels of extremity.

"Would you like me to go see where your blazer is? I must have put it in the wrong spot." I hadn't, but taking the blame sometimes saved me. I had learned the ways to please him. The more I did that, the less I paid for whatever it was he was convinced I had done.

His clean-shaven face was tan, and his teeth, which he had professionally whitened, were clenched as he stalked toward me. "Did I not tell you that today was important? You live here like a fucking lazy mooch who has ONE job, Carmella. Yet you are too ignorant to even do that right!" he roared before his hand cracked against the side of my face. "There are wealthy women from powerful families who would kill to be my wife. Women worthy to carry my name! Yet I chose you. A nobody from the swamps of Louisiana. You should be grateful that I gave you this life. FUCKING GRATEFUL!" He grabbed my arm and threw me onto the floor.

I said nothing. I knew if I did when he was like this, it only made it worse. Even begging for forgiveness seemed to make the monster inside him expand.

"I let your face and body seduce me, and I pay for it every goddamn day of my life!" He sneered the hateful words, then kicked me hard, taking my breath away.

The sharp pain that shot through me made it impossible to move. If I tried to even shift, the searing in my side would cause me to cry out, and he'd do it again.

"GET UP! GO GET MY FUCKING BLAZER!" he bellowed.

Closing my eyes, I inhaled deeply and forced myself to do as I had been told. The agony caused a cold sweat to break out all over my body. I found a focal point and breathed out and in through my nose. Keeping my eyes locked on the door that led to the back patio, where I would escape if I could. Imagining I was running for the door to freedom. That I would never see this house again. My secluded cabin in the woods with Bear the dog was there, waiting for me.

"If you would just try, Carmella—do something worth the life you've been gifted—then I wouldn't be so angry. You bring this on yourself. You know that, yet you do it anyway." He was talking softer now. Explaining himself. It was part of the routine.

I nodded. "I'm sorry. I'll do better."

He sighed heavily, as if he was weary from trying to teach me.

"Go upstairs and get my blazer, then just get out of my sight. I don't want to look at you wincing and being dramatic," he ordered me.

I did the best I could to stand up without crying out. I didn't make eye contact with him, keeping my head down as I hurried to the staircase. I wanted to get away from him as much as he wanted to not see me. I'd get his blazer, then go back upstairs and hide until he left. I would be kept here all day to clean, make sure everything he'd touched upstairs was back in its place, prepare the evening meal, and hope he came home too late to eat it.

If I had known then that it would be the last time I had to live in fear of Churchill Millroe, the pain would have been easier to bear.

ONE

*"Monsters could come in pretty packages.
I knew that only too well."*

RUMOR

I should have called the police. That would have been the sane thing to do. I glanced back at Hill's Mercedes I'd parked at a busy service station I stopped at before I ran out of gas in Florida. I scanned the area, looking for a sign to clue me in as to where I was exactly. The abandoned Mercedes wouldn't be noticed right away. This place was crawling with people. It was why I had chosen this as my stop. I had to calm down and think.

Where did I go from here, and how? I couldn't use anything that required my identification or credit cards.

There was a little less than a thousand dollars in cash stuck in my purse. I'd taken it from Hill's closet. It was where I had gone to hide shortly after I heard the door on our veranda crash open. I heard Hill's panicked voice and men demanding their money, saying something about him stealing from them or selling something that wasn't his to sell. I stood there, listening long enough to know Hill was in danger. The way he begged for them to let him fix it. The tremor in his voice. Part of me enjoyed hearing him terrified. He deserved that. To know how it felt. The other part knew I was in danger and had to hide before the intruders found me.

I barely got myself tucked away when the sound of the gun went off, and then I sat quietly, barely breathing while huddled in the storage cubby inside his walk-in closet. Footsteps got closer, and muffled voices I couldn't hear well through the walls came, then went. I stayed there for over an hour. When the silence continued, I made a plan. I would leave. This was my chance to escape. I never thought I would get this kind of opportunity to flee Hill. He'd made sure I had no money of my own or a vehicle. My phone had a tracker on it so he could see where I was at all times. So many nights, I had lain awake, believing that my freedom would come with my death. The day that he hit me too hard or not stopped choking me in time.

I had no family to worry about my whereabouts. No one to ask where I was or call and check on me.

I only had Hill. And from the silence, I realized he could no longer hold me.

So, I took the money, necessities, and I left in his car. Not even stopping to glance back at his body, sprawled out on the living room floor. I could see it from the corner of my eye, but I feared if I went to look at him, he'd open his eyes. He'd still be alive. He'd somehow take me with him to his death.

That had been five hours ago. Now that I'd had time to calm down, reality was starting to sink in. I'd run from a possible murder. Stolen my husband's car. Hill had people who would be looking for him. They'd not get an answer. They would come to find him. Dead. And I'd be gone.

The car had to be left, and I needed to figure out how to get away from here. Put distance between me and the Mercedes. Taking my suitcase, I rolled it toward the entrance of the service station, trying not to limp or let on that every step I took was painful. Maybe I could find someone who looked safe and ask if I could pay them for a ride. To…anywhere. Anywhere but Georgia. Or I could just ask them to take me to a bus station. That couldn't be too far. You could buy a bus ticket with cash, couldn't you?

A woman stopped talking mid-sentence to the man beside her to stare at me. Then, she gave me a sympathetic smile before whispering to him. I started to hurry away from them when another man who was walking toward the door narrowed his gaze as he studied me. He seemed upset by something. My appearance maybe? It was then that it dawned on me. Reaching up to touch the side of my battered face, I winced. I kept forgetting about how bad I looked. I had taken the time to cover it the best I could this morning while I was staying upstairs, out of Hill's sight. He didn't like seeing the marks from his hands. When he did, it often made him angry all over again.

That had been hours ago, and all my hard work at concealing it was wearing off. Not to mention, it was probably turning a dark blue by this point, and it was hard to cover that up. I hadn't glanced at myself in the mirror in a while. I knew my bottom lip was swollen. At least half of it from the way it felt.

My side was throbbing, and sharp pains shot through me when I moved, but I'd grown accustomed to that kind of pain. I was good at living with it. This past year of marriage had taught me how to block out the injury and keep going.

"Hey, darlin'," a man with a long red beard and beady eyes stopped me. His belly stretched his shirt, and he smelled of stale beer and pee. "Looks like you need some help. I got my rig right over there. I can take you somewhere if you're needin'."

Oh, hell no. I shook my head.

"I'm waiting on someone," I lied.

He took another step toward me, tilting his head to the side with a smile that made the hairs on my arms stand up. "Sure don't look like it. From the looks of you, I'd venture you're runnin'. No man should hurt a face that purty. I can take you anywhere you're needin' to go. You hungry? I'm gettin' a large pizza inside. I'll even feed ya. Free of charge."

He was too close now. I felt the panic starting to creep up my spine. I should have stayed in the car. Looked for a safe older woman from inside of its locked doors. Then gotten out and asked for a ride. That would have been the smart thing to do.

I shook my head. "No thank you," I replied, trying not to appear terrified.

He reached out for my arm, and I winced before he even touched me. I had to get away. I wasn't sure I could run though. Not while pulling my suitcase. I'd wrapped my ribs up this morning, but that only helped so much.

"Don't be scared. I'm real nice. My rig even has a comfortable bed. You can rest," he said, lowering his voice as he got closer.

I shook my head, feeling frantic. Did no one see this? Were people going to just ignore me and let this man take me?

"If you'll back up from the lady, that'd save us a lot of trouble." The deep timbre of the Southern drawl was unmistakably masculine.

I didn't want help from a man. Men were dangerous. But at this moment, I would take any distraction so I could get away.

The burly man with breath that smelled like eggs snapped his head around toward whoever had come to my rescue. "I don't think anyone asked you," he replied, annoyed to have been interrupted during his attempt at abduction.

There was a low chuckle from the other man. It wasn't a nervous laugh; it was an amused one. As if he thought this was funny. There was nothing funny happening here. I stepped back, and the oversize trucker was no longer blocking my view.

At times like this, there were many things a woman should do. Run would be the first thing. Yell for help would also be smart. An attempt to escape was at the top of the list. However, I was slightly stunned.

Tall, broad shoulders encased in a dark brown leather jacket; jeans that made sure to showcase his thick, muscular thighs and narrow hips; hair the color of ink; and eyes so blue that they seemed turquoise. The stubble on his face didn't mask his square jawline and high cheekbones. When a slow grin began to spread across his face, I realized he was watching me gawk at him.

"I'm gonna ask this nicely only once. Go on back to your truck and leave," the blue-eyed man said as he turned his gaze toward the trucker.

"I ain't scared o' some purty boy," he replied, turning around to fully face the other man.

This would be the time I should get away. Take my suitcase and go inside the service station. Someone in there could help me. I started to move when I heard the trucker make a strangled noise. Unable to help myself, I glanced back to see the blue-eyed man grinning as if he were having a casual conversation, but standing very close to the trucker, who was now making small gasping sounds.

"You've got five minutes to get your ass in that truck and leave," he drawled as his eyes glanced past the man to look at me. Then, he winked before turning his attention back to the trucker.

"Jesus H. Christ. You're fuckin' crazy," he stammered, then began walking away at a quicker pace than I would have thought he could, seeing as how top heavy he was.

What in the world had the other man done? The big body of the trucker had blocked my view. And why did I care? I needed to get my butt inside. Turning back to the door, I went to grab the handle when a large, tanned hand reached it first, then pulled it open.

I knew before I even looked who had opened it. I should ignore him, but I couldn't help myself. My eyes went in his direction anyway.

"After you," he replied with one of those respectful nods that Southern men seemed to have perfected.

Nervous for so many different reasons, I hurried inside, muttering, "Thank you," without glancing his way again.

As attractive as he was, I needed him to stop getting closer. He was a stranger, and he was a man. I didn't trust either.

Monsters could come in pretty packages. I knew that only too well.

· TWO ·

"She had no idea what a picture she made to all the fucking swinging dicks out there."

KING

She was skittish as fuck. The bruise covering the side of her face and swollen lip made the reason why real clear. Not to mention the way she was favoring the left side of her body. She was hurt in other places, too, and not just physically.

Getting her to trust me was going to be more difficult than I had imagined. Typically, women came to me willingly. I didn't have to do more than smile, wink, and they were putty in my hands. This one wouldn't be softening anytime soon. There was a fighter shining back in those pretty sea-green eyes of hers. She had seen shit. Lived through hell. And now that she had the hope of freedom, she wasn't letting anyone or anything stand in her way.

Problem with that was, she was a looker. All that thick caramel hair in long, wild ringlets, that heavy upper lip of hers, and don't get me started on the eyes. She would turn heads and draw attention from men. All kinds of men. Just like the bastard I'd been forced to shove my pistol into his gut to get my point across.

Stepping inside the store, I watched her as she surveyed the place. Her back ramrod straight, her hand gripped so tightly on the handle of the suitcase she was pulling beside her that her knuckles were white. The side of her lip that wasn't swollen and cut open was caught between her teeth. She was looking for someone. My guess would be anyone who appeared trustworthy and not of the male variety. Which left me standing back and keeping an eye on her from a distance. She spooked too easily, and if I tried to get her in my truck right now, she was likely to get back in the Mercedes and take off again.

She walked over to the snack aisle and picked up a bag of cashews, but her eyes never stopped scanning the area. I saw her lock in on an elderly woman who was walking out of the restroom. That particular lady had come inside with a younger man. Possibly her son. They were traveling together with a younger woman and two kids who were currently arguing over which gum they were going to buy.

When she took a step in the older lady's direction, the younger man turned and called out, "You want me to get you Raisinets, Gram?"

The older lady beamed. "Yes! And a bottle of that soda pop I like."

The woman's shoulders dropped, and she moved back, turning away, and faced the snacks again. Not taking my eyes off her, I made my way toward the drinks and pulled out a bottle of water as she continued searching the place. She picked up a bag of pretzels next and then walked over to the fast-food area, where they sold pizza, burgers, corn dogs, and fried cheese sticks.

A younger guy, I'd guess to be about college age, did a double take as he was waiting on his order. I saw the slow grin cross his face, and I rolled my eyes and muttered a curse. This was going to require me to step in again. She had no idea what a picture she made to all the fucking swinging dicks out there. They saw needy, helpless, alone, and their radar went off. Straight to their cocks.

He stepped closer to her and said something I couldn't hear. Whatever it was caused her to step away quickly and tense up. The guy laughed as if he'd made a joke and leaned close to her again. I could literally see her trembling from across the damn store. How did he not notice this? Shaking my head, I took a long drink of my water and waited. I needed her to be desperate enough to trust me. The more she had douchebags messing with her, the more likely she was to get inside my truck.

The guy held up his hands and shrugged, flashing her an *I'm harmless* smile. He was really bad at this. The kid needed to learn how to read a woman. She was about to run from this goddamn store with the unpurchased items in her hand and probably get chased down by security.

When he held out the pizza he'd just been given toward her and she shook her head, he took another step toward her and tilted his head as he spoke to her. She took another step back and bumped into a man on the other side of her who was ordering something. He glared down at her, then realized who had run into him. His face instantly turned to a pleased grin. Fuck me. Another damn trucker.

Her entire body went stiff as the man began to talk to her. I couldn't stand here and watch this anymore. Sure, I needed her to be at a point where I was the best option she had, but she was fucking shaking. They were scaring the hell out of her. It was too damn painful to witness.

"Hey, sis. You order the pizza yet? I'm ready to get out of here," I said with my best charismatic smile as I stepped between her and the younger kid. Him I could scare off with a scowl. The trucker, however, might require me to be a little more threatening. I had to be careful with that though. If she saw how scary I could be, I'd never get her out of this place. At least not willingly.

Her green eyes swung to me, and for a moment, I saw the relief there. It was only brief. The uncertainty came in real close and shoved that right on out of the way. But it was something. I was clearly the lesser of all the threats.

"N-n-not yet," she stammered, her eyes locked on me as if she was trying to see my soul. I hoped like fuck she couldn't because she'd realize just how dark it was.

"I'll get it. You never add the pepperoni anyway," I replied with a smirk.

"You're with him?" the trucker asked her.

I smiled at her, then shifted my gaze to his and made sure he saw the threat. "Yeah, she is."

His eyes went back to her, and I knew he was checking out her bruising. "Seems someone needs to be taking better care of her."

No shit. "Yeah. And they are now," I replied.

He leaned down toward her. "Are you safe? I'd be happy to take you if you need to escape."

She took a step in my direction. "I'm with my…brother…now."

The trucker didn't seem thrilled, but he wasn't going to cause an issue. The man on the other side of the counter slid a box of pizza toward me, and I took it. I hadn't come in here, planning on getting food, but now that I could smell it, I realized I could eat. I thanked him, then looked back at her.

"Ready? You didn't get a drink," I said, ignoring the trucker.

She blinked and stared up at me. I could see the indecision in her eyes, but I also saw that I was about to win this thing.

"I forgot to get my water," she finally said.

"If I let you get it, can you keep from getting hit on?" I asked teasingly as I took the cashews and pretzels from her free hand and placed them on top of the box of pizza.

The man on the other side of the counter laughed, and I shrugged, grinning as if I thought it was funny too.

She nodded, then looked around as if she was making sure no one else was about to accost her before going to the drink coolers to get her water. I stayed close enough behind her that I wasn't following exactly, but I was there if needed. I also wasn't sure if she was going to try and leave the store or come back to me. She hadn't seemed as if she was even sure what she was going to do next.

Luck was on my side because a middle-aged man who was trying hard to hold on to the little hair he had left, wearing a Florida State football jersey, zeroed in on her while getting his soda. She noticed his creepy-as-fuck smile, then spun around and bolted right back to me.

Score. I won.

"Ready? This pizza smells fantastic," I said.

She glanced around us, then turned her eyes back up to meet mine.

"Can I trust you?" she whispered.

"Yeah, sweets. I swear it," I replied, then nodded my head toward the register.

She didn't move. "I just need a ride to a bus station."

"Okay," I replied, although there was no way in hell I was leaving her at a bus station.

Did she realize how much worse it would be there than it was here?

She swallowed nervously. "You aren't going to rape and kill me?" Her question was so quiet that I barely heard it.

I leaned down toward her and held her gaze. "Have you looked at me, sweets? Not one time in my life have I had to force a female to have sex with me. I'm normally knocking them off me. As for killing…" I couldn't help but smirk. "I'm just here to help you before some other scumbag makes another attempt to pick you up."

She took a deep breath, but didn't crack a smile. It was as if she was thinking hard about what I'd said and deciding how much truth there was to it. When she finally let out a sigh and nodded, I wanted to fucking sigh too.

"Okay," she replied. "Let's go."

I grabbed her bottle of water. "Gotta pay for the food first," I said.

She reached for her purse.

"It's on me," I told her, then headed for the register.

"I have money," she said, hurrying to keep up with me.

"Good. You'll probably need it at some point. But not right now."

She didn't say anything, and when I looked down at her, she gave me the closest thing to a smile I figured I was going to get. Especially since her mouth was so busted up. "Thank you."

I nodded. "My pleasure."

• THREE •

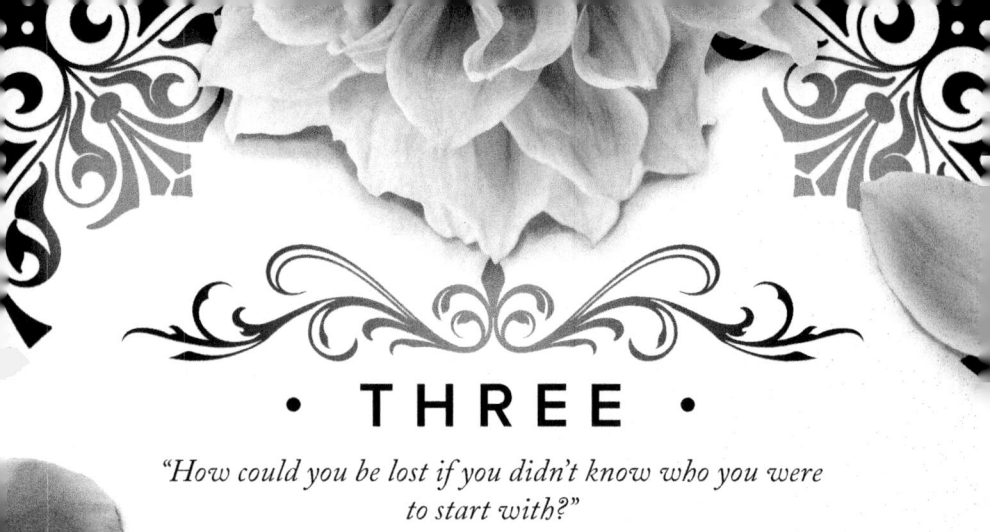

"How could you be lost if you didn't know who you were to start with?"

RUMOR

The woodsy scent of cedar with a touch of cinnamon filled the black Chevy truck as I climbed inside and sat down. I enjoyed the warmth of the aroma until I snapped out of it and focused on the fact that I had agreed to get into a stranger's vehicle. But it wasn't like I was having any luck with another option. I couldn't study the people and approach anyone for help because strange men kept talking to me. This was the only man who wasn't pushy and frightening. He'd helped me twice, and, well, he was right. He didn't need to resort to forcing a woman to do anything with him or for him. I was just an exception, and he didn't seem very interested in my appearance. He'd seemed more concerned than anything.

I heard my suitcase being placed in the truck bed, and then I glanced over at the driver's door just as he opened it and held out the pizza box to me. I reached out and took it, and then he climbed inside with the plastic bag that contained our waters and my random cashews and pretzels I hadn't really wanted. I'd just grabbed them to appear like I was shopping and not scoping out the place.

He took the waters out and placed them in the cupholders in the center console, then lifted his ridiculously blue eyes to meet mine. "If we're gonna share a pizza, we should at least know each other's name," he told me, then held out his hand. "King Salazar."

"Your…your name is King?"

I didn't think he was telling me he was a king, but I'd never heard of someone being named King before. Oddly enough, he held that name well. I wasn't going to tell him that though. Trusting a pretty face was something I would never do again. I hadn't gotten in this truck because he was hot. I'd gotten in it because he had proven to be helpful and kind. Nothing more. And, yes, because most women in there were checking him out, yet he hadn't seemed to notice.

He shrugged with a nonthreatening, amused smile on his face. "Yeah. My dad lost a bet."

How interesting.

I slid my hand into his. "Rumor," I said, then paused before saying my last name. I couldn't trust anyone with that information. "Beauregard," I finished, using the surname of my favorite foster family.

He gave me that killer smile that I was sure had women falling at his feet regularly. "It's nice to meet you, Rumor. Now, why don't we open that box and have a piece of greasy service-station pizza?"

The way he could so easily put someone at ease was a talent. One I needed to be careful with. Letting my guard down wasn't an option. Even if this was a nice guy, like I had just about decided he was, I was on the run. No one could be trusted with any of my truths. I'd given him the name I had before I was married. Hill hadn't felt that Rumor was appropriate. He said it was tacky and sounded backwoods. So, I agreed to have my name legally changed to Carmella. The name he had chosen for me. A name I came to hate so very soon after I said *I do*.

I never wanted to be called Carmella again.

Opening the box, I took out a slice and handed it to him.

He pointed at the glove compartment. "Napkins are in there. Grab us a few."

I did so, and he took one to hold on to the pizza while he ate it. I did the same. Never had grease tasted so good. I couldn't remember the last time I'd eaten anything like this. Hill had made me keep count of my calories, and I had to step on a scale every morning so that he could check my weight. I learned the hard way that sneaking around and eating food he didn't approve of would cause the scale to go up, and if it went up more than two pounds, I would pay for it. Painfully so.

I caught myself making a sound that was awfully close to a moan, and my cheeks flushed. Thankfully, he didn't say anything about it, and I kept my eyes focused straight ahead. If he was laughing at me, I didn't want to know.

"The closest bus station to here is about thirty minutes south," he said. "But I'm going north, and there is one about an hour in my direction that I can take you to instead, if that's okay."

I wanted to go south, but I also didn't want to make him go out of his way after he already helped me several times.

"North is fine," I replied.

"Great. I'll get home in time for my Maeme's Tuesday night chicken and dumplings and banana pudding."

The excitement in his voice made me smile. If he didn't have such a deep drawl, he'd have seemed much younger.

"Is that your grandmother?" I asked.

"Yep. My dad's momma. She raised me. Dad wasn't around much due to his work, and my own momma walked out on us in the middle of the night when I was two. I don't have much memory of her."

I had no memory of my mother or father for that matter, but somehow, his story felt worse. His momma had known him. Held him. Taken care of him. Then left after two years. What kind of person did that?

"That's awful," I said before I could stop myself.

He shrugged. "Not really. My Maeme is great. She's sweet as sugar, yet she is the only woman alive who can control my dad, and did I mention her banana pudding? Best thing you've ever put in your mouth. I figure there's no woman alive who outshines her. I was a lucky kid."

I sat back in the leather seat, finding myself relaxed for the first time since…I didn't know when. Hearing King talk about his grandmother made me forget my own troubles.

"She sounds really special," I agreed, then took another bite of my pizza.

King reached over and grabbed another slice from the box. "That she most definitely is."

I finished off my slice and wiped my hands on a napkin before opening my water to take a drink. King glanced over at me then, and I lifted my eyes to his involuntarily. I could see the question in his eyes before he even asked.

"Would you get all defensive and skittish on me again if I asked what happened to your face? Because if so, then forget it and pretend I asked if you'd ever ridden a horse."

Hearing him phrase it like that kept me from doing exactly as he'd suggested. It didn't mean I was going to tell him who'd hurt me. But I also didn't feel the pressure of having to tell him what had happened.

"I've never even seen a horse up close," I replied after a pause. I didn't look at him again because if he was disappointed that I hadn't answered the question he really wanted to know, I preferred not to see that.

"Ah, that's a damn shame. Everyone needs to experience the beauty of a horse up close," he replied, not letting on that I'd ignored his other question at all. He would never know how grateful I was for him letting it go so easily.

"Do you ride horses?" I asked him, finding myself more curious about him. His description and about his grandmother had intrigued me.

He chuckled. "Oh, yeah. I do more than just ride. My family is in the racing horse business. We raise thoroughbreds. They're a real work of art. It's something that never gets old, watching one grow into a winner. Seeing it and knowing that one is going to be the one. It's got the thing. What it takes. Something else," he said with real passion in his voice.

Hearing him talk about something he so clearly loved made me wish I had something like that. I couldn't remember what I liked to eat, much less what I liked to do. Having all my decisions, desires, wants taken from me and being forced to become someone Hill wanted me to be had wiped me clean. I no longer knew who I was.

Lost in my own thoughts, I fell silent. I didn't want to ask King anything more about himself. The more he talked, the more it became all too clear how empty I was. I'd called it lost, but it wasn't that. How could you be lost if you didn't know who you were to start with? I tried to think back to a time when I'd had dreams. Before all those had been snatched from me, and the fairy tale had morphed into a nightmare. One that I hadn't woken up from.

Family. That was all I could remember wanting. To belong. To be loved. To have a place where I was important, needed, accepted. There were no other things I could recall wishing I had. Just that. Something that most people were born with. Given the moment they were conceived. It was a gift that came with life. Except for me. It was an unattainable object I couldn't quite grasp.

The times I would get settled into a foster family and it would begin to feel safe—like this might be permanent, that I had a chance at a real family—it would be snatched away. A foster mother would get cancer, a couple would divorce, someone would lose a job and need to move. Then, as I got older, the men…they'd look at me or treat me inappropriately. Women no longer wanted me in their home. It had been a vicious cycle, and fate had been against me.

The blue lights flashing up ahead snapped me out of my thoughts as we slowed to a stop. My throat immediately constricted, and I gripped the door tightly. Unsure what I should do now. What if they were looking for me? Would they have found Hill already? Was there a search out for his missing wife? My heart slammed erratically in my chest. I had to do something. I couldn't stay in this truck.

"The way I see it is, we can get off at this exit and take a back road to my Maeme's or wait through this here roadblock to get you to the bus stop. I'm gonna let you make that call."

I tore my eyes off the lights and stared at him. He was watching me. His eyes told me nothing. He wasn't letting on if he knew I was about to have a full-blown panic attack.

The corner of his wide mouth lifted just a touch. "Maeme's banana pudding is real good. I think I said that already though."

Think. Think. Think. Breathe. Think.

I swallowed nervously and studied the situation up ahead. There was a good chance this had nothing at all to do with me. That Hill was still lying in that living room in a pool of blood. Dead. Where I had left him without a backward glance.

But could I take that chance?

"If I'm getting off, then I need to know now. If we start moving, it'll be too late," he warned me.

Jerking my gaze back to his, I decided I had only one option here. "Do you think your Maeme would mind me coming with you to dinner?" I asked.

A slow smile spread across his handsome face. "No, sweets. She'd be tickled pink. She loves feeding folks almost as much as she loves me. And that's saying a lot." He turned on his blinker. "Banana pudding then?"

I sucked in a breath, and then I nodded. "Yeah. Banana pudding."

• FOUR •

"My job was done."

KING

I let George Strait fill the silence instead of coaxing Rumor to talk. She was strung up tight again, and I knew she needed to be left alone to think. I almost felt guilty about the fucking cops. She'd been relaxed, talking, even smiling some. Then, she got a look at the police cars up ahead, and it was like a damn switch flipped. That had been the purpose, but still, part of me wanted to ease her again. I wasn't sure I could do it so easily this time though.

When we turned off I-20 onto the road that would take us to Maeme's, Rumor seemed to snap out of her thoughts and sat up straight.

"Where are we?" The panic in her voice didn't surprise me. She hadn't seemed to notice when we crossed the Georgia state line.

"Madison. Maeme is about three miles down this road, and then we turn off onto a country road that leads down into her land. She owns forty-five acres of pecan trees that she makes a nice profit off of every fall, among other things." That I was not about to get into.

· SLAY ·

Rumor would jump out of the truck and take off back to the interstate on foot if she had any idea exactly what all Maeme was involved in.

"We're in…Georgia," she said just above a whisper.

"Yep. Madison, to be exact."

"Oh God," she whispered, turning her head to stare out the passenger window.

"Hey, Madison ain't all that bad. I've lived my whole life here. It's a nice little place. I promise."

She didn't say anything, but she was clasping her hands so tightly together in her lap that I was afraid her nails were going to puncture her skin. The last thing she needed was more wounds. I still wasn't sure what else was hurt on her, but from the way she was sitting and being careful with her right side, I'd say her ribs weren't okay.

"I think maybe it would be best if you could drop me at a bus station close to here or maybe just at the nearest service station. I can find another ride," she said, then glanced at me warily.

I shook my head. "No, sweets, I can't do that. I already know what happens to you at service stations, all alone. And the nearest bus station is in Atlanta. It's rush hour, and as helpful as I am and as pretty as you are, I'm still not willing to face that shit. Just come on to Maeme's. Get you some dinner. You'll be safe. I'd be willing to bet there isn't a safer place in Georgia."

A panicked look came over her face. She was grasping at anything to change my mind.

"We're close to Atlanta?" she asked.

"Yes, but we are gonna be back on a big ole piece of land, way off the road, in a farmhouse where whoever you're running from isn't gonna come looking for you. If they did, then they'd have to deal with Maeme, and, well, that's something they wouldn't do for long," I assured her, then grinned. "Come on now. Relax. *You are safe.* I might not know what it is going on, but no one will find you. Whoever is looking, they won't look here."

Her chin snapped up, and she narrowed her eyes. "Why do you think I'm worried someone is gonna find me?"

I slowed the truck and turned onto the private drive that led to Maeme's house. "You've been hit. Someone used you as a punching bag, and that ain't a mark left by a woman. You have a suitcase you're carrying around, and you are so scared of men that you literally tremble when they get near you. I pay attention. You needed help. I noticed it the moment I laid eyes on you. So, I did what I had been raised to do. I helped." That was so far from the truth that hell should have opened up and swallowed me. What I'd been raised to do was not help. Not even close.

She said nothing as I pulled the truck up to the farmhouse I'd been raised in. It wasn't as big as my dad's mansion where he lived with his fourth wife, who was only two years older than me, and my five-year-old half-sister, but it was a three-story gothic-style farmhouse with a wraparound porch.

I parked and then turned to look at Rumor again. "We're here."

She studied the house and looked around at the rows of pecan trees surrounding us for as far as the eye could see. "This isn't a farmhouse," she said.

I shrugged. "Eh, it's close enough. You ready?"

She took a shaky breath, then nodded.

I climbed out of the truck and went to get her suitcase as she opened her door. I left the luggage to go help her down. Whatever injury she had under her clothes didn't need her jumping down. Not the way she was being so careful with it.

"Let me help you," I said.

She stared at my outstretched hand as if she wasn't sure she wanted to touch me. That was so foreign to me that I wasn't sure how to even deal with it. Grasping, I tried to think of something to say to convince her to trust me.

"If Maeme sees you getting out of my truck without my help, I won't get the banana pudding," I told her with a pleading look.

Her lips twitched as if she might smile, but she didn't. Finally, she slid her hand into mine, and I took all the weight I could as she stepped down. The wince on her face had me wishing I'd just picked her up, but that would have really scared the shit out of her.

"You okay?" I asked as she inhaled sharply through her nose.

She nodded. "Fine."

No, she wasn't. She was hurt, and if I couldn't get her to let me see it and help, then Maeme was gonna have to do it. Someone needed to see how bad it was. If she had cracked ribs, she needed them seen to. I headed over to get her suitcase and picked it up.

"Just in time, and you brought a guest," Maeme called out from the front porch. "What a nice surprise!"

The instant ease to Rumor's shoulders made me want to laugh. My grandmother had a way with people. She could work a crowd. Dad said I had gotten that from her. God knew I hadn't gotten it from him.

"Maeme," I called out as we approached the porch. "This is Rumor. I found her needing some assistance down in Pensacola. Thought you might like some company and another mouth to feed."

Maeme's smile widened as she put her hands on her hips. "Lord, what a pretty thing you are. I hope this one was a gentleman. He isn't always. But I raised him the best I could. Now, come on in here and let me get you some sweet tea. I just made a fresh pitcher," she crooned, walking over to put her hand on Rumor's back.

When Rumor flinched, Maeme froze, then looked from me to Rumor. "Is more than that lovely face of yours hurt?" she asked with a frown.

I expected Rumor to deny it, as she had with me.

"Yes," she replied.

Maeme shook her head. "A man who will lay his hand on a woman as sweet as you deserves a bullet in his head. Now, come on and let me tend to you."

Rumor walked inside, and Maeme looked back at me, then nodded her head once.

My job was done.

• FIVE •

"I'd dug myself a deep one by running."

RUMOR

From the way King had spoken of his grandmother and the house he had grown up in, I'd expected something smaller…and more farm-like. This was not a farmhouse. Well, maybe in one of those *Home & Gardens* magazines, but not in real life. The house wasn't even decorated like a grandmother. Sure, there were photographs on the walls, and it had a homey, lived-in feeling, but in an elaborate interior-decorator way.

"King, put her suitcase in the blue room," Maeme instructed him. "I'll bring her up there in a moment to check on her injuries. The others should be here in about ten minutes or so for dinner. You just make sure everyone waits on us in the dining room and stays out of the pudding."

The others? What others? King hadn't said a thing about others. My eyes swung to see him walking toward the staircase. He didn't turn around and look back at me. He hadn't mentioned others. I'd thought this would be a hidden place I could stay until he could get me to a bus station.

"I, uh, there is no need to take my suitcase upstairs," I blurted. "I wasn't going to intrude. King said we were coming here to eat while the traffic was heavy. Then, he'd take me to a bus station."

Maeme's eyebrows rose, and her hands went to her hips. The petite woman looked surprisingly intimidating. Her short platinum bob was elegant, just as was her delicate bone structure. She was an attractive woman that I would guess was in her mid-seventies. Since King looked to be around thirty and she was his grandmother, I couldn't imagine she was still in her sixties, although she could pass for it. Her cornflower-blue eyes were nowhere near the intense color of King's, but they were lovely just the same.

"In your condition? No. That will not be what happens. Someone has hurt you. I can see it clear as day. You will stay here and let me help you heal. Tomorrow, after a good night's rest and a full belly, you can tell me exactly why you're running, and I will fix it," she informed me.

Her blue eyes narrowed as if there was no room for argument. But she had no idea what she was asking. I could not bring what could possibly be coming for me to her doorstep.

"Don't argue with her," King told me from the staircase.

I swung my gaze to his, pleading silently for his help with this.

He shrugged and nodded his head toward his grandmother. "When Maeme says she will fix it, she does."

"You promised," I argued.

The corner of his lips curled up. "Don't believe every pretty face you meet, sweets. You should know by now, that's a terrible fucking idea."

"King Chasen Salazar!" Maeme snapped angrily.

"Sorry," he replied obediently, but the glint in his eyes said no such thing.

Realizing I'd lost what I thought was my way out of here, I decided to turn back to Maeme. It was clear that she called all the shots.

"I have family in Louisiana," I lied. I might have grown up in foster homes from Saint Helena Parish all the way down to

Jefferson Parish, but there was no family for me there. It was just the only place I knew to go.

The way Maeme studied me felt as if she could read every lie out of my mouth. "Maybe so, but that family let you get in this kinda shape. Can't say they're doing their job. Family protects. You come on up those stairs with me. There's a bathroom that will be all yours. I'm gonna see what we are dealing with under that shirt of yours, then let you get cleaned up and comfortable." Then, she motioned for me to follow King up the stairs with a stern *no arguments accepted* stance.

I was angry with him. He'd fooled me, but he hadn't hurt me. There was a difference. I followed King up the stairs. He didn't say another word to me or even glance back in my direction. It was ridiculous to feel hurt by his betrayal when I had bigger problems. Real issues. But I was.

We stopped at the second floor and went to the first door on the right. King opened the door and walked inside. Maeme was directly behind me, and I had no choice but to go inside the room. Not surprisingly, it was a beautiful bedroom with a king-size canopy bed sitting in the middle of the room on a raised platform. I assumed she called it the blue room because the walls were paneled but painted a soft blue. The bedding was a crisp white, as was the chiffon draped over the canopy. The windows had matching chiffon curtains that pooled on the floor. A white antique dresser and dressing table sat on opposite walls, and a lovely blue-and-white striped chaise lounge chair with a fluffy blue throw over the back of it sat in a corner with a floor lamp made of crystals to its side.

"Put her suitcase on the luggage rack in the closet," Maeme told King. "Then get downstairs before the boys arrive."

The boys? The others were boys? Something else King hadn't told me. I should assume from here on out that everything he'd said was a lie.

"Yes, ma'am," he replied, opening the door on the left wall and walking inside, then turning on a light.

I could see from here it was a large walk-in closet.

"The bathroom is this way," she informed me, walking to the door on the opposite side of the room and opening it. "Come on in here and show me what else has been done to you. I have supplies to ease the pain and some medicine that'll help too. Just need to know what we are dealing with. Might require a doctor."

Panic seized me again, and I shook my head, backing up. The thought of running from this room and house played out in my head. King would catch me, and I had no vehicle to get far even if I tried.

"I can't go to a hospital or doctor for that matter. I need to just leave. I think it will be best for everyone. I can call a taxi. I don't need the bus—"

"Take a deep breath and calm down, Rumor," Maeme said, closing the space between us and touching my arm lightly. "Ain't no one going anywhere. Not even the hospital. We have a friend who is a medical doctor. He makes house calls. He is also real discreet. He will come here, fix you up, eat my chicken and dumplings, enjoy my banana pudding, and be happy as a clam to do it."

"I can't pay for that," I argued, wondering what kind of doctor would come here and work on a patient without equipment.

"And you won't need to. He will do it as a favor," Maeme informed me. "King, you can go now."

I turned to watch him walk out of the room without a word. He closed the door behind him, and I took in a shaky breath.

What had I gotten myself into? I could have kept trying to find a woman to help me. Those men weren't that big of a problem. It wasn't like one of them was going to abduct me from the store in front of all those people. I was scared and alone, weak and terrified. He had approached me at the right time.

"Take off the shirt and show me what has you holding that side like it hurts to breathe," Maeme directed me. It was said in a kind tone, but the demand that left no room for argument was also clear in her voice. It was amazing how she could sound like a kind grandmother but have a fierceness that had you obeying her.

I was also worn down. It was clear she wasn't going to listen to me. I had to get through this, and in the morning, I'd find a way to leave.

I placed my purse on the dresser, then unbuttoned my blouse, only wincing when I had to shrug it off my shoulders. I'd done the best I could with athletic wrap this morning that I kept in my closet for times when Hill went beyond bruising me.

"Let me," Maeme said with her eyes locked on my ribs.

The pain in her gaze as she began to gently remove the wrap was the first time I'd had anyone genuinely care about me. I felt my eyes begin to burn, and I blinked, fighting back the tears. I would not cry on this woman.

Closing my eyes, I inhaled deeply as the cool air hit my skin. I was afraid to look at the damage that had been done. I knew by now that the bruising would have set in.

"Son of a bitch," Maeme muttered.

I opened my eyes as she was studying me, shaking her head with a look of fury on her face.

"I'm not a doctor, but I've seen enough broken ribs to recognize one when I see it. I'm gonna wrap you up with something a bit better than this, but why don't you go stand in a hot shower first? It'll make you feel better. Wash every bit of that bastard's touch off your body. I'll go get you some pain medicine that's strong enough to ease the pain with a glass of sweet tea that I promised. Don't you worry. We are gonna handle this. You're safe now, honey."

Even though I knew this sweet grandmother meant well and probably believed everything she was saying, I was aware that she couldn't handle my problems. I'd dug myself a deep one by running. I could still go back. Tell the truth and hope the police believed me. I could call them now and tell them what I'd done and why. But then a battered wife who ran would look like the number one suspect. I didn't have money for a lawyer. I wasn't on any of Hill's bank accounts. He had given me one credit card, and it had a two-thousand-dollar limit.

"Come on now. I'll get you a towel and get the shower going," Maeme said gently. "Everything is going to be okay, Rumor."

No, it wasn't, but I nodded regardless. I'd let her help me tonight. In the morning, I'd leave. Thank them for their help and walk out the door to get in a taxi. I could pay in cash and hopefully have enough for a bus ticket and motel room. I couldn't let this nice lady be held accountable for my actions.

· SIX ·

"Keep your chin up. Life will get better."

RUMOR

When I stepped out of the shower, there was a glass of iced tea and a pill lying beside it. I didn't question it. The pain had gotten worse even if the rest of me felt refreshed from the warmth of the shower and the lavender scent of the body wash Maeme had given me to use. There was a plush white robe hanging on the hook that hadn't been there when I got in the shower. Assuming Maeme had left it for me, I slipped it on, then dried my hair with a towel the best I could, only using one hand, then ran a brush through it.

Facing whoever was downstairs eating sounded like more than I was up for at the moment. I was grateful to Maeme for her hospitality and willingness to help, but I had to think. Plan. Prepare for what I was going to do next. Without my cell phone, I didn't have a way to actually call a taxi without help. I kept forgetting that. I would need to borrow a phone to get any kind of taxi service.

Opening the door, I stepped into the bedroom and found Maeme sitting on the chaise lounge, near a man with a thick beard and friendly eyes, wearing a white oxford button-up and khaki pants. I paused my gaze from shifting between the two of them. Maeme stood up and stopped whatever she had been saying to the man.

"Rumor, this is Dr. Drew. He's been a family friend for nigh on forty years. He's here to check you over and to join us for dinner."

I listened to Maeme, then turned back to the doctor. How had she gotten a doctor here so quickly? I had only been in the bathroom maybe thirty minutes at most.

He smiled and gave me a nod. "It's nice to meet you, Rumor. I hear you've been worked over."

He was studying my face, now blue and purple with the makeup completely gone. My lip was cracked on that side as well and swollen more than I had realized.

"Yes, sir," I replied.

He gave me a sympathetic smile. "Maeme believes you have a broken rib or two, but if I could see for myself…"

He didn't have an X-ray machine, but I figured being rude and pointing that out wasn't the best thing to do.

"Okay," I agreed.

He nodded to the bed. "I left you a gown to slip on. Then, Maeme will bring you to the examination room."

Wait, what? My focus swung to Maeme, who just smiled as if what he had said made complete sense.

"We will be right down," she informed him.

He gave another nod, then headed for the door to leave. I watched him until the door closed behind him, and then I looked back at Maeme.

"Go on and slip that on. It's like any hospital gown. Leave it open in the back, and you can put the robe over it. Then, we will take the back stairs, so no one sees you."

"Where are we going?" I asked.

"The basement. We've got the equipment down there already set up that Drew will need to examine you."

I shook my head, confused. "You…you have an X-ray machine in your basement?"

She gave me a bright smile. "The boys get hurt on those horses so often that it's just easier to have it available to us."

Her explanation still made no sense. King had told me about the horses, but where were they? All I had seen outside were pecan trees.

I nodded though, deciding this wasn't really my business. I should be thankful that they had something like that available for me to use. When Maeme didn't move to leave, I figured she was going to wait on me to slip on the gown. I picked it up from the bed, then went back to the bathroom to put it on.

When I walked back into the bedroom, she was standing beside the door.

"Let's go," she said, opening it, then waving for me to exit the room first.

We went in the opposite direction of where we had earlier. A narrow set of stairs was tucked away at the end of the hallway behind a door that was unnoticeable since it blended in with the walls.

I followed her down the stairs that led into a brightly lit area with white walls, ceramic tile flooring, and three brown leather sofas that were set up in a U-shape with a rustic hand-carved table in the center. A flat screen television covered the wall the sofas were facing.

We walked past the seating area and came to two doors. The one on the right was open, and Maeme went inside. Glancing back, I scanned the area to make sure there was no one else down here. I found my curiosity was getting the best of me.

The room I followed Maeme into was small, sterile, and did in fact have an X-ray machine in there, along with an examination table and a wall of cabinets.

"You can hang your robe over there on the hook," Dr. Drew informed me. "Then, if you will, come stand right over here. I'm assuming there is no chance you could be pregnant."

I shook my head. "No. I get a Depo-Provera shot every twelve weeks."

He nodded. "Good. When did you have it last?"

"Seven weeks ago," I told him with more certainty than I felt. I had kept track of it on my calendar at home and I wasn't positive about the timeline without looking at it. But then it wasn't like I had to worry about getting pregnant anytime soon if ever.

"Go ahead and step outside, Maeme," he instructed. "This won't take long."

I stood in front of the machine and moved my arms the different ways he asked. The more his bushy eyebrows came together in a frown, the more I felt my anxiety building. By the time he let out a heavy sigh and told me we were finished, he appeared to be scowling.

"You have a broken rib and a fractured one. I expected as much. But this isn't the first time. There are multiple healed fractures on your clavicle and humerus, as well as your third and fourth ribs," he said, studying me.

I said nothing. He was a doctor, and he was going to want me to go to the police. File a report on a dead man. One that I had left to lie in our house, bleeding out, alone.

"There is scar tissue, some things that should have been seen to properly, and it's clear that it was not. Are your ribs and face the only areas I need to be checking? What about past injuries? Your head? Anything that might cause you issues later?"

I shook my head. He was going to mention the police. My hands fisted in my gown, and I struggled to come up with a reason why I couldn't do that. Why I wouldn't.

He gave me a tight smile. "Very well. But if at any time you think there might be, just tell Maeme. She'll make sure I am here to check it out. I'm going to wrap it properly. Maeme told me she gave you an eight-hundred-milligram ibuprofen. That will take the bite off, but it's not strong enough for you to get proper rest. I'm going to leave you something that will ease you better."

I stood there silently as he began to wrap my ribs. Not one word was said about the police. Filing a report. He didn't push me to show him where I had been hurt in the past. He simply finished his task. Maeme stepped back in the room, and she looked over at the X-ray he had taken. Her eyes narrowed, and the angry gleam in her gaze made me think she knew exactly how to read what she was looking at.

"Not the first time," she said, swinging her eyes to meet mine.

I didn't respond.

She nodded and straightened her shoulders even more so than they had been. "Thank you, Drew. I'll take her on up to get dressed, and we will see you in the dining room."

Once we were alone, her eyes locked on me. "You're gonna be okay. You'll heal, and this will be the last time you have to go through this. Keep your chin up. Life will get better."

I wish she could control fate with her commands as easily as she seemed to control everyone else.

• SEVEN •

"You not gonna spoon me out some too?"

KING

"You get caught in that banana pudding, and not a one of us will be safe," Storm Kingston said as he opened the fridge to get a beer.

"It's just a bite," I replied.

"Get me a beer," Wells Jones told him as he pulled out a stool from the bar and sat down. "I'm starving. How much longer we got to wait?"

"Why are we not eating yet?" Thatcher Shephard asked as he strode into the kitchen, still wearing his cowboy hat, which would piss Maeme off more than me tasting the pudding.

"Doc D is doing an X-ray on her ribs," I told him, then turned to Storm. "Toss me a beer, too, while you're at it."

"Do I look like a motherfucking bartender?" he shot back, annoyed, but reached into the fridge and took out another beer anyway.

I smirked, reaching up to grab it. "Thanks."

"Fuck off," he replied.

"Anyone talk to Wilder? He was supposed to be breaking into the bastard's bank accounts and draining them," I asked.

"You worry about your job. Wilder has it under control," Thatcher replied.

"My job is done," I pointed out. "Successfully so at that."

Storm rolled his eyes and pulled out a stool beside Wells. "You had the easiest job. Flash your pretty-boy smile and do the charming shit."

I chuckled. "You'd be surprised. She wasn't easily moved by my smile or charm."

"Bullshit. She's getting a motherfucking X-ray in the basement. I'd disagree," he shot back at me.

I shrugged and washed off my spoon before Maeme saw it. "I swear. She was tougher to convince than I'd anticipated. I'd convinced a Christian into a threesome easier."

Storm let out a cackle of laughter. "When do you have threesomes? Doesn't that master kink shit you like only work with one bitch at a time?"

"Is she as hot as the pics we saw of her?" Wells asked, leaning on the counter and raising his eyebrows, ignoring Storm's obnoxious questioning.

I shrugged, unsure why hearing Wells call her hot bothered me. We'd all made comments about her looks when we got all the information about Churchill Millroe. But that had been before I met her. Now, it seemed wrong. She was an abused woman. Yes, she was smoking hot, but she had been hurt in more ways than just physical.

"Yeah. Could have done way better than that piece of shit she's married to. One side of her face is pretty messed up, but it'll heal," I replied.

"Body? Tits—small or big?" Wells asked.

"Doesn't matter," Thatcher drawled, then took a drink of his beer.

"He's right," I added. "You go there, and it won't just be Maeme you have to deal with. Not part of the job."

"Blaise will be here tomorrow," Thatcher said. "He might have her moved to Ocala."

It wasn't the boss I had been referring to, but I let that go. Wells was too damn close to a motherfucking narcissist himself. I wasn't about to let another man hurt her. She was vulnerable and nowhere near tough enough to handle Wells. That was all it was. I wanted her safe from other assholes.

"Wilder coming with him?" Wells asked.

Thatcher smirked and cut his eyes toward Wells. "He's a newlywed. Doubt he's gonna leave that pussy since he's been wanting it for more than a decade."

"Thatch, don't start shit," I begged.

We had real things to deal with. Getting Wells all worked up over the past was pointless. Wilder Jones was Wells's cousin, and Wilder had just married Wells's first love, Oakley Watson. Not only that, but Wilder had also taken her away from Wells over ten years ago. Wells claimed he was over it, but he and Wilder had never been close again after it happened. Thatcher knew that, and he thrived on conflict.

"What? Wells is over it. Sebastian isn't here to fuck with," Thatcher replied, grinning smugly.

Oakley had also dated Sebastian once upon a time. He'd proposed, and she'd broken things off.

Wells shook his head. "That shit doesn't get to me anymore. Wilder and Oak belong together. She was never good for me."

"No, you weren't good for her," Thatcher replied. "Cheating bastard."

Storm chuckled, and Wells shot him an annoyed glare.

"I was a fucking kid," he grumbled.

That much was true. They had been in high school back then. Sebastian, on the other hand, had dated her years later. Yet he seemed to handle the fact Oakley and Wilder were married better than Wells.

"Is the dining room table set?" Dr. Drew asked as he walked into the kitchen.

I straightened from leaning against the sink. "You done?" I asked.

He nodded. "Yeah. And if Maeme gets up here and that table isn't set, you're all getting an earful. Thatcher, take off the damn hat. You know she's gonna be mad if she sees it on in the house."

Everyone got into motion. I turned and grabbed the plates. Storm opened the fridge and got out the gallon pitcher of sweet tea. When I headed to the dining room, Thatcher had taken off his hat and was getting the flatware from the drawer, and Wells was carrying the pot of chicken and dumplings.

"I'll get the collards," Doc D said, heading to the stove.

We all made at least two trips, getting the rest of the supplies for the meal. I checked the oven and found the cornbread warming in the cast iron skillet and a casserole dish full of mac and cheese.

"I got the cornbread. Someone grab the mac," I called out and headed back to the dining room.

When I stepped inside, I paused at the sight of Rumor standing there with her damp curls and clean face. Goddamn, the bruising was much worse than I'd assumed. Her swollen, cracked lip looked as if it had some medication on it now. Those sea-green eyes of hers met mine, and she looked almost relieved. As if seeing me was something she needed. Damn, that wasn't a good thing, but I'd be lying if I said I didn't like it.

Off-limits. For a list of reasons a mile long.

"You ready for those dumplings I told you about?" I asked her while setting the cornbread on the table.

She dropped her gaze, and I saw her eyes widen at the spread. It had been a couple of hours since we'd shared the pizza, and I was starving. I wasn't so sure about Rumor though. She didn't look like she ate much.

"All right, boys," Maeme said, getting everyone's attention as they made their way back to the dining room. All eyes were on my tiny grandmother, who stood with her hands on her hips. "I expect your best behavior."

She turned to Rumor then. "This here is Storm," she told her, waving a hand in his direction. "Then, we have Thatcher." She paused and looked back at Rumor. "He's got a dark soul, but he's still a good boy." Which was a damn lie. Thatcher was a fucked-up son of a bitch. "You know King." She gave me a pointed look like she had some things to say to me in private. "That there is Wells."

Her steely gaze met each of ours. "Boys, this is Rumor. She's gonna be staying with me for a while. I expect her to be treated like *family*."

Everyone nodded and said their, "Yes, ma'am," but my focus was on Rumor, who looked like her anxiety was on the rise again.

When her eyes met mine, I gave her a reassuring smile before taking a seat. Maeme had her hands full. I hoped she realized it. The look in those pretty green eyes said she was planning on running. Not that she'd get far, but it was going to be a full-time job, watching her until she calmed her ass down.

"Storm Kingston," Maeme called as he reached for the skillet of cornbread. "I know you ain't reaching for something before the blessing is said."

He pulled his hand back. "No, ma'am."

She nodded, then gave us all a pointed look that meant we'd better bow our heads while she blessed the food regardless that Thatcher had killed a man today, then shot another; I'd lied my ass off to convince a woman to get in my truck; and Storm had held a knife to a man's throat to get information from him, then made the man piss himself. Sure, if there was a Lord, he really cared about us thanking him for the food we were about to eat. Made complete sense. Not that anyone would point that out to Maeme.

When she said, "Amen," we all fell in line and repeated it before hands shot out and grabbed at the different offerings filling the table.

Pausing with the pot of dumplings in my hand since I'd been sure to set them directly in front of me, I glanced over at Rumor. She seemed to have paled as she watched us all, wide-eyed. I really fucking hated the bruise on her face. It made me want to hurt someone.

Standing up, I walked over to her, carrying the dumplings. She followed me with her eyes until I came to stand behind her.

"You gotta have some of this," I told her, taking the first spoonful and placing it on her plate. "Eat up."

She tilted her head back to look up at me. "Thanks."

I smiled and nodded before walking back to my seat. Thatcher was watching me with a smirk. I shot him a scowl, then sat down.

"You not gonna spoon me out some too?" he asked me.

"Shut up," I replied with a warning glance.

He leaned over and took the collards, still looking amused. Crazy bastard. Most of the time, we allowed his shit because he wasn't what you would call sane. There was something inside him that didn't quite work like everyone else. He was detached. A little too much so.

Looking back down the table at Rumor, I saw her pick up a piece of cornbread and take a bite. She needed to lather that thing up with butter. Maeme was thinking the same thing because she took a pat of butter and reached over to spread it onto Rumor's cornbread. I couldn't hear what she said to her since there were three different conversations going on at the moment. But the small smile that touched her lips somehow helped me relax. She was gonna be fine.

EIGHT

"I bet his dick was small too."

RUMOR

The sunlight flooding the room greeted me when I opened my eyes. I lay in the soft bed with lavender-scented sheets, staring out the window overlooking the lines of pecan trees outside. When I had lain down last night, I had thought sleep wouldn't come. My plan to figure out how I was going to leave today hadn't happened. Not only had I fallen asleep, but I had done it so quickly that I barely remembered much after getting in bed.

The throb in my side became a sharp pain with every breath I took. I needed to get up and take an ibuprofen to take the edge off, then get dressed. Tossing the covers back, I sat up slowly, hissing through my teeth. It wasn't until my feet hit the floor that I realized, today, I wouldn't have to go make Hill breakfast. There would be no anxiety while I waited to see what his mood was this morning. No chance that I had done something wrong. I wouldn't have to pretend I was happy to see him or that I cared about his day. There would be no list of things texted to me that he expected me to accomplish. I was free. Perhaps being lost and running from the law wasn't the ideal situation, but at least I wasn't controlled. Locked away in a world, alone, with no way out.

Standing up, I made my way over to the bathroom, taking slow, easy steps. The bottle of ibuprofen that Maeme had left for me in the bathroom last night was my first order of business. I needed to be able to focus and not be so controlled by the pain. Then, I could hatch a plan. What I would say to Maeme to get her to understand. Part of me felt as if I could tell her the truth and she wouldn't judge me. That she would help me get to the bus station. But there was the other part of me that said there was no way this woman was going to help me stay on the run from a murder I hadn't even committed. She'd think I should tell the police. Confess as to why I had done this.

No. I couldn't tell her. I had to get out of here though. If there was any chance that the police could find me, I was not dragging Maeme and King into this with me when all they had done was try and help a beat-up woman who they assumed was running from her husband or boyfriend.

There was a bottle of water left for me beside the ibuprofen, and I quickly washed down the pills before brushing my teeth. It took longer than normal to get myself looking presentable. The makeup didn't cover my face as well today. The swelling on my lip was better, and the ointment that I'd been given for it helped where it was busted.

I decided wearing a sundress would be easier with my ribs, so I slipped on the only one that I had packed and found a lightweight cardigan to cover my arms until the sun warmed things up outside. Spring in Georgia could be tricky when it came to dressing.

Once I had all my things packed back in the suitcase and I made up the bed, I opened the bedroom door and stepped into the hallway.

There wasn't a clock in my room, and without a watch or a phone, I had no idea what time it was. The sun was bright enough that I knew it wasn't too early. I made my way down the wide staircase and paused to look at the portraits on the wall.

There was one of a teenage King with a football uniform on, holding a football between his hands. Even then, his smile seemed to say, *I know I'm charming and beautiful.*

The next portrait was of an even younger King on a huge black horse. He had a cowboy hat on and was in mid-gallop. It was a stunning photograph.

"That boy was born loving to ride," Maeme said from the bottom of the staircase.

I turned to look at her, and she smiled up at me.

"If he wasn't throwing a ball back, then he was on a horse," she said with a soft laugh. "I miss those days." Then, she waved a hand at me. "Come on down. Let's go have some breakfast and talk about what we're gonna do. I reckon you can think of little else. I'm sure you've concocted a story that you think will convince me to let you leave. Might as well save your breath. I'm not hearing it."

I walked slowly down the rest of the stairs, stopping at the bottom to meet her eyes. "You've been so kind to me. I will forever be grateful, but—"

"Not listening to it," she interrupted, holding up her hand. "I said to save your breath. You're gonna sit and have breakfast, and I'm gonna tell you what's going to happen." She started toward the kitchen. "Are you a coffee or tea drinker in the mornings?"

Unable to think of anything I could possibly say to this woman, I replied, "Coffee, please."

She glanced back over her shoulder and gave me an approving nod, as if I had chosen correctly. I hadn't been aware that was a test, but it felt as if it had been in a way.

The delicious smell of things I hadn't eaten in a long time for breakfast met my nose before we even made it into the large, bright kitchen.

"Bacon, Conecuh sausage, biscuits, tomato gravy, cheese grits, and scrambled eggs," she said as she walked over to the large island bar in the middle of the room. "It's not as formal as dinner was last night. Just get yourself a plate and fill it up."

Then, she picked up a plate and held it out to me. I reached for it and took in all the food that was sitting out.

"Eat all you want. King and Storm came in and ate earlier before they headed over to the ranch. Don't reckon the others are coming, or they'd have already stopped by," she said, picking up a slice of bacon and taking a bite of it.

I hadn't thought I was hungry until now, but everything looked so good and completely off the list of items I was allowed to eat. Taking a slice of bacon and a biscuit, I stopped at what I assumed was the tomato gravy. I'd never heard of it, but it smelled nice.

"Tomato gravy. My granny's recipe. It'll have you getting a second biscuit just to soak it all up."

Okay then, why not? I took the ladle and poured some over my biscuit, then took a small spoonful of the grits and some eggs. My breakfast was normally two egg whites, a half cup of blueberries, and one slice of low-carb whole wheat bread, no butter.

"Sugar and cream in your coffee?" Maeme asked.

"Uh, do you have any Splenda or Stevia?"

She grinned. "Can't say I do. But I have some fresh honey."

"Sugar will be fine," I replied, then added, "And the cream too." I always used almond milk, but I already knew that wasn't going to be in her fridge.

"Have a seat at the bar," Maeme said as she put a cup of coffee down in front of an empty stool, then went to refresh her cup.

I took the seat and waited, unsure if we were supposed to pray or not. Last night, it had seemed important, and I didn't want to insult her after she was so kind to me. She didn't add anything to her coffee, and it didn't surprise me that she drank it black. Maeme might look soft and sweet, but the woman was tough. She had controlled a room full of tall, muscular, intimidating men last night with one glance. I had expected boys, but they had all been men and older than me at that.

"Go ahead and eat up. I'll do most of the talking," she said, walking over to stand on the other side of the island from me.

No praying over breakfast. Got it.

I picked up my fork and decided I would try the biscuit with tomato gravy first. If it was terrible, I'd get it down, then wash away the taste with the items I knew I would enjoy. Besides, I needed to eat good now because I wasn't sure when I would get another chance to eat a real meal again.

"You've been abused," she began. "Your bare ring finger has a tan line. So, the bastard is your husband. I've seen this before, and I know it when I see it. No use in lying to me. You're on the run. You have no family to run to, or you would have called them already. You took off and were so desperate that you went to a service station, looking for a kind soul who could give you a ride."

My appetite was gone instantly. I placed my fork beside the plate and put my hands in my lap as I stared at Maeme.

She used her hand and motioned toward me. "Eat. You need it. You look like a strong wind would blow you away. That's part of the abuse. The control he craved. I bet his dick was small too. Anyway, I'm not going to let you leave. You need family, and you need protection. I can give you that. I can even give you a step more. There is a small cottage on the back right side of my property that backs up to the Shephards' ranch. You met their oldest son, Thatcher, last night. Our families go back to the early 1900s. Security is tight, and no one gets back there who isn't supposed to be." She paused and took a sip of her coffee, then reached to take a biscuit from the skillet.

I was speechless. All I could do was sit there and stare at her. Unable to believe what she was saying. The temptation to let her tell me what I was going to do and forget the reality of my actions yesterday was there, but I couldn't. I knew that. I couldn't help wanting to though.

"The house is furnished. It's not much, but it is clean, safe, and so far away from the road that it is basically hidden. No one has lived there in a few years, but I keep it cleaned regularly for when it might be needed. I'm going to have King come by later and move your things out there. You make a list of groceries you would like, and he will bring those too. You need to hide, and I'm going to hide you."

This was when I should tell her that I was hiding, but not from my husband. I was hiding from the police. She didn't want to harbor a fugitive—or whatever I'd made myself look like. As wonderful as this house in the woods away from the world sounded, it wouldn't be right for me to take it.

"Yes, my husband hurt me. But it's not necessarily him I am running from. It's complicated."

"I don't want to know. Your secrets are your own. I am telling you that you are a woman without a family who needs a safe place to hide. That's all I need to know. Now, eat and relax. No one is going to find you. But if I let you leave here and go to a bus station or some other crazy idea you have come up with, they'd find you. Whoever is looking. You stand out, honey. You would be back in the shit you're running from before the day was done."

I dropped my gaze to my uneaten breakfast. She was right. I would need my identification to get on a bus. My cash would run out soon. I was hurt and would be an easy target to anyone. If she was so sure she could hide me, how long would that last? I couldn't stay hidden forever, but while I was healing, I could use the time to think of a more permanent solution. Would that be so bad? No one knew I had gotten in King's truck. Or who I was. How would I be traced here? I doubted there was any connection to lead the police to this place. At least not right away. They'd need a lead, and that would take time.

"Okay," I replied, looking back up at her. The words tumbling out before I could stop them.

This was wrong, but she wasn't really leaving me any choice. I would just get myself in better shape, then leave. They'd be safe here. I wouldn't let them take the fall for my actions. I'd get out before it happened.

"Thank you. I don't know why you want to help me, but I am forever in your debt," I told her.

She walked around the island and placed her hand over mine. "God didn't bless me with a daughter. But if he had, I'd like to believe that if she was in trouble, someone would step in and help her. You need family, and that I can provide."

I felt a lump of emotion form in my throat. I'd lived my life looking for someone to give me what this woman was having to force me to accept. I nodded, unable to say anything just yet.

"Good. That's settled. You have all you want to eat. I'll get you a pen and paper so you can make a grocery list. There's not a washer and dryer at the house, but you can do all your laundry right here."

"Thank you," I whispered, feeling as if I would never be able to say those words enough.

She smiled, then took another drink from her cup.

Voices suddenly broke the silence, and she set her cup down. "Reckon Thatcher and Wells are coming to eat after all."

As she walked over to take down more plates, King walked in the room, followed by Thatcher and Wells, just as she had predicted. King's eyes met mine, and he smiled. When he entered a place, it was as if he had this magnetic pull that came with him. The mood lightened, and everything seemed to revolve around him.

"Good morning," he said, making his way over to me. "Maeme talked you into staying yet?" he asked, then picked up my untouched bacon from my plate and took a bite.

"If you take one more thing off her plate, I'll toss your cocky butt out of my kitchen," Maeme scolded him.

He winked at me, then took another bite.

• NINE •

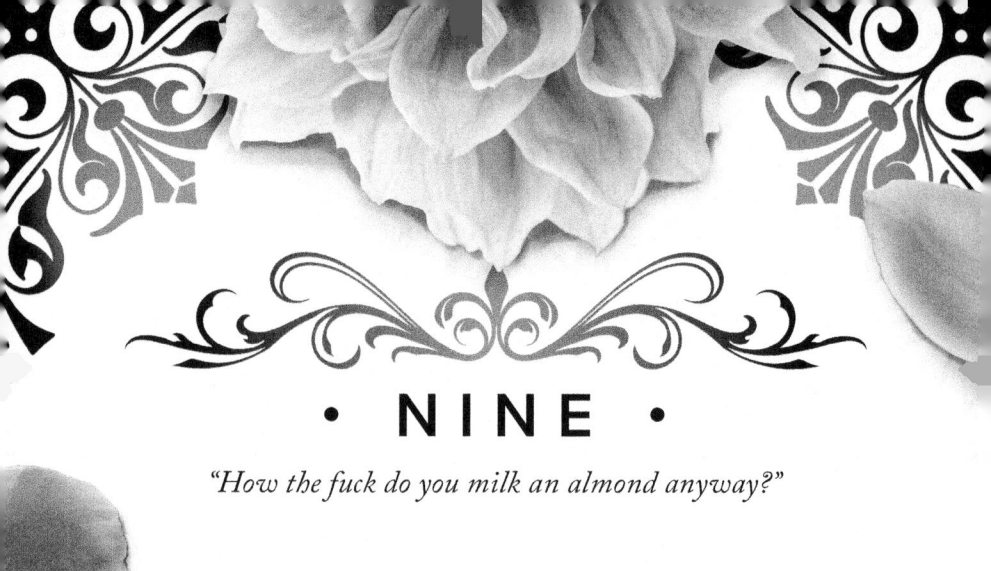

"How the fuck do you milk an almond anyway?"

RUMOR

Hidden back in the thick of pecan trees sat a white clapboard house with a front porch. Maeme's house couldn't even be seen from back here. Maeme had told me its floor plan was a shotgun house, and I had no idea what that meant, but I was looking forward to finding out. The front porch was tiny with enough room for the single rocking chair and a little side table that had a lantern on it.

"Here it is," King said. "What do you think? I know it's small—"

"It is perfect," I breathed, reaching for the door handle as his truck came to a stop.

"I wouldn't go that far. She did tell you it doesn't have a dishwasher."

I laughed then, and the sound was foreign to my own ears. "I don't care. I will happily wash the dishes."

I pushed open the truck door, ready to jump down and go look inside. I couldn't remember the last time I had been excited about anything. But this…this was almost as if Maeme had plucked the image out of my dreams and placed it here. I just needed a dog now. Not that I would get one. I couldn't stay forever.

"Whoa, wait a second. Let me help you down. Broken rib, remember?" King said as he got out of the truck, then made his way around to my door.

He held out a hand, and I noticed a black leather bracelet on his wrist as I slipped my hand into his for the extra support stepping down. I let go of him the moment I was on the ground. His grip wasn't painful, but it was strong. He was twice the size of Hill. Taller, broader, more in shape. He had to work out. Lift weights.

"I'll grab your suitcase. You can go on ahead and check it out. It's unlocked."

I didn't hesitate as I made my way along the pea gravel drive to the paver stones that led to the porch steps. There were four of them. My lips ached from the smile I couldn't keep from spreading across my face. Reaching for the outer screen door, I opened it before taking the doorknob of the heavy wooden door. I fought back a giddy laugh as I went inside.

The first room that greeted me was a yellow-and-white kitchen. It was bright and cheery. There was a refrigerator to the left, along with a sink and just enough counter space for the dish drainer to sit. The stovetop-and-oven combo completed that side. In the center of the room was a round table with a ceramic tile top and two mismatched chairs. Then, on the right was what looked like a wood-burning stove, and the window on that side of the room had an air-conditioning unit in it.

The screen door opened behind me, and I turned to see King walking inside with my suitcase and a bag of groceries.

He seemed so out of place in the small kitchen as he grinned at me and raised his eyebrows. "Well? What do you think?"

I let out a soft laugh. "It is beautiful."

He set down the groceries on the table, then nodded his head to the wooden stove. "That's the only source of heat in the house. There is a shed just out the back door, full of dry wood for it. If you need help working it, I can give you a lesson." Then, he pointed to the window unit. "You have two of these. One in here and one in the bedroom. They can keep it nice and cool in the summer. You'll find opening the front door and the back door in the fall and spring will allow a breeze to blow straight through the place, keeping it a pleasant temp. That's what the screen doors are there for."

I nodded, already loving the idea of fresh air in the house, but not sure if I would be able to have unlocked doors while inside.

He tilted his head toward a quaint arched doorway that was directly across from the front door. "That takes you right into the living room."

Ready to see more, I walked into the next part of the house. The overstuffed green sofa was the only seating in the room and sat against the far-right wall, just underneath the windows. A coffee table and a twenty-inch television that was on top of what I think used to be the bottom half of a vanity table were the only other pieces of furniture in the room. The rug in the center of the room covered most of the hardwood.

"Rug is new. Maeme had me bring it over this morning. The hardwood gets fucking cold in the winter. The house doesn't sit on a concrete slab, so the cold air blowing under the house can freeze your feet when the temps drop."

I figured King was exaggerating, but I appreciated the fluffy blue rug nonetheless.

Just like with the arched doorway, there was another one directly lined up with the front door. If you stood at the front door in the kitchen, you'd be able to look right through to the back door of the house. King motioned for me to continue on as he picked up my suitcase and started that way.

It led right into the bedroom. A white iron-framed queen-size bed with a chenille coverlet—which had pink, blue, and yellow daisies on it—was in the middle of the room under two windows that overlooked miles of green grass, a building out in the far distance, and horses. There were several horses. I walked over to the windows to see the horse closest to me in a round pen with a man out there with him. They seemed to be circling each other. I'd never seen anything so beautiful. The dark brown horse was huge.

"That's the ranch. Shephard Ranch, to be exact. Thatcher's family owns it. You'll see them out there, working with the horses, pretty regularly," King informed me.

"The horse is gorgeous."

King chuckled. "Thoroughbreds are beautiful creatures."

I studied the rest of the room. In the far-right corner sat a clawfoot tub with a showerhead and a curtain that wrapped all the way around it. A pedestal sink and white wicker shelves for bathroom supplies were to its left. Thankfully, there was a closed-off corner with an actual door that held the toilet. The idea of using the bathroom in my bedroom, even if no one else lived with me, would have been odd. Another window air-conditioning unit was in the bottom half of the window that looked into the backyard.

The other side of the room had a white dresser with three drawers.

King walked over and opened a small closet on the opposite side of it.

"This won't fit much, but you have the extra rack space there." He nodded toward the clothing rack that stood beside it. On each side of the bed were round tables. One held a lamp, and the other was just the right size for a book to sit and maybe a glass of water at night.

The back door to the house was on the other side of the clothing rack. King unbolted the lock and swung it open.

"Wood is right there," he said, then stepped back for me to look out.

There was a concrete stoop with three steps, and to the right sat the small shed that held the wood. Behind the house were more lines of pecan trees, then a wooden fence stopped them about one hundred yards away. More of the Shephard Ranch, I assumed.

"You think you can be happy here?" King asked me.

I looked out over the property. It was stunning. I would be tucked away in my own little haven.

"I love everything about it," I said, feeling so many emotions that it was almost overwhelming.

"Good. I'll go get the rest of your groceries," King replied behind me.

I listened as he walked back through the house and took another deep breath of the fresh air before stepping back inside and closing the door. I looked at the bolt, and although I felt like I was safe out here, I wouldn't be leaving the doors open for the breeze. I locked the door back up firmly, then headed back to the kitchen.

King brought in two more bags and was heading back to his truck. He couldn't be getting more. I'd given Maeme a very short list of necessities. They would have fit in one bag. The eighty dollars I had left with the list wouldn't have covered three bags full of groceries.

Opening the first bag, I looked inside to see the blueberries that I had put on my list, along with apples, oranges, strawberries, raspberries, and grapes, which had not been on my list. All this fruit alone would have cost almost eighty dollars. Frowning, I turned to the next bag to find my egg whites and wheat bread I had put on the list, along with a dozen eggs that I hadn't.

King walked back inside with two more full paper grocery bags. I stared at them, then at him as he set them down with the others.

"I didn't order all this. I only gave Maeme eighty dollars. This is all way more than that."

King shrugged. "The list was too short. You need more than that. I looked at what you wanted and used it as an idea of what you liked. Then added a few things you should have put on there. Like the Oreos and real milk."

"What? How much did all this cost? And I ordered the almond milk. What if I have a dairy allergy?" Which I didn't, but that wasn't the point.

"You ate the cornbread with butter on it last night. Both of those had dairy in them," he replied with a smirk. "And I saw you eating the cheese grits at breakfast. Dairy. Not to mention, you had creamer in your coffee. The only creamer Maeme has is dairy. You can't properly eat Oreos without real milk. How the fuck do you milk an almond anyway? It just sounds nasty."

I sighed. "Okay, fine. I can have dairy, but this…this is a lot of food. How much did it cost?" I was trying to be frugal. This was not being frugal.

"Doesn't matter. Take it up with Maeme if you have a problem with it. She paid for it, and good luck getting her to let you give her any more money."

I peeked into the next bag, and there were the Oreos he'd spoken of, along with a multitude of other items I hadn't asked for. "This is too much food for one person, King."

He frowned. "No, it's not. You don't have to eat it all today. Pace yourself."

I would not get upset about this. It was done, and I needed to be thankful. Let it go. If this was what Maeme wanted, then there wasn't much I could do to stop her. She had made it clear that when she wanted something, she got it. And I couldn't even be upset about that. This house was more than I would have ever dreamed up in a million years.

"One more thing," King said and pulled out a phone from his pocket, then held it out to me. "You need a phone. My number is in there, and so is Maeme's. It's untraceable, and before you argue with me, this is something Maeme ordered. You might as well take it."

I reached out and took the phone from him. "Thank you, really. I know I've been difficult, but I have reasons. I just didn't want to bring anyone else into my mess. But I appreciate it."

He smiled then. That distracting one he had. The one in the photos on the wall at Maeme's. "You're welcome, sweets. If you need anything, call."

I nodded, and then he turned and headed out the door. Leaving me here in my new sanctuary. It all seemed too good to be true. I'd never known people this kindhearted existed in the world. I just had to be sure I didn't take advantage of it. I would do everything I could to make it up to Maeme and King.

But first, I was going to settle into my temporary home.

· TEN ·

*"They see your cocky ass coming
a mile away."*

KING

Sitting across from the man who had been the cause of my name, I took a drink of the whiskey in my glass.

Barrett Kingston, Storm's father, had made a bet with my father thirty-four years ago that my dad lost. Technically, my dad was supposed to name me Kingston because he'd lost to Barrett, but my mother had been furious, seeing as she had planned on naming me Bash. In the end, she had settled for King. It was one of those stories I'd heard a million times, and I couldn't say I was mad about it. I liked my name. What kind of fucking name was Bash anyway?

"Where is Stellan?" my father asked as he stepped into Stellan Shephard's office.

He seemed annoyed that we had all been called here, and Stellan not being here yet was going to be an issue.

"Pour yourself a drink and stop scowling, Ronan," Barrett said to him. "Stellan is on his way. He went in the lead car that escorted Blaise back to the airstrip. Before you ask about their whereabouts, Thatcher and Storm are in the follow car, and Monte is in the library, downloading files that Wilder sent him."

Dad sighed and shrugged out of his jacket, then made his way to the bar, only giving me a brief nod as he passed. I didn't bother to respond. I just took another drink and cut my eyes over to Wells, who was arguing with his father, Roland, about the fact that his younger brother, Teller, wasn't more involved yet in the family business. Teller was only nineteen, and, sure, we'd had to step up at that age, but why make Teller? He could actually enjoy college without the stress of the life he'd been born into just yet. Wells saw it differently though. He'd not gotten to finish his four years at the University of Alabama as QB one because of his responsibilities to the family. He was still fucking bitter about it too.

"Maeme tells me that the wife was abused regularly," Dad said, taking the seat to my left.

I turned my attention to him. "Yeah, the X-ray is fucking brutal."

Dad's scowl deepened. "Should have let Thatcher kill the bastard."

"He will, but first, we need to get the money," Barrett pointed out.

"We got all his money and his wife. A week is more time than he should have been given," Dad replied.

"We left him bleeding out, Dad. He can't do much at the moment. He's in the hospital," I reminded him.

Dad took a drink, then put a cigar in his mouth to light it. "Pansy-ass," Dad said, his teeth clenched around the cigar.

"We also need more information from him," Barrett added. "We need names, other properties he sold and profited from that he didn't own."

"We can find that out while he's strung up in the cellar," Dad said.

Barrett shrugged like that was a given. Which it was. I myself was looking forward to getting my own revenge on Churchill Millroe. I wasn't going to tell them that though. They'd get the wrong idea and assume I was planning on fucking Carmella Millroe—or Rumor, as she wanted to be called. It was her name before she changed it after all. But Beauregard wasn't. She'd thrown that name out there, and I was curious as to where she'd gotten it from. I couldn't exactly ask her that though.

"Maeme has her settled in the shotgun house then?" Roland asked, walking over to us and leaving Wells looking annoyed.

I nodded. "Yeah. She seems less like a flight risk now. She likes the place. Doesn't mean she won't try and run as soon as she's healed."

"She's strung tight," Wells said. "Even with Casanova over there."

I smirked. "I got her here, didn't I?"

Wells shrugged. "Yeah, but Maeme made her stay. You had nothing to do with that. Losing your touch with old age. I might have to step up and take your place as Prince Charming."

Barrett chuckled. "You might have the looks, kid, but you don't have the charm. They see your cocky ass coming a mile away. King here has the talent to hide it."

The door opened, and Storm came inside, followed by Thatcher. They were laughing about something—well, Storm was, and Thatcher had a small tug on his lips, which was as close to amused as he got. Storm's gaze met mine, and he grinned bigger.

"There's Mr. Wonderful," he said.

I raised my eyebrows. "Glad you finally realized it," I replied.

He laughed and shook his head. "Not me. I know you're an asshole, but it seems our hurt little sparrow is blinded by that pretty-boy face of yours."

I straightened in my seat and studied him. "What are you talking about?"

He glanced over at Thatcher, who was headed to the bar, not at all interested in the conversation. He sank down on the seat to my right and sighed. "Well, Maeme sent me back to the cottage with an apple pie she had made for Rumor—that's what we are supposed to call her, right?"

I nodded and narrowed my eyes, wanting him to finish whatever he was going to say.

"She wouldn't open the door for me. Talked to me through the damn door. Asked where you were in fact. Told me to leave or she would call you. If we hadn't been called here, I might have sat down on that rocking chair and let her call you. That would have been a fun little turn of events."

"Don't fuck around with her. She's been abused, and she's scared shitless."

I glared at him. He knew this. We all did. Why didn't he take it more seriously? She needed to be handled delicately.

"And you don't fuck around with her either—even if she wants you to," he replied, wagging his eyebrows at me.

"I don't plan on it. She might be married to a goddamn narcissistic bastard, but she's still married. I don't do drama and baggage."

"She'll be a widow in about a week," Thatcher said, leaning back against the edge of the desk and crossing his ankles.

I gave him a warning look. He would never take the time to even attempt to gain her trust. But I didn't like the insinuation. That got a deep chuckle out of him.

"We have real shit to discuss. We aren't here to talk about pussy," Roland said just as the door opened, and Wilder's father and Roland's older brother, Monte, walked inside.

Monte held up some papers in his hands. "Got what we needed. His accounts have been drained, and all his money is sitting in one of our accounts in Switzerland. He'll find out soon enough."

"Guess we will be torturing and killing sooner rather than later," Thatcher drawled, looking entirely too pleased.

"Bloodthirsty, brother? You just shot the man two days ago," I pointed out, not that I wasn't ready to hear Churchill beg for his life and wail in agony.

Thatcher cut his gaze to mine. "Don't act like you aren't ready for her to be a widow."

I stood up. "I want her free of that piece of shit, and I want him to pay. But that's it."

He smirked. "Sure. That's all you want."

I wasn't going to argue. He was trying to bait me. I knew him too well. Unlike the younger guys, who always fell for his shit and let him get them worked up, I was unphased. Instead, I just chuckled and shook my head before going to fill up my glass. Our meeting had just been extended.

"Boss made it clear—no one fucks her," Monte said, his eyes leveled on me.

Fine. I hadn't planned on it.

ELEVEN

*"I didn't like men.
I wanted to stay clear of them."*

RUMOR

I had spent the last four days tucked away in the little cottage, and I'd found more than just my body healing. The peaceful beauty was good for my soul. I knew this was temporary, but I clung to the serenity, soaking it in and hoping it was enough before I had to leave it behind.

Maeme had stopped by every day with something she'd made. I had more food than I would ever eat, but I found myself being able to enjoy it without fear of gaining a pound or two.

Yesterday, I had even braved going outside for a walk. There were two horses out for me to watch from afar. The breeze was cool, but the warm sunshine made it the perfect weather. The trees were already green, and the grass was lush and felt like velvet under my bare feet. It'd felt as if I were in a utopia, created in my own imagination.

The first two nights, I had feared I would wake up and this all would have been a dream.

This morning, when I had opened my eyes to hear the birds chirping and the sunshine pouring through the windows, I had smiled so big that my lip stung. The swelling in it was gone, but where it had broken open was still on the mend. Walking into the cheery yellow kitchen, barefoot, wearing whatever I wanted, and making my own cup of coffee with no fear—it'd made me want to weep with joy. If only I could stay in this house like this forever. It would be a perfect life.

I couldn't let myself think like that. It was hard not to, but I knew this would come to an end. Staying would never be an option. If I pretended like it was, it would be harder in the end.

Taking my cup of coffee, I stepped out onto the front porch with a shawl over my shoulders I had found at the top of the bedroom closet. Sitting out here with the fresh morning air was becoming my favorite thing to do. Especially after waking up.

I just sat down and got comfortable when I saw the front of a familiar truck heading down the path toward the house. Running back inside to hide from King the way I had with the others would be rude. I didn't know them. I'd only met them that first night at Maeme's. Technically, I didn't really know King either, but he had swooped in to save me when I had no one. I was here in this perfect corner of the world because of him.

His truck came to a stop a few feet in front of the house, and I watched as he stepped down from the shiny black Chevy. That smile of his spread across his face, and he gave me that head nod he was so good at, then tilted his cowboy hat back on his head so that I could see his eyes before he headed toward me.

"Morning," he called out.

I pulled the shawl closer together over my tank top. I didn't have on a bra yet, and I didn't want to appear inappropriate.

"Good morning," I replied.

King put one boot on the first step and leaned his elbow on the railing. "You seem to be settling in just fine," he said. "House treating you good?"

I nodded. "Yes. It's wonderful."

His smile spread. "Good. Glad to hear it. I know Maeme has been bringing you food, but I was gonna see if you wanted to go with me to her house for breakfast. Sunday morning, she normally does it up right. She even makes these homemade waffles that are so damn fluffy and soft that you can't stop at just one."

I tensed. Maeme's house and meals meant the others. I hadn't seen them since Thatcher and Storm had brought the apple pie over. I'd been rude, but they had surprised me. I didn't trust Thatcher. He was different. Terrifying really. In a way I couldn't quite label. Seeing them after that didn't sound appealing at all. I just wanted to stay here, alone.

"I think it is better if I don't. I would be in the way, and if it's a family meal, I shouldn't—"

"If I go back and tell Maeme what you are about to say, she's gonna drive back here herself and haul you to her house. Now, don't make it hard on me. She sent me to get you, and I don't want to let her down. Those waffles sure are something, and you can't stay back here alone all the time. It'll be good for you to be around folks. Visit."

He was hard to tell no, but I had a feeling he knew that. It was probably why Maeme had sent him. He hadn't come back here to get me of his own free will. When he had picked me up at the service station and given me a ride, I doubted he had known he'd end up being sent to convince me to do things all the time. It made me feel guilty.

Sighing, I nodded. "Okay. Let me just go inside and change."

I stood up, and it was hard not to notice the way his eyes traveled down my body.

I wrapped the shawl tighter around me and hurried into the house. I knew every flaw my body had. Hill had made sure of it. He pointed out my problem areas and told me the exercises I needed to do to fix them. Although they were never fixed. He'd always blamed me for not trying hard enough. The sleep shorts I was wearing revealed too much leg. Having King look at my legs made me feel exposed. I hadn't thought about it when I wore my sundress, but then I hadn't caught him looking.

Reminding myself that I did not care what King thought of me or my body, I tried to focus on getting dressed quickly. I grabbed my jeans and a long-sleeved blouse. I would have to change later when the day was warmer, or I would sweat in this. But for now, I needed it. Slipping on my shoes, I headed back out to the front porch.

King was waiting on me right where I'd left him. He smiled brightly, then tilted his head toward the truck. "Let's go eat," he said before walking that way.

I followed behind as he went to the passenger door and opened it for me. His hand was already held out for me to take, palm up. Even his calluses were attractive. His hands were big, tanned, and used to hard work. Hill's hands had been smooth and unblemished. He got manicures and pedicures regularly to keep them from looking bad. Yet those soft hands had hurt me painfully so many, many times. How much more damage could hands like King's do?

When I lifted my eyes to look up at him, he smiled, and there was a kindness there in those turquoise depths that was unmistakable. Could he ever hurt a woman? After being raised by someone like Maeme? She wouldn't have allowed such behavior. Unlike Hill's mother, who I'd been told adored him when she had been alive. I'd never met her, but he spoke of her as if she had worshipped him and I should do the same. Maeme loved King, but she did not worship him. There was a difference. I'd witnessed it the little time I had seen them together.

I slipped my hand into his, and he helped me into the truck, making it almost too easy. Once he had my door closed, my gaze followed him. King Salazar was too perfect. There had to be a flaw somewhere. Yet even the way he carried himself, with a confidence I envied, was attractive.

I dropped my eyes to my lap when he opened his door and climbed inside the truck. Letting the scent that I was beginning to associate with King—cedar and cinnamon—appeal to my senses wasn't helping matters.

I had to stop this…this…whatever it was I found myself doing. King was a man. I didn't like men. I wanted to stay clear of them. I didn't trust anyone stronger than me. Perhaps it was just the fact that he'd rescued me in a sense. I was drawn to him because he had led me to my first safe place. I didn't live in fear here, and it was all because he had given me a ride.

That had to be it. Letting myself dwell on him in any way was pointless—not to mention unhealthy. King was friendly. Nothing more. I didn't need to develop any fixation where he was concerned. I knew I was damaged, and I'd read about how someone who had been in my position could get confused when faced with kindness.

"What have you been doing out here all day?" he asked me, breaking the silence.

"Reading, cleaning, enjoying the peacefulness."

He glanced at me. "Reading? Maeme has a library in the house. Do you want me to take you to it so you can pick out some books?"

I had brought two books with me, and I had found one book in the cottage. Having something new sounded wonderful. I stared over at him, and he was smiling. My heart did a little flutter thing in my chest, and I fisted my hands in my lap. I had to stop that.

"Yes, please. If she wouldn't mind, that is. I would bring them back and take very good care of them."

He chuckled, and why that sound was so appealing I didn't want to think about too deeply.

"Maeme will be fucking thrilled you want to use her library. You can come and go as much as you like. I'm not big on reading, but she sure as hell wanted me to be."

Not big on reading. That right there should be a flaw. Unfortunately, I couldn't make myself like the man any less because of it.

· TWELVE ·

*She didn't know the need I had
for owning someone.*

KING

Maeme's dining room table could fit twenty people. The only time it was full was on Sunday mornings. Not everyone made it for breakfast. If they did, twenty places would not be enough. However, it was rare that all twenty spots weren't filled. Sometimes, the stools at the kitchen island bar were also full. The youngest were always sent to the kitchen.

Seeing all the vehicles outside, I already knew who would be inside before we walked through the door. Voices carried through the house, and when Rumor stepped inside, she immediately moved closer to me, her body strung so tightly that it was hard to miss.

I placed a hand on her shoulder. "I know they're loud, but everyone is family. It'll be fine. I promise," I assured her.

My words did little good. She didn't move away from me. In fact, she seemed to move in even more so. I couldn't say I disliked it either. Knowing she trusted me enough to touch me was sure as hell different than when she had been skittish around me.

With my hand now on her back I leaned down close to her ear. "I swear you're gonna be okay, sweets."

She nodded and continued to stare straight ahead while she stayed pressed close to my side. A deep laugh I recognized as Barrett's caused her to flinch. As much as I was enjoying her borderline clinging to me, it made me fucking furious that she'd been abused. The sick bastard who had done this to her was going home from the hospital tomorrow. He wouldn't be there long though. We were waiting on him.

"There are a lot of people," she whispered, looking toward the direction of the dining room.

"Yeah. Always is on Sundays. It won't be the entire family, but at least half. Maybe more."

A slight tremor went through her body. I wouldn't have even noticed it if my hand hadn't been resting on her back. This was becoming more difficult than I would have imagined. And not just for her. I was struggling with it myself. The idea of forcing her to go face everyone while she was this fucking terrified about it wasn't appealing me to me either. Part of me wanted to take her back to the damn cottage and leave her there, where she was happy. She clearly felt safe there.

The front door opened behind us, and Rumor jumped, startled, then plastered herself to my side, grabbing my shirt in her small fist in the process. As if I might leave her here. I glanced from her trembling body to see Storm walking inside. His eyes went from her to me. Amusement curled his lip, and I glared at him. This was not the time for his fucking jokes.

"You remember Storm," I told her in a gentle tone.

She nodded but just barely.

"Everything okay?" he asked, raising an eyebrow at me.

"Yeah. We will be in there shortly," I informed him. Hoping he took the clue and left us.

He glanced back at Rumor. "Okay," he replied, then walked away from us.

Once he was out of sight, Rumor's body slightly eased, and she let out a small gasp, then released my shirt, dropping her hand quickly. Even though she wasn't looking at me, I could see the blush on her cheeks. She hadn't even realized she had a death grip on me. Not that I was complaining. She didn't know the need I had for owning someone. My master kink when it came to fucking. She was playing to it, and my body was reacting. I had to stop that shit.

I studied Rumor while I thought it over. Sure, I liked it. Her needing me. Typically, I didn't like my females clingy, but this wasn't the same. I was finding I enjoyed this. Knowing that she trusted me and I was the one she was pressed up against. Fuck. This was probably going to mess me up. But what the hell was I supposed to do about it? I sure as shit wasn't going to push her away. She was hurt far deeper than the physical injuries to her body. This had to be dealt with gently. She was fragile.

And, yes, while she could trust me to protect her, that was all she needed to be trusting me to do. Because at the end of the day, I would never touch her. I needed things that she couldn't handle. Dark things that someone with her emotional damage would never be able to understand. I'd also manipulated and lied to her to get her here.

"Everyone in that dining room, I trust. I would never take you somewhere I thought you would be in danger. Maeme trusts them. You're safe, Rumor."

She took a deep breath and moved back away from me just enough so that we were no longer touching. I missed the way she felt against me, and I had to fucking get that shit out of my head. Wasn't happening.

"Okay," she replied, then lifted her eyes to meet mine.

The trust shining in them tightened my chest uncomfortably. Jesus Christ. This shit had gotten tricky real fucking fast.

Pressing my hand on her back, I nodded my head toward the dining room. "Let's go get some of those waffles I told you about."

She smiled then, and it took every ounce of my self-control to tear my gaze off her and start walking. Leading her to a room full of people. I was going to hand her off to Maeme, then get some space. Far enough away that I didn't smell her sweet scent that reminded me of vanilla.

THIRTEEN

"That library needs to be put to use."

RUMOR

The long dining room table was full, and it sounded as if there were also people in the kitchen. King had placed me beside Maeme and a lady who introduced herself as Annette Kingston. She was married to Barrett, and they were Storm's parents. That much I could remember. The others, however, started to get confusing. Except for Ronan Salazar. King's father. He was nothing like his son. In fact, he was intimidating and unfriendly-looking.

Maeme spoke to him as if he were one of the younger men she called the boys. He was her son after all, but it still surprised me. His icy gaze made me even more nervous than I already had been. I tried my best not to look in his direction, but it was hard because King was two seats over from him, and I found myself wanting to look at King. Even though he had dropped me off with Maeme and basically gone to the farthest end of the table away from me, not giving me a backward glance.

I tried not to think about it too much. Facing a crowd was something I had never been good with, even before Hill. But life with Hill had made it almost unbearable. I hated that about myself. I wanted to be normal. If only I could smile, have confidence, enjoy life instead of wanting to hide in the shadows and go unnoticed.

"Sorry I'm late! Traffic from Atlanta was a bitch," a female said, and I turned my attention to the blonde walking into the room. She was stunning. As in thick, long platinum hair, big blue eyes, full, pouty pink lips.

"Language, Lela!" Maeme scolded.

The blonde swung her gaze to Maeme, and she smiled brightly. "Yes, ma'am," she replied, and even her voice had a sexy timbre to it.

"I didn't know you were coming, darling," Annette Kingston said beside me. The pleased tone in her voice was clearly affection.

"I wanted to surprise you," Lela replied, then walked over and bent down to kiss Annette on the cheek. "Surprise, Momma."

Momma. Lela was Storm's sister. Much younger sister, I guessed. She still had the youthful glow to her. Life hadn't handed her any struggles yet. But then seeing as she belonged to this family, I wasn't sure it ever would.

Lela then stepped over and wrapped her arms around Barrett Kingston's neck and pressed a kiss to his head. "Hey, Daddy," she said as he reached up and patted her arm.

She turned then, and her eyes locked on me. I saw the curiosity as she stood back up.

"A new face that I don't know," she said.

"This is Rumor," her mother informed her. "She's a guest of Maeme's, staying out at the shotgun house for a while." Then, Annette turned to me. "Rumor, this is my oldest daughter, Lela."

Lela's lips curled up on each side. "I wish I didn't have to go back to Atlanta so soon." She glanced over the table, then back to me. "Things should get interesting around here."

"Go on and get you a plate. Nailyah and Teller are in the kitchen, eating with Birdie. There's a stool left for you," Maeme told Lela.

Lela beamed. "Birdie is here!"

"The brat hasn't even come in here to see me yet. I didn't know she was here," King said, pushing back his chair and standing up.

Lela tilted her head and gave King a smile that made my stomach knot up. "Before she gets all your attention, I'd better get some."

King walked over to Lela and wrapped an arm around her neck, then pressed a kiss to the top of her head. "Come on, gorgeous. Tell me about college life," he told her. "I want to hear all the good shit too."

They left the room, and Annette sighed contentedly beside me. "I have all my kids home today."

"Ah, Mom. I didn't know you were expecting me to come visit," Storm drawled. "I feel so wanted."

"You have work to do," Barrett replied. "You know what she means. You're all in Madison. Not an invite to come to my house."

"Barrett"—Annette's voice sounded angry—"our son is always welcome at his home."

"He eats our food and puts his feet on the goddamn furniture like he owns the place."

"Barrett!" Maeme scolded. "The Lord's name is never to be used in vain at my house. You know that."

My gaze swung back to the door that King had walked through with Lela. I wondered who Birdie was and how long he would be gone. Then, I realized I was obsessing over it and tried to shut it out. This wasn't my business. I had to remember not to dwell on King and what he did.

Conversation picked up again, and I took another bite of my food. The waffles were as delicious as King had promised, but I found myself missing my cottage, the more I sat there. I felt out of place. I kept my head down and finished my food, surprising myself with how much I had eaten. When King came back in the room, I heard him talking, but I didn't look at him—or anyone for that matter.

"Ready to go check out the library?" King asked close to my ear.

I jerked my head, snapping up from being startled. I hadn't known he had stood up, much less was behind me.

"Don't scare her to death," Maeme snapped at him. "Sneaking up on folks."

I took the napkin from my lap and placed it on the empty plate, then stood up.

When I reached to pick up my plate, Maeme placed her hand over it. "No. Leave it. You go on with King and pick out as many books as you'd like. That library needs to be put to use."

Ready to escape the room, I thanked her for the meal, then followed King from the room. This time, he didn't touch my back, and I found that I missed that. When he had done it earlier, I'd felt secure. I couldn't blame him for being careful not to touch me this time. I'd all but mauled him when Storm arrived. He was probably afraid I'd do it again.

"That wasn't so bad, was it?" he asked as we crossed the foyer and made our way over to the other side of the house.

I hadn't enjoyed it, but I'd survived, unscathed.

"It was a lovely meal," I replied.

"Sitting beside Annette was purposely organized by Maeme. She's good with reading people and knowing what makes them comfortable."

I thought back to the meal, and I could see that. She hadn't pushed too much and had been careful to give me space, but not make me feel unwelcome.

"Whereas Luella—she was the blonde across from me, Wells's mom—she's got no fucking filter. Clueless to anyone else or anything unless it affects her."

I hadn't studied the table closely, but I had listened to conversations. I knew who he was talking about simply because her voice stood out. She'd been louder and very focused on herself.

"Annette was very nice," I agreed.

King shot me a crooked grin, then opened the door we had stopped at. When he stepped back and waved his hand for me to enter, my eyes locked on the inside. Books covered the walls from floor to ceiling. There was even one of those rolling ladders attached so that you could reach the top shelf.

"This is amazing," I breathed as I went past him and into the library.

Inhaling deeply, I felt a smile spread across my face so big that it hurt my still-sore lip. I didn't care. I was happy. I was ecstatic. There were thousands of books in here. It would take me a decade to get through all of them. Not that I would be here that long, but the thought of a never-ending supply was the most wonderful thing I could think of.

"Fuck," King muttered, and I spun around to see what was wrong.

He was studying me with a stunned look on his face. I wondered if my lip had started to bleed and reached up to check, but it felt fine.

"This makes you happy," he said, and then a soft expression touched his face.

I nodded. "Yes, it does." I let my eyes wander over the titles and colorful bindings. "It's the most beautiful thing I've ever seen."

"Yeah," he whispered, then cleared his throat. "Go on and take as much time as you'd like. Stay all day if you want to. If I'm gone when you're done, Maeme will drive you back."

Before I could respond, he was almost out the door. I opened my mouth to thank him and say goodbye, but he was already closing it behind him.

Had I done something wrong? Or was he just in a hurry?

It didn't matter. I was here. In my own little heaven.

FOURTEEN

"The little shithead was entertaining."

KING

Glancing back at Storm and Sebastian, who were covering the main floor, I found myself wanting to study the place. There was no reason for me to want to explore the fucking house. At least not one I wanted to admit. But I was curious. This was where Rumor had spent the past fifteen months of her life. This had been her home. One that had been a hell for her.

Turning my attention back to the stairs, I followed behind Thatcher, who was taking them two at a time, as if he was in a hurry to get this over with. He was always the bloodthirsty one, but I had to agree with him this time. I was ready to see Churchill Millroe suffer.

A nurse was closing a bedroom door, and her back was to us. Thatcher moved quickly and wrapped the gag around her mouth before she could turn around. She began to fight back, and I slipped the cloth bag over her head as he grabbed her arms more roughly than necessary, then tied her wrists with the rope he had brought. Her muffled screams were making her inhale the soaked chloroform gag she had on, which would speed up her unconsciousness.

Throwing her over my shoulder, I headed to the nearest closet and shoved her inside, then bent down to bind her ankles before closing the door and leaving her in there.

Thatcher was already in the master bedroom, standing over Churchill Millroe, who appeared to be sleeping. This had been Rumor's bedroom too. I wondered which closet was hers. If I could get some more of her things without her questioning where they'd come from, I would. Unfortunately, my being here was something I'd never be able to tell her.

"There was a nurse downstairs and a housekeeper. Both have been sedated and tied up. Sebastian said he would take the chloroform gag off the one up here when she finally passes out," he informed me.

Which meant the only person left in the house was the man we had come for. Sebastian slapped him hard across the face, causing his head to snap to the side. Churchill's eyes flew open as he let out a strangled shout, and Thatcher slapped him even harder. He began to try and move, but his current pain medication had him so sedated that he had little control over his body. It was almost too fucking easy.

"Yo-you got your money. You got all my money!" he cried out, his body shaking as his eyes darted from Thatcher to me.

Thatcher hit him again, and blood trickled out of his nose as he began to cry. That was just pathetic. Son of a bitch was crying like a damn baby over being slapped after he beat the hell out of Rumor.

"We aren't here for the money," I told him, walking over so that he could see me clearly. I wanted my face to be one of the ones he went to hell remembering.

"Wh-what m-more do y-you want?" he stammered. "I have n-nothing else."

"Information and revenge," I replied, then grabbed his hair and jerked his head back so that his neck was at a painful angle. "But it won't be easy. It won't be quick. It will be long and agonizing." I glared down at him.

"What revenge?" he choked out, unable to talk clearly. He already knew the information we wanted.

I leaned down, inches from his face. "For Rumor."

His eyes widened even more, and I saw the understanding slowly sink in.

"You done? I'm ready to get him out of here. I'm fucking starving," Thatcher drawled.

Letting his head go, I stood back up as Thatcher tied the gag around him. I waited while he then kicked up the morphine from his IV enough to completely sedate him before unhooking it and stepping back so I could toss the bastard over my shoulder.

Sebastian was standing outside in the hall with the chloroform gag that had been on the nurse we left in the closet, swinging it around and looking bored. He glanced from me to his older brother. "Storm is out back with Wells in the Escalade."

I started down the stairs and tried not to get caught up looking at the photos on the wall or the touches I knew had been Rumor's doing. Knowing she'd lived here and what she had suffered in this house infuriated me. I wanted to begin beating the man thrown over my shoulder now. See him bleed out, listen to him beg for mercy.

Sebastian went ahead of me and opened the door to the kitchen, where he went to the fridge and grabbed a beer before going to get the back door for us. I heard him crack open the can and shook my head, unable not to smile. The little shithead was entertaining. Nothing like Thatcher. Two brothers couldn't be any more different.

The back of the Escalade opened, and I threw the bastard inside before closing it. With one last glance, I felt relief that he would never touch Rumor again. She was safe. I'd made fucking sure of it.

• FIFTEEN •

"Not sure what went wrong in his DNA."

RUMOR

I was going to take more books this time. The four I had taken Sunday only lasted for three days. I had woken up early and walked the one mile from the cottage to Maeme's. She was thrilled to see me and even insisted I have a cup of coffee with her and try one of her blueberry muffins. It was nice to feel normal. I had felt guilty about turning down her invitation to come to dinner Tuesday night. She had called me and said she'd come get me, but I had lied and said I had a headache.

Now back in the library, I wanted to inhale the smell of books, run my fingers over the bindings, and stay lost in here forever. No fear of the future or what was to come. My ribs were feeling much better, and Maeme had said the doctor was coming tomorrow to take a look at them. My lip were healing, and the bruising on my face was almost gone. All that being said, I knew my time was running out here. Soaking in every moment I had left was important. I might never have this again. A safe place to be. I didn't want to miss a moment of it.

I reached for a book on the third shelf near the left side of the door that I had noticed Sunday just as the door opened. Expecting to see Maeme, I froze when an unfamiliar face entered the room. I wasn't sure if I should scream or remain calm. Just because I had never seen him didn't mean he didn't belong here. There were a lot of people in this family of Maeme's, and I didn't quite understand all their connections, but the man was attractive. Somewhat familiar, but I wasn't sure why. I'd definitely recognize that face if I had seen it before.

The small grin that touched his lips seemed amused yet friendly. I wasn't the best at judging one's character though.

"You must be Rumor," he said, causing me to exhale in relief. He knew my name. He wasn't some stranger off the street or law enforcement, looking for Carmella Millroe. "I'm Sebastian Shephard. You've met my brother, Thatcher."

I tensed up again. Thatcher wasn't someone I wanted to be alone with, and that went for anyone closely related to him. When I took a step back, Sebastian appeared confused, and then he chuckled.

"I should have clarified that I am the sane younger brother. I'm nothing like Thatch. Not sure what went wrong in his DNA."

The way his grin crinkled the corners of his brown eyes, which were free of the troubled darkness in Thatcher's, led me to believe he was telling the truth.

"It's, uh, nice to meet you," I replied.

He glanced around the room and sighed contentedly. "This is my favorite place."

I didn't say anything, but I studied him. He seemed to be inhaling the smell of books much the way I had. Interesting.

When his eyes locked back on me, he gave me a sheepish look. "Mind if I stay? I'm here for a few more days, and I like to have something to read when I need to get away from it all."

I shook my head. "No. Not at all. Please, I will just get my books and leave you in peace."

He walked over to me, his eyes on the books in my hand. "Do you like horses, Rumor?" he asked, lifting his gaze back up to meet mine.

I shrugged. "I like to look at them. I've never been close to one or ridden one."

He narrowed his eyes, yet his smile stayed in place. "Hold on," he said, then walked across the room and scanned a row of books before pulling one out. When he turned back to me, he held it up. "Read this. I think you'll enjoy it." He told me, then placed the book on top of my others.

I looked down at the book he'd given me. "*The Ride of Her Life* by Elizabeth Letts," I read aloud, then saw that it was a true story. A memoir. I smiled before asking, "And you've read this?" It seemed very unlikely.

He blushed and lifted his shoulders in a small shrug. "Yeah. But if you tell anyone, I'll deny it."

I laughed then, surprising myself. This man was not at all what I had expected. He was at least six feet tall, muscular but leaner than King was. His lips weren't as full, but his face was handsome. He was clean-shaven, and his square jaw made the rest of his features more masculine.

I realized he was grinning at me, and I covered my mouth, feeling bad about laughing. "I'm sorry."

"No. You can laugh. I'm secure enough in my masculinity to handle it. Just make sure you keep this our little secret. The guys would use it as a weapon for their entertainment."

I nodded and held the books to my chest. "I swear to never tell a soul."

He let out an exaggerated sigh of relief. "Now, you read that, and the next time I'm back in town, I'll take you to the stables. When your ribs are better, I'll teach you to ride. You can ride Malta. She's a sweetheart and perfect for learners."

The thought of getting to ride a horse was exciting and terrifying, all at once. Although I shouldn't think about it too much. There was a good chance I would be gone by the time he visited again. I nodded and said nothing more. I didn't want to get into my having to leave soon. He'd have questions that I had no answers to. Not yet.

"Sebastian," a familiar voice said in a deep timbre that made my heart speed up.

Swinging my gaze to the door, I saw King leaning against the frame, looking at Sebastian.

"Hello, King. What brings you to the library?" he asked cheerfully.

King shifted his gaze to me. "I came to see if Rumor would like a ride back to the cottage."

Getting to be around King was too appealing to turn down. It was also concerning that I had become so happy about seeing him. It had been three days since I'd seen him last, and I would be lying if I said I hadn't thought about him every one of those days. Wondering what he was doing, where he was, if he thought of me at all. None of those being healthy things for me to be focusing on, but I couldn't seem to stop it.

"I, uh, yes, that would be nice. Thank you," I replied.

He cut his eyes back to Sebastian and gave him a smirk before straightening his stance, then walking over to me. "I'll carry the books. I was glad to see you back in here, but Maeme said you walked. You could have called me or texted. I'd have come to get you."

Don't look him in the eyes. Don't do it. I blinked and caved as I met his gaze. Those eyes of his made my stomach feel funny.

"I didn't mind the walk. It was a nice morning."

The softness in his expression made me want to curl up against him like a cat. What was wrong with me? I had to get a grip.

"It was nice to meet you, Rumor," Sebastian said, reminding me he was here. I had forgotten so easily.

How was it that King could walk into a room and immediately become the center of attention? Everyone else seemed to fade away when he was there.

Turning my gaze back to his, I smiled. "It was nice to meet you too. And thanks for the book recommendation."

He nodded his head, and King's hand touched my lower back. It was a miracle I didn't shiver under his touch.

"Later, Sebastian," King called out to him as he led me to the door.

"You sure you were ready to go? I could wait for you if you wanted to look some more."

I shook my head. "No. That's okay. I was about to leave and give Sebastian alone time, deciding on what he wanted to read."

"That was nice of you, but Sebastian can go do actual work. Like he's supposed to be doing. He doesn't have time to be reading."

I tilted my head back and looked up at King. He leaned forward then and opened the front door, not taking his hand off my back in the process. I did the best I could not to try and smell him because that would be weird.

"Can't say you're wrong about it being a pretty day," he said once we were outside. "Feels like spring."

We had another week before it was officially spring, but he was right. It did feel as if it was already here. I loved spring. The green trees, the flowers, the new life. It had always made me happy, growing up.

"As a kid spring, seemed like a hopeful time." I said the words without thinking.

"What kind of hopes did you have as a kid?" King asked me.

I hesitated, not sure how much I should share, but decided saying it to someone would feel like a release of sorts. And I trusted King. It had been a very long time since I had trusted anyone. Even Hill had worked to gain my trust, and I'd been cautious. Never telling him too much. Afraid if he knew, he'd never accept me. Want me.

"Oh, you know, to have a family. Somewhere to belong." I tried to say the words lightly but heard the heaviness in my tone.

King's hand on my back flinched, but he said nothing. I wished I could take it back. That wasn't the kind of thing he'd expected to hear. I'd overshared. Made it awkward.

"You'll have that one day. I swear it."

There was a fierceness in his tone. It almost made me believe him. Forget the facts. The truth I was pretending wasn't waiting for me. If only his words held the power to make my wish come true.

SIXTEEN

"This shit gets messy."

RUMOR

As sunny as it had been the past few days, it made the suddenly dark sky and cold wind that was blowing seem out of place. The wood-burning stove had been going since I had started it this morning. The house had been freezing when I woke up.

I walked into the living room to listen to the local weather report while wrapped in a blanket. The kitchen was much warmer, but the television was in here.

A storm was coming this way, and I wanted to think I had faced worse things than a storm alone. I didn't want to be a wimp, but the more the weather forecasters warned that it was going to be a strong one, the more nervous I seemed to be getting.

I glanced over at my phone and considered calling King. I hadn't seen him since he'd brought me back from Maeme's two days ago. He had said to call if I wanted a ride to her house, and I was starting to think maybe I did.

Chewing on my lower lip, I debated if I should or not. Maeme hadn't called me or driven down here. She must not be worried about it. Maybe I should just turn off the news and read. Forget about the weather, and it would blow over soon enough. If I fell asleep before it hit, then I could sleep through it.

The gravel crunching under tires caught my attention, and I hurried back to the kitchen just in time to see King stepping down out of his truck. I wasn't sure if I was more relieved or excited to see him. I hurried to the door to unlock it and get it open by the time he reached the top step.

It was almost unfair the way the man made a pair of boots, jeans, and a brown leather jacket look so good. I tried not to gawk at him and kept my eyes on his face. This thing I had developed for him was getting out of control. I knew better than to feel anything for a man.

"Storm's coming," he said as he walked toward me, carrying a brown paper sack in his left hand.

I stepped back and let him inside. "I know. I've been watching the weather."

My kitchen felt tiny when he was in it. His gaze went to the wood stove, and then he smiled. "I see you figured it out without help."

I nodded. "I had one like that in a…home, growing up." I had almost said *foster home* and caught myself.

"You know, I am beginning to wonder if you're ever going to need me at all. You've yet to text or call me."

I bit my bottom lip to keep from smiling like an idiot. Did that mean he wanted me to text and call him? Why was it making me so happy? Had I not just told myself I had to stop thinking about King like this? He was a man. I had to leave here soon. I could never be honest with him.

"I was considering it just now, but you showed up before I could make up my mind if I should be worried or not about the weather."

The pleased smile that made his eyes light up was not helping me with my unwanted attraction to him.

"That makes me feel needed," he replied. "It's nothing to worry about, but I thought I'd stay here until it blows over. I didn't want you riding it out alone in case the power goes out. Not that you'd mind that, but from my experience, women aren't real crazy about being alone in the dark."

I hadn't thought of that, and I wasn't sure there was a candle in this place. I hadn't looked for any. "Thank you. I don't think I'd like being out here in the dark."

"All right then, let's eat while we have light," he said, holding up the paper sack in his hand. "The best burgers and hot fries you've ever put in your mouth."

He'd brought food. Burgers and fries. He wanted me to eat burgers and fries with him. I had to stop myself before throwing my arms around his neck. Every time I thought I had this under control, he did something like this. Something no one else had ever done for me.

"I'll get some plates and set the table," I replied.

"Set the table? That's not the way you eat burgers from the Doghouse," he informed me. "These burgers must be eaten out of the bag, on the sofa, in front of the television."

I hadn't eaten anything on the sofa since I had been a kid. Smiling at the idea, I nodded. "Okay, then I'll get the drinks. I have water, milk, and orange juice. Oh, and I still have that wine that you bought with the groceries."

He smirked. "The wine."

"I don't have wineglasses here."

"Good. Bring the bottle," he called over his shoulder as he walked into the living room.

I took a deep breath and gave myself a mental scolding for going all fluttery in my chest when he was around. "It's just dinner with a friend," I whispered as I went to get the wine and a bottle opener.

Taking my time, I uncorked it before meeting him in the other room, then took out two regular drinking glasses from the cabinet.

Pausing as I entered the room, I realized I hadn't considered that we would be sitting so close on the sofa together. It was an average sofa, but the table in front of it was on the smallish side. King had taken out the burgers from the bag and placed them on the table, along with a large container of what appeared to be fries, covered in sauce and crumbled cheese. He'd stuck two plastic forks in the fries and placed them between the two burgers.

"I got plenty of napkins. This shit gets messy," he said, looking up at me.

I walked over and set the bottle between the two burgers. Then gave him one of the glasses before setting the other in front of me.

He reached for the bottle. "Too proper to just drink out of the bottle, huh?" he asked with a teasing lilt to his voice.

I shrugged. "I wasn't sure that was what you meant, and, well, I do have glasses, just not actual wineglasses."

He poured wine into my cup, filling it over halfway, before he filled his to the top. I laughed, and he cut his eyes over to me.

"What? It just keeps me from having to refill it so much."

I nodded and took my glass to take a sip.

King picked up his burger and took a large bite, then grabbed the remote control. It was hard not to just watch him. The way his jaw flexed as he chewed and the muscles in his neck moved. Why was I doing this? Men could dominate. They had the power to control. King had saved me, but hadn't I thought Hill was saving me once too? When I'd met him at the diner where I was waiting tables, wondering where I was going to sleep that night. My roommate hadn't paid her part of the rent, and I couldn't afford all of it. The landlord had given us two weeks, and my roommate had vanished during that time.

How many times had I wished he had never walked into the diner? How many times had I wished to be homeless instead of the life he had placed me in?

Yet here I was, reacting to another man in ways I never had with Hill. I was getting funny feelings in my chest. He had been showing up in my dreams. I had to get some control over it. Stop it. I was leaving soon. How easily I kept forgetting.

I began to eat while King went through the stations on the television. Then, he pressed something, and Netflix came up. I didn't know how he had done that, but it didn't really matter. I rarely watched the television. I preferred books.

"Action, romance, thriller, horror—what's your preference?" he asked me.

I finished chewing and swallowed before replying, "Doesn't matter. Whatever you want to watch."

A loud clap of thunder outside, followed by hard rain that was blowing against the east side of the house, startled me.

King raised his eyebrows. "Might not matter soon. I doubt the electricity out here holds out for long."

I continued to eat, and he put the remote down, then stood up and went to a window to observe. The lightning outside was so bright that it lit up the living room brighter than the lamp in here ever did. The thunder that trailed it was startling as it vibrated through the house.

"I'll unplug the television. Wouldn't want that to get hit," he said to me before going over to it. "Do you have anything important plugged up? Computer?"

I shook my head. The only computer I had ever been allowed to use was the desktop that Hill had put in the office. Not his office, just the office in the house. One that was rarely used.

King walked through the rest of the small house before returning to the sofa and sitting back down. "Everything looks good," he informed me, then picked up his burger. "So, what do you think of the burger?"

"It's delicious," I assured him.

His pleased grin before he took another bite was mesmerizing. Jerking my gaze off him, I stared down at my food before reaching for my glass of wine and taking a long drink.

"Weather making you nervous?" he asked.

I shrugged. "A little," I lied.

With King here, I wasn't even thinking about the weather. I was too focused on how close he was sitting, how good he smelled, and how he made me almost lightheaded when he smiled.

He took the bottle of wine and filled my almost-empty glass this time. "Drink up," he said, then nodded toward the glass. "You'll be relaxed in no time."

Wanting that to be true, I drank some more.

King took a fork and jabbed it into the fries, then held it out to me. "You haven't tried these."

Obediently, I opened my mouth, and he slipped the fork inside. I was sure I had never been fed before. It was almost as if someone was taking care of me. I liked it. I shouldn't, but I did.

His blue eyes watched me closely as I chewed. He was right; these were really good. The buffalo sauce and what I assumed was goat cheese since it didn't have a strong bite to it mixed well together. I swallowed, then smiled at him, unable not to. He looked so anxious to know what I thought.

"Wonderful," I told him, although that was probably too strong of an adjective. Being fed by him was the wonderful part.

The lights flickered as rain beat against the windows and thunder rolled across the sky.

King set the fork down and stood back up. "We are gonna need some light soon," he said, then headed in the direction of the bedroom.

I heard a door open and figured it had to be the closet. Then, I heard something else open and waited, staring at the doorway for him to reemerge. The doors closed, and then he came walking back in with two oil lamps.

He held them up. "I'll get these lit."

Those had not been in the closet. I would have seen them before.

"Where did you find those?" I asked him.

"Secret storage inside the closet," he replied before he disappeared with them into the kitchen.

I hadn't known about a secret storage inside the closet. He hadn't shown me that when he gave me the tour. Why did they have it, and what all was in it? Just lanterns? That seemed odd.

Both lanterns were lit when he returned to the living room, and he set one down on the coffee table and another on the table where the television sat. He was almost back to the sofa when the electricity went off with the newest round of thunder.

"Just in time," he said as he sank back down on the sofa beside me.

"Why is there a secret compartment in the closet?" I asked, leaning back on the sofa with my glass of wine, then crossing my legs.

King's gaze dropped to my legs a moment before lifting to my face. The mischievous gleam in his eyes made me smile.

"To keep the lanterns, extra supplies, that kind of thing," he told me, then reached for his glass of wine. "I heard Doc say your ribs are healing perfectly. How's the pain?"

The doctor had done another X-ray on Friday. Talking about it only reminded me that my time was coming to an end here. I still had no plan for what I would do next. I hadn't been able to bring myself to watch the news and see if there was anything about Hill's death, missing wife, or accusations that I had killed him. I felt as if I were living in my tiny bubble, but I knew, soon, this information was going to be on the news, and someone here was going to see it. Maeme possibly. I had to face reality and figure this out.

I took a long drink from my glass. "The pain is barely an ache now. Which means I should start planning what to do. I can't thank y'all enough for letting me stay here and helping me the way you have, but there are things…I just need to prepare to leave. Soon." Saying the words were easier than I had imagined. Perhaps it was the wine's effect on me.

King sat back up and took the bottle of wine to refill my glass. "You still plan on leaving then?"

"Yes…I can't live here, and I don't want to bring my trouble to your door."

He'd known I wasn't going to stay, but he seemed bothered by the fact that I was leaving. Reading too much into that was a path I didn't need to take, but my mind was taking it anyway.

He turned his attention back to me and studied me for a moment. "It would be a real bad idea for you to leave, seeing as your husband was found shot in his home. A colleague of his found him, but his wife, Carmella Millroe, was missing, as was his

Mercedes. He was taken to the hospital, survived. His Mercedes was found at a Buc-ee's just outside of Pensacola, Florida. Then, one day after he was sent home from the hospital, he disappeared." He paused and used his glass to point at me. "That pretty face of yours is all over the news. So is his. You leave here, and someone will recognize you."

It felt as if the blood had drained from my face as I sat, staring at him. He seemed too calm about the fact that he was housing a fugitive. Why hadn't I checked the news? Why had I convinced myself that it was okay? That if I ignored it, the facts would go away?

"I…I…you know. I should have told you the truth. Maeme… she's been so kind to me. She let me stay in her house. I need to go. I'll hide somewhere else. I can't let them come here. Bring her into this."

I started to stand up, but King placed a hand on the top of my thigh and stopped me.

"Churchill Millroe was found hours after you left. It was on the news, as was your face, the night you arrived here. Maeme doesn't miss the news. Ever."

I stared at him. She had known. They all had. Yet here I was. I shook my head, confused as to why they would allow me to just stay here.

"Why? Why would she have me stay here? If they find me here, it will incriminate her, you, everyone."

"Because you were beaten. You were the one who was hurt. And I highly doubt you shot the son of a bitch, but if you did, then he deserved it. I've told you already that this is the safest place for you. No one will get to you here. No one."

My throat burned as my eyes glazed over. They had known all along, and they believed me. They hadn't known me, but they had stepped in and helped me. Trusted that I hadn't done it. Someone cared. Several people in fact.

King reached out to me. "Come here." His voice was husky as he pulled me to him. I went willingly.

I needed the comfort. The emotions unraveling inside me were overwhelming.

When the first sob broke free of the cage I had been trying to trap it in, King wrapped his arms around me and held me against his chest. I clung to him as the pain, fear, relief, hope all released at once. I wasn't alone. For the first time in my life, I wasn't alone.

· SEVENTEEN

"I'd never been one to ignore temptation"

KING

The sobbing had grown quiet, but I wasn't ready to let go of her just yet. Getting my own fucking head straight after this was gonna be difficult. She'd been ready to leave, and Maeme had agreed that when she seemed as if she was planning on going, we had to tell her this much. It wasn't a lie exactly. Her face had been on the news, but it hadn't been in over a week. The fact that Churchill was missing was never reported. The boss had handled that with one call.

The past eleven days, she'd changed. She smiled more often. She didn't seem to be constantly tense and on edge. I'd sat and watched her out on the front porch with a book in her hands more times than I cared to admit. I enjoyed seeing her relaxed. She felt safe here, and I wanted to believe part of that was because of me. Not that any of this was something I needed to think too hard on. Rumor would always be off-limits to me. Even if Blaise hadn't made that very clear, she would never be for me. What I needed, what I wanted, was something she could never understand.

"I'm sorry." She sniffled and pulled back from me, wiping at her face.

"Don't be," I replied, unable to help myself as I reached over and got the last of her tears. "You've been through hell, and it's over. That's a lot of shit to process."

The more I had uncovered on her, the more I'd realized she wasn't fragile, like I had assumed. It takes a strong spirit to live through the abuse she'd suffered—and not just from Millroe. Her abuse had started before him. When I found the other two men at the foster families who had hurt her, I would kill them too. Slowly.

She let out a heavy sigh, then turned to look toward the windows. The storm had eased some, but the rain was still battering against the house. "How long do I stay here?" she asked, her voice just above a whisper.

"That's not something for you to worry about. You've been good here, right? It's been comfortable, and you've found things to do."

I already knew she appeared content when no one was around. There hadn't been a day when I didn't check in on her from afar.

She nodded. "Yeah," then a soft laugh escaped between her lips. It was hard not to stare at them and imagine the things I'd like to do to her mouth. "This place is wonderful. I just…I can't just stay here. I will run out of money soon, and I need to pay for rent, pay for groceries."

"Maeme doesn't need or want your money. She wants you safe. That's all. Don't get focused on all the details. Accept this and know you being back here is what she wants."

The rest she couldn't know. When she did, she'd hate me for it. She'd hate us all.

When she turned her focus back to me, it felt like someone had kicked me in the gut. The trust shining in them I didn't deserve, but, damn, I wanted to. Her sea-green eyes were so full of things they didn't need to be. Not when directed at me.

I dropped my gaze to her lips. The top one being slightly fuller than the bottom. She was naturally beautiful. I'd seen it in the photos before I met her, and even when I had found her swollen and bruised, it hadn't hidden it. Men had still flocked to her, and she'd been so clueless as to why.

Her lips parted, and a small quick intake of breath brought my attention back to her eyes, only to see she was staring at my mouth, just as I had been hers. I'd never been one to ignore temptation. I enjoyed taking what I wanted, when I wanted it.

I cupped her face and ran my thumb over her bottom lip. She shivered and leaned closer to me.

Several things ran through my head in that moment. Unfortunately, the reason why I could never touch this woman was leading the pack. I had been ordered not to, and she needed more than I would ever give her. I wanted things she couldn't handle.

The look in her eyes right now was killing me, but I'd done this. Being here and letting her see the good side of me. Pretending around her. Not letting her know who I really was. To save her from feeling any more, I had to stop this bullshit. I would not hurt her. She couldn't feel things for me. If she was starting to, then that was on me, and I had to put an end to it before it was too late. It was time she got to see the real me. Not the nice guy I was showing her.

I dropped my hands from her and moved back, unable to look her in the eyes. If she was upset, I wouldn't be able to forgive myself. This was for the best. This was what she needed even if she wasn't aware of it.

Standing, I turned to look out the window. "Storm's over. I need to go check the property," I said, breaking the silence, then focused on the door. Escaping. Getting out before I messed up even more.

EIGHTEEN

"Something a touch larger."

RUMOR

There had been no Sunday breakfast due to storm cleanup, and I wasn't sure if I was relieved that I didn't have to face King or disappointed. He'd not been back since he had run out three days ago after I thought he might kiss me. I had found myself looking for his truck and going outside more often than normal.

Yesterday, there had been someone out, riding a horse, and I had watched them for over an hour. Something about the way the rider sat on the horse reminded me of King. I had been sure it was him, but if it had been, he'd have ridden over to the fence and spoken to me, right?

I had replayed the scene on the sofa a million times, it seemed. He'd looked at me as if he was going to kiss me. He stared at my lips like he wanted to. Or had it all been in my head? Had it been me wanting him to kiss me so badly that I imagined he wanted the same? It was driving me crazy, thinking about it. If he had wanted to, wouldn't he have stayed or at least come back to see me?

None of this was making sense, and the more I worried over it, the more I began to realize it was pointless.

He knew what I'd done. He knew I was married. I shook my head, attempting to clear my thoughts. Stop thinking about King. Why would I even allow myself to think about a man after what I had lived through? It was careless.

Today, I needed to do some laundry. That was productive. It was something other than thinking about King. It would keep me from thinking about texting him. Although he had mentioned that he expected me to. Perhaps I should.

NO! I had to stop this.

I would wash the clothes, although I had to get them to Maeme's somehow. That would be a reason to contact him. But seeing as he hadn't stopped by, I feared he was avoiding me. Walking a mile, carrying my clothing, didn't sound like a good idea. I considered washing them by hand and using the clothing line out back to dry them as I stood on the front porch with my cup of coffee.

A new horse and rider were out today, and it sounded as if they were getting closer. I turned to watch and realized they were headed directly for the fence that separated us. Maybe that was him. Curious, I stepped down the stairs just as they reached the wooden barrier. The rider reached up and took off his cowboy hat, then waved at me.

Sebastian Shephard. I hadn't seen him again since the library.

I waved back just as he motioned for me to come over. I set my cup down on the railing, then made my way down the stairs and across the yard. Sebastian had put his hat back on his head and was saying something to the horse as he leaned down over it.

"How'd you like the book?" he asked me when I was close enough.

"It was fascinating. I read it in one day," I admitted. But then I'd been reading most books in one day lately. I had enough time for it.

He was clearly pleased to hear it. His smile said as much.

"What book are you reading now?"

"*Of Mice and Men*," I replied. I had read it before, back in high school, but I was curious as to how I would enjoy it now.

"*Guy don't need no sense to be a nice fella. Seems to me sometimes it jus' works the other way around. Take a real smart guy and he ain't hardly ever a nice fella,*" Sebastian said, quoting a line from the book.

"Impressive," I said, surprised that he remembered the words like that. I read a lot, but there weren't many quotes I could pull up from memory. I could recognize quotes most of the time.

He shrugged. "Why don't you come with me to see the horses?" He patted the massive black one he was on. "Sword here is a beauty, but we've got more where he came from. Even a new colt."

I chewed on my bottom lip nervously. I wasn't sure he knew about me. King did, and Maeme did. What if Sebastian didn't watch the news and someone in his stables did? I would draw attention to myself. As much as I wanted to see the stables and the horses, I couldn't do that to him or Maeme…or King.

I shook my head. "I don't think that's a good idea. I need to stay back here…hidden." I stopped, not sure how much he knew about my still being at Maeme's.

"There's a gate behind the trees in the backyard. I'll get you from there, and we will head over to the stables. No one will see you who could cause you any harm," he assured me.

"I'd need to talk to Maeme about that. She…she's being really kind, letting me stay here, and I'm not sure what all you know, but I don't want to cause any problems for her," I explained, hoping that would be enough to stop his pushing for me to go over there.

He smiled at me then and leaned forward slightly. "I've already cleared it with Maeme. And I know why you're here. There are no secrets in the family. Besides, if we all know, then we can all protect you. Being with me is as safe as being here in this house."

I stared up at him, not sure if I should even be surprised anymore. They all knew I had left my husband bleeding out from a gunshot wound? They were all okay with that? Just because I'd had some broken ribs and a bruised face?

"Walk right on back there, and I'll meet you," he coaxed.

I hesitated, but the slight pleading look in his eyes, as if he wasn't sure if I was going to do it or not, and the thought of going to the stables won me over.

I nodded. "Okay, but I don't think I'm ready to ride a horse."

The smile that broke out across his face made me glad I'd agreed. "Probably a bad idea with your ribs. I'll get down, and we will walk him back."

I nodded, and then he turned the horse and rode him back around the circular pen. While I walked around to the backyard, I watched where he was going so I would know where the gate was located. I considered going inside to text Maeme, but I didn't think that Sebastian would lie about having asked her already. Trusting was something I struggled with and had sworn I wouldn't do again. But this family had helped me in a way no one else could. If I was going to trust again, they were the ones I should do it with.

By the time I reached the gate, Sebastian was there, standing against the fence opening. His horse obediently stood back behind him, and although I was sure that I wouldn't be charged by the horse, it still made me nervous, being this close to it without a barrier between us. I shifted my focus between the thoroughbred and Sebastian.

He held out a hand to me. "Come on. I swear you're safe. Sword looks like a beast, but he's a good boy. Well trained."

I took a step toward Sebastian and looked down at his hand, but didn't take it. Holding hands with him wasn't something I was comfortable with. He seemed to understand and dropped his hand back to his side, then closed and latched the gate behind me.

"It's a bit of a walk, but you can see the horses out along the way," he told me.

My curiosity about the Shephard Ranch got my attention, and I fell into step beside him. The horse walked on his other side, slightly behind us. I fought the urge to look back and see if he was watching me.

"How many horses do you have?" I asked Sebastian.

"Right now, we have twelve thoroughbreds that we own, five that are boarded, and a few quarter horse mares," he told me. "Although I believe we are selling a thoroughbred this week. We raised it to sell. He isn't a champion, but he will hold his own in a race."

He pointed toward a large circular path that was about one hundred feet away from us. I looked in that direction and saw a horse being ridden so fast that dust was flying behind them as the rider leaned down low over the horse.

"That's Bloodline, who we hope is our Preakness Stakes winner. Carmen, our best jockey, is on him today," Sebastian explained.

I had no knowledge of horse racing, but I was assuming Preakness Stakes was a race. I simply nodded, watching in amazement at the speed they were going. We continued walking, but I kept glancing back over to the two, even after the jockey slowed the horse down.

"Is this what your family does? I mean, as a job. You raise horses?" I asked, curious as to how someone could afford to have all this land and horses.

He shrugged. "Yeah, but I mean, we own other things too," he replied vaguely, and I decided not to push.

But what other things did they own? I would be lying if I said I wasn't interested in this.

Up ahead, a stunning house came into view. It appeared to be built of multicolored rocks and had a thatched roof with several gables.

"Is that your house?" I asked, squinting so I could see it better.

He laughed. "No. That's the stables. Well, the main one. There are two other buildings, but you can't see them from here. They are on each side of that one, making the shape of a U."

I stopped walking and stared at him.

When he realized I wasn't beside him, he paused and looked back at me. "What is it?"

I pointed at the building. "THAT is a stable?"

He grinned while he nodded his head. "Yeah."

I stared, agape, at the sight. "If that is where you house horses, what kind of house do you live in?" I asked him.

He cleared his throat as I looked back at him.

With a tilt of his head, he raised his eyebrows slightly. "Something a touch larger," he replied.

Why did I think it was much more than a touch larger?

I started walking again. I had thought the house I'd lived in with Churchill was big, but it wasn't as impressive as the stables here. These people had to be billionaires. But with horses? Really? You could be that wealthy, racing thoroughbreds? Clearly, I was clueless about this world. When he had said they owned other things, I was wondering if he meant hotel chains, banks, shopping malls, that sort of thing.

"Why do you need so much room for the horses?" There had to be more than horse stalls inside that mansion.

He rubbed his smooth jawline and sighed. "Well, there is a mudroom, laundry room, tack room, and two different office spaces. One for the stable manager and one for us to use. A game room with a bar, where we host parties sometimes. A large patio with a hot tub and firepit is in the center of the three buildings. Two bedrooms upstairs with private en suites, a gym, a full kitchen with a dining area large enough to feed twenty or so. And of course, the most important thing, twenty-five horse stalls."

"Wow," I breathed. I hadn't imagined that stables would consist of all that.

We were getting closer, and I noticed the area was surrounded by bricked paving. Red brick flooring all around the outside. Someone called out to Sebastian, and he raised a hand to wave, but he didn't stop. I could see a man wearing a black cowboy hat coming out of the side of the first building with a large brown horse behind him.

Another man walked over and took the reins from Sebastian, then led Sword in the opposite direction.

I was in complete awe by the time we reached the doors to the stables. They stood over twelve feet tall and were rounded at the top, wooden, with a hand-carved design of some kind of symbol on each one. Sebastian reached for the black iron curved handle and pulled it open, then held it for me to walk inside.

To say the inside was more breathtaking than the outside was an understatement. This place was fit for royalty. I stood there, turning in a slow circle, looking at everything I could and feeling as if I would never see it all.

"Let me take you to the game room, and we can get a drink. You probably should sit down after that walk. I don't want Maeme mad at me for causing you to do too much with your ribs healing," he said.

I wanted to argue and continue on a tour of the place, but I simply nodded. A drink would be nice, and my side was hurting more than it had been the past few days. As we made our way down the center of the place, I tried not to miss a thing. The ceilings were high, but they were smooth wooden planks, much like a hardwood floor would look. Ceiling fans and recessed lighting were scattered about in a pattern, but the center of the open area was a gorgeous chandelier. Not what you'd expect in stables.

"The colt is just up ahead. We will go there after you sit for a few," Sebastian informed me. "This way," he then instructed, turning right and toward a door smaller than the front doors but identical in looks. All the doors inside were.

A woman's scream stopped me. I turned my head toward the door we had just passed, and my heart began to slam against my ribs wildly. Another scream. I took a step back and sucked in a breath. What was happening?

"OH GOD, YES!" she shouted loudly.

I frowned. She'd been screaming in pain, hadn't she? Now, she sounded as if she were…

"Sorry about that. Just keep moving. Seems someone needed to let off steam," Sebastian replied, and I turned to him to see he was trying not to smile.

Another scream of pain. I tensed. Something bad was happening. No one screamed like that from pleasure.

"She's fine. I promise. I know it sounds bad, but she's enjoying it. He wouldn't be doing it if she wasn't. Let's go," he said to me, then pulled open the door and waved his hand for me to enter.

I wasn't sure I should be here. No one enjoyed being hurt. Screaming was not a good thing. Did she need help? I shouldn't have come here. I started to back away and shake my head. I couldn't run.

"HARDER, SIR!" the female voice shouted.

My eyes flew open wider as I stared at the door. What on earth was happening in there?

"Come on, Rumor. Trust me, that's going to just get more intense," Sebastian told me.

More intense? I shook my head, not understanding any of this, and turned to look at him.

"What…why is she screaming?" My voice was barely above a whisper.

He let out a heavy sigh. "Because she likes rough sex. Being tied up and whipped is my guess since that is supposed to be a tack room. But I swear to you that she went in there willingly and wanting it. They always do," he said, then gave me an apologetic smile. "I didn't know he was in there, or I wouldn't have brought you this way."

Who was *he*? I started to ask and stopped myself. I didn't want to know. I just wanted to leave.

"Come on. You can't hear that in here, and you need to sit down. Rest a bit."

Unsure, I stared at the inside of the room as he waited for me to move. Leaving would be dramatic, and I did want to see the rest of the place. But why would someone want to be whipped and tied up? I didn't understand that at all.

Finally, I gave in and went into the game room. When the door closed behind Sebastian, the sounds of the woman were gone. I wanted to forget what I had heard, and I also wanted to get an explanation for it. I knew people had rough sex and did kinky things. I hadn't been living under a rock. But I didn't realize it was so painful that it would cause someone to scream like that. Wasn't it about pleasure ultimately? Did she truly want to be hurt?

"What can I fix you to drink? I have everything you could want," he told me, walking over to the bar setup, equivalent to that at a nice restaurant.

Was there anything this place didn't have?

"Water," I replied.

"Still or sparkling?" he asked me as he stepped behind the bar and went to take a glass off the rack.

"Sparkling."

While he proceeded to fix drinks, I took in the room. It was the size of my cottage. A pool table, a black leather sectional sofa, a screen that covered the left wall—which I assumed was supposed to be a television maybe, although I'd never seen one like that. A fireplace that was so large that it almost covered the back wall with four black leather chairs set around it. Then a round card table with eight chairs surrounding it sat in the center of the room.

"Here you go," Sebastian said as he came up beside me. "Let's go sit down."

I took the glass from him and took a sip as I followed him to the sectional sofa. He motioned for me to take a seat, then sat opposite of me, giving me plenty of space. I appreciated it. The things I'd heard were still making me jittery. I didn't like that a woman was being whipped across the way from us. Even if she wanted to be.

Realizing I hadn't thanked Sebastian for my water, I started to when the door to the game room opened, and I was left speechless. A shirtless King walked inside with a pair of jeans hanging on his hips enough to show off a very impressive set of abs. He was barefoot as well and appeared to be sweating, as if he'd just worked out. As I sat, stunned by the view, unable to stop looking at him, he headed toward the bar before glancing in our direction. When his eyes met mine, he stopped and studied me for a moment.

"Lost some of your clothing, have you?" Sebastian asked him.

King swung his gaze to Sebastian. "What is Rumor doing here?" The way he said it sounded as if he was angry about my coming here.

Was I not supposed to leave the house?

"I broke her free. Maeme knows," he replied, then smirked before taking a drink from his glass.

King looked back at me, and his jaw clenched before he continued toward the bar. "I see," he finally bit out.

He wasn't happy about me being here. I didn't like that feeling. King was always so nice. I hadn't meant to do something to upset him.

"I-I can leave," I stammered, standing up.

"Sit down," Sebastian told me. "Ignore him. I do."

That might be the case, but I didn't sit back down. If King didn't want me here, then I didn't want to be here. I could find my way back to the gate behind the cottage. I didn't need anyone to walk me there. King grabbed something under the counter and then stood back up. His eyes cut back to me. The look in his eyes made me nervous. I should have stayed at the cottage.

"Sit," he barked, and I started to do just that but stopped myself.

What was wrong with me being here? This was Sebastian's stables. Not King's. He didn't decide who came here, and Maeme had said it was okay.

I narrowed my eyes as I looked at him and straightened my shoulders. "If I sit, then I will do so because I want to. Not because you ordered me to so rudely."

I heard a smothered laugh from Sebastian, but I didn't take my eyes off King.

He walked back from behind the bar with a longneck bottle of beer in his hand. His eyes stayed locked on me as he studied me. I felt my heart begin to race, and I questioned if it was smart to talk to a man his size that way. Sebastian wasn't wimpy by any means, but King was taller, broader, and his arms were...well, his arms were thick and corded with defined muscle. I couldn't tell what the tattoo on his left biceps was, but it wasn't unappealing.

"And do you want to sit?" he asked me before taking a long pull from the bottle while keeping his eyes on mine.

I swallowed hard, unsure of what I should say next. Should I apologize? No. Absolutely not. Just because I was currently feeling a little lightheaded from the sight of King and his perfectly sculpted body didn't mean I had to allow him to boss me around.

"I came here with Sebastian to see his stables. So, yes, I believe I do," I replied and sat back down. I could feel Sebastian watching me, but I was unable to stop looking at King.

A slight twitch of his lips was the only softening on his face. He didn't actually smile, but it seemed like he wanted to. "Then, by all means, sit."

"That's enough, King," Sebastian said from where he still sat, leaned back with his right ankle propped on his left knee and one of his arms stretched out over the back of the sofa.

King shifted his attention to Sebastian. "I thought you were leaving today."

"Change of plans," he replied.

King's entire body seemed tense as he stared hard at Sebastian, but he said nothing. I felt as if they were having a silent conversation. Were they cousins? This family that Maeme had was confusing, and no one had actually cleared up who was who for me.

The door opened behind King, and I watched as an attractive blonde woman with long, straight hair draped over one shoulder walked inside. She had on a pair of minuscule cutoff jeans and a black crop top that showed her flat, tanned stomach and pierced navel. Her eyes went directly to King, and she smiled before sauntering in his direction.

"You were taking too long," she said, running a hand up his tattooed biceps.

King glanced at me, and for a moment, I saw what I thought was regret in his gaze before it dropped to meet hers. "I didn't tell you that you could get up, did I?" he asked in a hard tone that startled me.

She shook her head and stepped back from him, then dropped her gaze to the floor. "No, sir. I'm sorry," she replied softly.

He reached up and ran his hand over her head, as if to reassure her. "Go back to where I left you and wait."

She nodded. "Yes, sir," she replied before turning and leaving the room quickly, without another word or glance in our direction.

"All right, Rumor, let's you and I go on that tour, shall we?" Sebastian said a little too brightly.

I lifted my gaze to his. A sick knot formed in my stomach as a slow understanding of what I had just witnessed began to connect. The screaming had been her. King had been in there with her. That was why he was shirtless, barefoot, and sweaty. He'd been…beating her?

The smile on Sebastian's face didn't mask the apology in his eyes. He hadn't wanted me to know who had been in that room. I trusted King. He'd saved me. Brought me here. They all knew that.

Did Maeme know he did that to women? And why would he do it? What was the purpose? Was he like Hill? Did he like hitting women?

I was unable to stand up.

The sound of a door slamming made me jump, and I spilled water over the rim of my glass as my eyes swung back to the door. King was gone. He had left.

"I'm sorry about that. With what you went through, that shit has to strike a chord. He's not mad at you. He's upset that you heard it," Sebastian told me, stepping in front of me. "Come on. There's a lot more to see."

I shook my head and sucked in a deep breath. "No. I…I think I want to walk back to the cottage. If you don't mind," I told him, standing up and holding my glass out for him to take.

As he took it, he sighed heavily. "I understand. I'll walk you back."

"No," I blurted. "I want to go alone. I'll be fine. I remember the way."

"Rumor, I'm not going to hurt you. No one is. I swear it."

I nodded. "I know. I just…I just want to go back alone."

He looked at me as if he wanted to argue, but finally stepped back. "I get it."

Good, because I didn't. None of what I had just learned made sense. Sure, the girl hadn't been bruised, nor did she walk as if she were in pain, but I had heard her screaming. He'd talked to her like a child. Sebastian had said she was being tied up and whipped. That was all something that made no sense to me. I had assumed people who did that were role-playing. Not actually causing someone real pain. It was a kink thing that I would never get. But the whole control thing I'd seen was unhealthy. Wrong.

I started toward the door and paused to glance back at Sebastian. "Thank you for bringing me," I told him, feeling rude about the way I was running off.

He set our glasses down and smiled at me. "He only does it to women who want it. He doesn't force anyone."

He was defending King. Okay, fine.

"Women want that? She was screaming," I pointed out.

Sebastian shrugged. "I don't get it either. I'd be lying if I said I did. But trust me, King has never had an issue with finding women to do his bidding. Sometimes, he has a couple doing it at the same time. They like it. He chooses them carefully." He stopped and shook his head. "Look, I shouldn't be talking to you about this. It's his business. Not mine. I just don't want you to be terrified of him. He would never touch you that way or any way. He knows what you've been through and that you aren't the kind of woman who would be on board with that shit. He will always treat you respectfully."

So many different things were racing through my head. I wasn't sure which one to be most concerned about. Was it that King did those things to women during sex, or that he liked doing it with more than one at a time…or that I was someone he'd never touch?

I had thought for a moment the other night that he was going to kiss me. I'd wanted it too. It had shocked me and excited me. But he was never going to kiss me.

I masked the disappointment and managed a tight smile.

"I understand," I told him, although I really didn't. Not at all.

NINETEEN

"Some things she was better off not knowing."

KING

"Dude, if you hit the punching bag any harder, it's going to burst open," Sebastian said behind me.

I paused for a moment before slamming my fist into it one more time. The look on Rumor's face wouldn't get out of my fucking head. I hated it. I hated that I had put it there. Why the hell had Sebastian brought her here? This wasn't a place for her. This was where we lived, burned off steam, fucked when and how we wanted to. It was not somewhere for Rumor to be. The women who came here knew the score. They had been prepared and were approved to step foot on the property. They weren't fragile, abused wives who needed to be handled with care.

Breathing hard, I let my hands fall to my sides before glaring at him. "You shouldn't have brought her here."

He held up his hands. "I didn't know you were gonna be having one of your twisted fucks in the tack room in the middle of the goddamn day."

I tossed the boxing gloves down and stalked over to my water. "Doesn't mean it was okay for you to bring her here. This isn't something she needs to see. This life. Who we are. You think she saw this place and doesn't have questions now? What happens when she decides to start asking questions?"

I gulped down the rest of the water in my bottle, wishing something would calm me down. Anything. I was wired, and I was never this fucking wired up after tying up a woman, whipping her with my leather strap, then fucking her while she hung by her wrists from the lead hook.

"She looked lonely," he said. "She reads all the damn time and stays at the shotgun house. It's sad. I felt bad for her. I figured we could talk books and I could show her around. Become her friend. She needs to trust someone other than you and Maeme." He cleared his throat. "Especially now."

I threw the bottle down and started toward him.

He backed up and shook his head as he watched me. "Dude, you know it's true. You didn't have to be so fucking angry when you saw her. It didn't help. Then, Sedona came in the room, and you went all Master on her. It was a lot for Rumor to take in at one time."

I inhaled sharply through my nose and fisted my hands at my sides. Hitting Sebastian wasn't going to fix this. He was right. I'd handled it wrong. I couldn't switch on my charming persona. I walked in, saw her there with Sebastian, and didn't fucking like it. Then, Sedona had come in the damn room and made shit worse. This wasn't supposed to happen. Rumor trusted me. Not someone else. I didn't want it to be someone else.

"She's off-limits," I reminded him.

"No shit. I'm aware of that. I wasn't making a move on her."

That simmered me down somewhat. Not enough, but at least we weren't about to end up beating the hell out of each other.

"Give her a little space, then go talk to her. She just needs to get her head around what she saw—or heard rather."

I didn't want to give her space. I'd been giving her space. I had planned on going by and checking on her later today. It was one reason I had Sedona come over to fuck. I'd thought if I was sated sexually, I wouldn't end up kissing Rumor, like I almost had the other night.

"What did she hear?" Thatcher asked.

I turned to see him striding into the gym in a pair of athletic shorts and tennis shoes. His pierced nipple still seemed out of place on him. He was the last one of us I would have expected to pierce his fucking nipple.

Sebastian glanced at his brother, then back at me. He wasn't going to answer it.

"Me fucking Sedona," I replied.

An evil grin spread across his lips. "She heard her screaming? Or you hitting that ass with your strap?"

I started for the door. I wasn't in the mood for Thatcher.

"What? You're gonna drop that shit on me and not give me the details?" he called out.

I didn't look back. I knew Sebastian would tell him what he needed to know after I was gone. There was work to do today, and I'd already wasted enough of my time. I'd get focused and too busy to think about the way Rumor had looked at me.

Once she had some time to digest it, I would go over and talk to her. Maybe take her something to eat again. Although she didn't seem to like to eat that much. She did like books. I could pick her out some and take them over. Or go get her and take her to the library. Fuck, I didn't know what to do. I wasn't used to trying to do nice things for women. They obeyed me. Did what I told them to. It was what I liked.

Rumor wasn't my type, and she never would be. But we had been on our way to being friends. Even if I was lying to her about almost everything happening in her life. It was for her safety even if she didn't know it. Some things she was better off not knowing.

· TWENTY ·

"I will regret it for eternity."

RUMOR

I finished hanging the rest of my clothing on the clothesline just as the sun was beginning to set. Washing them in the tub by hand had been a much-needed distraction. Hopefully, the book I was planning to start next would be equally distracting.

Every time I had thoughts of King and the way he'd been with that woman, it got me all twisted up. The one thing that was really bugging me was the way she had walked up to him and touched him. The look in her eyes, like she wanted nothing but to be near him. That wasn't a woman who was scared of a man or tolerating one. I should know.

She had been…enamored with him. She didn't tense up when he scolded her. She'd seemed…to enjoy it.

I was finding myself trying to figure that out more than anything else. As much as I didn't like it, I kept coming to the same conclusion: King was sexy and charming. He was hot. She was willing to do anything he wanted so she could be with him.

Was that what she got out of it? What they all got out of it? Since she was clearly not an exclusive thing. Or was she? Sebastian had said King was with different women, but he didn't say King wasn't just with her right now. Were they dating?

Jerking open the back door, I walked inside, angry with myself for not being able to stop my train of thought. I was going to read. First make myself a sandwich, then read. Get lost in a story that wasn't reality and forget all about King for a while at least.

I was almost in the living room when a knock at the door snapped me out of my thoughts. I looked straight ahead through the doorway leading into the kitchen to see Sebastian through the window. He lifted a hand to wave, and I let out a weary sigh. He'd come to check on me. I was not going to get to shut King and his kinky sex life out of my head as soon as I'd thought.

Walking through the kitchen, I unlocked the door and then the screen before pushing it open.

"Hey," I said in greeting.

He ran a hand through his hair and smiled. "I, uh, came to check on you. Make sure you made it back okay."

"I did. Thank you, and I'm sorry about running out today. It was rude," I told him. That had been bothering me too. How I had acted. It just hadn't bothered me as much as it should have. Unfortunately, King seemed to be the center of my thoughts.

"No worries. It was a lot, I'm sure. Seeing as…well, what you've been through. It has to look different to you," he said.

I nodded and let out a sigh. "Yeah. It definitely does or did. I don't know anymore. She seemed to be happy with it, and who am I to judge?"

He laughed then and raised his eyebrows. "Yeah, King has always been persuasive."

That much I knew. He'd gotten me in his truck when I was at my most vulnerable. I wasn't sure there was another person alive who could have convinced me to get in a truck with a strange man that day. Or any day really. I was cautious. I didn't take chances. I knew the consequences. But King…he'd been different.

"I've experienced that," I replied.

Sebastian nodded. "Yeah."

Stepping back, I waved a hand for him to come inside. "I was about to make something to eat and read. But if you want to come in, I'll find something better than a sandwich to feed you."

He seemed to hesitate, then finally walked inside the kitchen. "You don't have to feed me. The cook at our house has dinner made. I was about to head over there and eat. But you could come with me. We've got a pretty impressive library, too, with reading areas that will make you want to stay awhile. There is no chance that King will be, uh, well…" He trailed off.

I thought about it for a minute, and at first, I was going to say no, but another library and seeing his house was a temptation. If his house was bigger than the stables, that would get my mind off things. It might be the only chance I ever got to seeing a mansion. A real one, which was what I was expecting.

"Okay," I agreed. "That sounds nice. If you're sure it'll be okay with your family."

He let out a small laugh. "My parents are out for the evening. The cook made dinner for Thatch and me. She makes enough for an army though. There will be plenty."

In that case, it sounded like a great idea.

"I'll go grab my sandals," I told him, then made my way to the bedroom.

My tennis shoes were at the back door, dirty from walking outside so much today and then being in the backyard, hanging clothes. I slipped on a pair of Tory Burch flip-flops, then glanced in the mirror. My hair was a bit messy from blowing in the wind. Curls were everywhere. I went over to the cabinets in the bathroom and found a hair tie to pull my hair up the best I could.

Stepping back, I assessed my clothing and decided a hoodie over my tank top would be better since the evening air was cool. The white linen shorts I was wearing worked with the blue hoodie that had a stack of books on it and the words *I'm with the banned* underneath. It had been a gift from a coworker for my birthday three years ago. Hill had hated it and called it tacky. Getting to wear it when I wanted was freeing.

Sebastian was texting on his phone when I walked back into the kitchen. He glanced up, then read my shirt before breaking into a smile. "That's awesome."

I nodded, pleased with his reaction. "Thank you. I happen to love it."

He slipped his phone back into his pocket. "As you should. Let's go, shall we?"

Sebastian let me go out first, then followed me out. The silver Porsche parked in front of my house shouldn't have surprised me. But it did.

"Nice car," I said, looking back at Sebastian.

He smirked. "Thanks. You know much about cars?"

I shook my head. "I drove a 1998 Honda Accord that didn't crank most days, and I had to talk to Patricia real nice to get her to stay running when I stopped at red lights. Then, I married, and…I drove a Mercedes…on days I was allowed."

Sebastian was silent for a moment, and I wished I'd left the latter part out.

We almost reached the Porsche when he stepped in front of me and opened the passenger door. "Patricia sounds like she was special."

I nodded, relieved that he hadn't asked any more about Hill. "She was. We were tight."

He was smiling when he closed the door behind me.

I studied the interior of the car while I waited for him. Everything—from the leather seats to the console—was a brick color. I'd never seen anything like this. It was far superior to Hill's Mercedes. This was another level of luxury. Even the leather seats were softer, smoother, like butter.

Sebastian opened his door and slid inside. "Well, this will mean little to you, but this is a custom 2024 Porsche Panamera 4. I designed it myself. Ice-gray metallic exterior, barrique interior, all the bells and whistles." He stopped and patted the top of the steering wheel. "Haven't named her, but now, I feel as if I should."

I laughed, and he winked at me before starting the engine and backing up.

"Want to take it for a spin before we go to the house? See just how fast it can go?"

I was tempted, and for a moment, I almost agreed. But what if a cop pulled us over? That would be bad.

I shook my head. "No. That's okay. I think just going to the ranch is all the fun I should have tonight."

He shrugged. "Very well. But you're missing an experience."

"I'm sure I am, and I will regret it for eternity," I replied.

When we passed Maeme's, I caught myself looking for King's truck, and when it wasn't there, I felt a stab of disappointment I had no business feeling. I wondered if he was going to keep his distance from me now. My chest felt heavy at the thought, and I wished it didn't. I wished I didn't care at all.

"How are you related to Maeme?" I asked him.

He turned into the massive arch that read *Shephard Ranch*, then glanced over at me. "That's an interesting question. You see, we aren't technically related. The Shephards and Salazars have been in business together for a very long time. Before even our fathers were born and their fathers."

That was odd. "In business with the horses?"

He nodded. "Yeah, among other things. It's like a corporation, if you will. Our families and the Jones and Kingstons are all inside the same one. There are a couple others as well, but they don't have homes in Madison. They're in other parts of the South. But here, it's our four families that run the Georgia side."

I sat up straighter in my seat. "What things do you own?" I asked. "I mean…if it's not my business…"

I felt my face warm. I was being nosy, but I wanted to understand their dynamic. Why they all came to Maeme's on Sundays and acted like one big family. It was strange yet nice at the same time.

"It's okay. I don't mind," he assured me. "We own a couple of restaurant chains, hotels, casinos, A few malls, corporate buildings. Quite a bit of corporate real estate."

That explained the stables then. They were billionaires. The kind Hill did business with. He handled corporate real estate in Atlanta. I wondered if they knew him. They had seen the news, so if they knew of him, then wouldn't they have mentioned it? Maeme would have said something, surely. I decided against bringing it up.

"I've been overseeing things in Vegas for a few years. One of our casinos and handling the purchase of another one. But I'm thinking it's time to come home. That life was fun for a while, but when I go back, I start missing this place almost immediately."

I could understand that. Even if they weren't all blood, they might as well be. Having a family that big must be incredible. I wouldn't want to leave it either. You'd never feel lonely or lost. Someone would always be there for you when you needed it. If this had been my family, then I'd have had someone to call the first time that Hill had hit me. They would have saved me, and I wouldn't be in this mess.

The lights outside caught my attention, and I turned to look at what we were approaching. It was phenomenal and lit up like a castle. The stone exterior matched the stables, but it was all just more. Much more. There was even a turret on each end of the mansion, making it appear even more castle-like.

"Whoa," I breathed as he pulled the car around to the side of the house and down into what appeared to be an underground parking garage. There were at least ten other vehicles parked under here. "And I didn't think it could get any more impressive," I muttered as he pulled into a parking spot.

He cut the engine and opened his car door. "We like cars," was all he said.

I stepped out of the Porsche and looked at the other expensive vehicles of all kinds. Sports, SUVs, convertibles, all luxury. Shaking my head in amazement, I turned back to see Sebastian standing there, watching me with his hands tucked in the front pockets of his jeans.

"Ready?" he asked. "Or we could take one of these for a spin. Your call."

I laughed and started in his direction. "No, that's okay. I think staying here is the best idea."

"All right," he replied. "This way."

We walked over to what I thought was a solid stone wall until I heard a click, and a door slid open to reveal the inside of an elevator. I wanted to laugh at how insane this was getting, but I didn't. I stepped in behind Sebastian, and he pressed a code instead of one of the buttons, and the doors closed.

"How many floors is it?" I asked him.

"Four," he replied. "And a basement."

The doors opened back up, and a wide hallway with a marble floor stretched before us. He waved for me to go out, and I did, doing my best not to gawk, but finding it almost impossible.

"This way to the kitchen," he said and started to go left.

We walked through two different hallways, through a large sitting room with a roaring fire in a fireplace bigger than I had ever seen, then down another hallway before we reached what no one I had ever met would call a kitchen. It was much too elaborate to be labeled as such.

"Minna made a Mexican spread." He went to the buffet set out with silver covers over serving dishes that were sitting over warmers. "Fajitas," he began, looking under one, then continued, "enchiladas, refried beans, tamales, mole," until he took off the last cover. "I hope you're hungry."

"That is for two people?" I asked.

He shrugged. "More or less. Some of the guys might stop by later and eat. Never know for sure. What's not eaten Minna will pack up and take home with her. She hates to cook for her family since she cooks here all day, so she takes the leftovers."

That made a little more sense. At least this food wasn't wasted.

"She'll have the cold stuff in the fridge, trayed up for us," he said and walked over to open a commercial-sized refrigerator that had been camouflaged to blend in with the cabinetry. He pulled out a long silver tray and set it on the island bar. "This should be it. Grab a plate and fill up," he said with a smile.

What kind of world had I walked into?

• TWENTY-ONE •

"Okay, so maybe I let her have too much."

RUMOR

I licked the salt from my lips that had been on the rim of my margarita glass, then giggled. Sebastian was critiquing *Ocean's Eleven* and what they should have done differently while I drank my third margarita because he kept filling my glass without asking if I wanted more. It seemed he got funnier the more I drank.

After we had eaten our dinner in the kitchen, he had taken the pitcher of margarita left by Minna and led me to a theater in their house. It had five rows of long brown leather sofas that were made up of reclining seats. We sat in the second row, and he pulled down a divider between our seats that had holders that fit our glasses. There was a table that came under the seats and popped up in front of us, where he put the pitcher, along with tamales. He had said he might get hungry again.

I was not getting hungry again. I was stuffed. But I figured he might.

The last time I had been to a movie theater was when Hill and I were dating. He'd taken me to many places. It had been part of his grand scheme to get me to marry him. Just so he could beat me and control me. I shoved that thought away. I was having fun. I hadn't had fun in a very long time. I couldn't remember the last time I'd had fun. I was sure the margarita was helping me with this, but I did not care.

"There you are," a deep voice said, and I startled, sloshing my margarita, but not spilling it—thank goodness. "You didn't answer my text."

I looked back to see Thatcher walking toward us and blinked, realizing my vision was a tad bit blurry. But the moment my eyes locked on King, they seemed to clear up quickly. He was scowling, and I wondered what had happened to make him look so unpleasant.

"You found me," Sebastian replied, barely glancing at the other two. "What do you want?"

Thatcher walked into the row and sat down on the other side of Sebastian. "Nothing. Just curious. Well, King was the one who was curious. He couldn't find Rumor, and you were the last one seen with her."

I frowned. Who had seen me with Sebastian? Did he mean at the stables? And why had King been looking for me? A shadow came over me, and I tilted my head back to see King taking the seat beside me. I took a drink from my glass and studied him over the rim of it, then found myself laughing again. I didn't know why exactly. He was still scowling and looking all mean, but it was funny.

"How many of those have you had?" he asked me, reaching for my glass.

I moved it back away from him. "I don't know, but you can't have it," I informed him.

"Three," Sebastian said. "Give or take. Mostly give."

King held out his hand for my glass, as if I would give it to him. "That's too many. Minna makes those strong. Hand it to me, Rumor."

The way he spoke to me like I was a child should make me mad. I should tell him to kiss my ass. But I snickered and took another drink, watching as his brows drew together.

"Now, Rumor." His tone deepened.

I swallowed the salty sweetness and shook my head. "I am not one of your little...obedient females. I don't...don't have to do anything you say."

I heard a deep chuckle behind me, but I didn't turn around to see which of them was laughing at me.

"Okay, so maybe I let her have too much. But she was relaxed for a change," Sebastian said.

I nodded. I was relaxed. I agreed with him.

King reached for my glass again, and I tried to snatch it away, but he took it from me too quickly.

"Give it back!" I demanded.

"No."

"You are not my daddy!" I informed him.

He paused and raised an eyebrow, then set the drink down on the other side of him without taking his eyes off me. "No, I'm not." His voice sounded husky as he studied my face.

I crossed my arms over my chest and huffed, then turned to stare at the screen. We had been doing just fine without him here. We didn't need him and his bossy ways. This wasn't his house. It was Sebastian's house. Thatcher's, too, but I didn't think I liked him very much, so he didn't count.

I turned to look at Sebastian. "Can I have your glass?" I asked him.

His gaze lifted to look behind me, and he pressed his lips together, then shook his head as he returned his attention to me. "I'm sorry. I don't want you to be sick and hate me in the morning."

That was how it was going to be? Fine. I would just leave. I stood up and felt slightly off-balance for a moment and reached to grab something to steady me when two large hands wrapped around my waist.

"Easy," King said close to my ear.

I shivered and turned my head just barely to peer up at him.

His jaw was clenched again, like he was mad. Second time today that I'd seen angry King. Nothing like the King I'd grown accustomed to. The King I liked. As a friend, of course. I was married, or I was a widow—I wasn't sure exactly.

"I'll take you home," King said, then wrapped an arm around my waist and started to lead me away from the others.

"Wait," I said, trying to turn back around but he stopped me. With a frustrated sigh, I glared at him. "I need to tell Sebastian bye and thank him for tonight."

"He heard you. He's been thanked. Let's go," King replied, the tic in his jaw unmistakable. Even if I was slightly tipsy.

"This is rude," I told him.

"He understands," King said, pushing me to move forward.

I tried to jerk free and stalk away from him, but I stumbled, and then I was no longer on my feet, but in the air. Or rather in King's arms. He was carrying me. I looked up at him and wished his face weren't so nice and his arms weren't so muscly and his abs weren't so ripped.

The corner of his lips twitched. "Ripped, huh?" he asked, glancing down at me.

I covered my mouth with my hand. "I said that out loud?"

He smirked. "Yep. The muscly arms and nice face too."

Crap. I closed my eyes and already knew I was going to be really humiliated in the morning. Right now, he smelled too good. Like cedar trees, freshly cut, and cinnamon. It was a sexy scent, and I wanted to bury my face in his neck and inhale.

"What was that about cinnamon?" he asked, and I gasped, covering my mouth again.

The cool night air hit me in the face, and I realized we were outside already. How had we done that so fast? Where was the underground garage?

"I don't park my truck down there. It's out here."

Clearly, I could not keep my mouth from speaking my thoughts. "I can walk," I told him.

"No, you can't. You already made that clear."

I slapped at his chest. "You're mean. I thought you were nice, and you are not nice, King. You are mean. You do mean things."

He stopped and dropped his gaze to mine. "I'm not mean. I'm angry right now at Sebastian for getting you drunk."

I shook my head. "You…you…you like to hit women."

His eyes didn't leave mine. "No, I don't. I spank them, but only the ones who want me to. I tie them up because they want it and ask for it. I'm not mean."

I swallowed hard as his blue eyes seemed to glow under the moonlight. "Why do you want to spank them?"

The corner of his mouth lifted slightly. "Because I like it when they give me control. When they submit to me. When they trust me to give them pleasure and want me to take them to the brink of pain. Pleasurable pain."

I felt hot. All over. I needed to take off my hoodie and stick my head in a freezer maybe.

"I would never hurt a woman, Rumor. I only fuck women who want the same thing I do."

I stared at him, unable to say anything more. I believed him. I'd seen the blonde today. She had clearly wanted him. Even though she'd been screaming.

He started walking again, and then he opened the truck door and set me inside of it. I laid my head back on the seat, and he reached in to buckle me. I didn't bother telling him I could do it because I wasn't so sure I could. Maybe I had drunk a little too much.

When he closed the door, my eyes followed him as he walked around the front of the truck. The seat was warm, and it smelled like him. My eyes felt heavy, and I closed them, letting the comfort seep in as I drifted away.

TWENTY-TWO

"He was just kinky."

RUMOR

Before I opened my eyes, I realized my mouth felt as if I had swallowed cotton balls. I tried to create saliva and felt the slight ache in my head. As I squinted against the sunlight pouring into the room, last night came back to me all in one big rush.

I'd gone to Sebastian's, eaten Mexican food, drunk margaritas, watched a movie, then King…had come and gotten me. Carried me to his truck. Told me…he spanked women who wanted it. Women who submitted to him for pleasure.

I sucked in air through my teeth and sat up. The last thing I remembered was getting inside his truck. Studying my clothing, I found that I was in the tank top and bra I'd had on underneath my hoodie, but my shorts were gone. I was in my panties.

Had I undressed myself? My eyes scanned the room, and I found my hoodie neatly folded, along with my shorts, on the end of the bed. Drunk me wouldn't have folded my clothes so neatly. I doubted sober me would have even done that. Had King undressed me? Was he here? I looked at the other side of the untouched bed, and I wasn't sure if I was relieved to see I had slept alone or disappointed.

Shaking my head, I stood up. I was not disappointed. I would not be. King was not for me. No one was for me. I might still have a husband who would be hell-bent on finding me and possibly killing me.

I started to walk over to the sink when I noticed a glass of water and two white pills on my bedside table. Aspirin. I reached for them and then took the water to wash them down. King had definitely done that.

Okay, so he wasn't mean. He wasn't abusive. He was just kinky.

I let out a groan and decided I needed coffee before a shower. Reaching for my shorts, I slid them on. Then, I took my glass and made my way to the kitchen, then stopped when I walked into the room. The coffeepot was full, and there was a plate covered in foil on the table with an empty cup beside it. On top lay a note. I walked over to pick it up.

Take the aspirin, drink all the water, and eat. I only brought over the greasy stuff. It's best for a hangover.

—K

I might have reread it two more times before placing it beside the plate and taking the foil off. Bacon, biscuit and regular sausage gravy—not the red tomato stuff—a sausage patty, and some cheese grits filled the plate. There was no way I was going to be able to eat all this, but I would eat some of it. He was right. I needed to get food in my stomach. I glanced down at the note again and found myself smiling. Even if he had forced me to leave last night, he'd carried me in, asleep, undressed me, and put me in bed. Then, he went and made sure I had coffee made, food to eat. He had even left me some aspirin.

I took the empty cup and walked over to the coffeepot. None of this mattered. My feeling things for him. Attraction or whatever was pointless. Even if I were into getting tied up and spanked, I was not in any place to have a relationship other than friendship with anyone.

And he knew that.

Once I was seated at the table with my coffee and plate of food, I heard the crunch of gravel that meant someone was driving up. I took my cup and went to look out the window. It was King. He was climbing down from his truck, and I watched as he walked toward the porch. I let out a sigh and waited until he knocked on the door before going to open it.

I smiled at him through the screen door and held up my coffee. "Thanks for this. And everything."

He opened the screen, and I stepped back for him to come inside. "Figured you might wake up feeling shitty. Thought I'd help out."

I let out a small laugh, trying hard not to think about the fact that he'd seen me in my panties. My face felt warm regardless, so I turned and walked over to the table.

"It's been a while since I drank like that," I admitted, sitting back down in my chair.

"You weren't a bad drunk. You didn't even puke on me," he said, his voice sounding amused.

I lifted my eyes to meet his. "I fell asleep in your truck."

"Eh, so I had to take off your clothes. Get a look at you in your little pink panties. I've been forced to do worse things."

I bit my lip and dropped my gaze back to my plate. I really hoped he was joking and that seeing me in my panties wasn't that bad. But I'd been married to a man who complained about my body and how I looked, so I was sensitive about it. Maybe Hill had been right. Maybe my hips were too wide and my thighs were too thick.

"Rumor," King said, and I looked back up at him, forcing a smile I didn't feel. "You know I'm joking, right?" he said.

I managed a nod. I had not known he was joking, but he seemed sincere. He wasn't someone who I thought would point out a female's flaws to her.

He walked over and pulled out the other kitchen chair, then sat down, never taking his eyes off me. "Something in those eyes of yours is telling me you didn't."

I wasn't sure how to respond to this, and now that I had made it completely awkward, I simply stared at him. I had to think of something lighthearted to say or change the subject.

"Fuck," he muttered, then placed his elbows on the table and leaned toward me. "I looked at you way longer than I should have. I even ran my hand between your thighs. Was that morally grey, yes. But you're too damn tempting. I held your shorts to my fucking nose so I could smell you. When I finally got home and in the shower, I had to jerk one out, thinking about what I had wanted to do to you, but hadn't."

I sucked in air, realizing I had been holding my breath. *Oh my God.*

He picked up my fork and held it out to me. "I shouldn't have told you that, but I can't stand the idea of you thinking I didn't enjoy the view. Now, eat."

I reached out and took the fork, not sure I could eat. I was still struggling to take in oxygen properly. If I tried to eat right now, I would probably choke. Since he was watching me, I had no other choice. I gave the biscuit and gravy more attention than necessary as I used my fork to cut a piece off.

"Maeme mentioned you hadn't been there to do laundry. Thought you might need a ride to the big house. I could take you to exchange your books too."

I shook my head. "I washed my things in the tub yesterday and hung them out on the clothesline."

The mention of my books reminded me that Sebastian and I never made it to his library. The margaritas had played a hand in that.

"Seriously? Why didn't you call me or send me a text?"

I lifted my gaze back up to his and shrugged. "I didn't want to bother you."

He groaned, then leaned back in the chair, crossing his arms over his chest. "Would you stop worrying about bothering me? Goddamn it, I gave you a phone for a reason."

Explaining to him that I had been trained not to bother a man because of Hill was hard. I didn't like admitting it. The more I was away from the life I had been living, the more my eyes were open to just how brainwashed I had been. Hill had changed me completely. He'd taken away my personality. I had lost a part of who I had been, and I didn't know how or if I would get that back. I could very likely end up in prison.

"I will make a mental note of that," I replied, then put a piece of biscuit and gravy in my mouth. If I ate, then perhaps he would leave. Having him watch me was making it difficult.

"You do that. And don't hand-wash your clothes again. I'll be fucking insulted."

I nodded and continued to chew.

"About what you said last night," he started, and I swallowed, then shook my head.

"No. We do not have to talk about that."

He sighed, and then a small grin played on his lips. "You called me mean and accused me of hurting women. I explained it, but you were drunk, so I wanted to make sure you remembered it and understood things."

I set my fork down beside my plate. "Yes, I understand. I've read *Fifty Shades of Grey*, like the rest of the world. It's just…I guess, with what I've experienced, it makes that seem fictional to me. I never really considered people really liked that."

A deep rumble came from his chest, and he cocked an eyebrow at me. "Not the rest of the world. For the record, I've not read it. But I did see the movies. And that isn't exactly what I do. I don't have a special playroom, and I don't keep a submissive. That's too much commitment and work."

That confused me a little. I'd loved the books, but I wasn't going to tell him that. They were better than the movies, but then that was always the case. The reason I had loved them was because of his commitment and the way he took care of her. He made it something I could understand her wanting. But if King wasn't giving that to the females he did these things to, then why would they let him do it? Just because he was gorgeous?

"I can see your mind working over there. Ask me. Say it," he coaxed.

I pressed my lips together for a minute and studied the table before meeting his gaze. "I was just trying to figure out what was in it for them. If you aren't in a committed relationship and you don't take care of them, protect them…" I trailed off, not able to find the right words to say this.

He smirked. "Not everyone is looking for a commitment. Some of them just enjoy sex that way. What you read is a romance novel. It's not reality."

No kidding. I'd already learned that men in books were better. The real kind let you down, betrayed you, hurt you. I much preferred the ones created from the mind of a female.

When I said nothing more, he stood up and tapped the table twice with his knuckles. "Eat up. Rest. Text me or call if you need anything."

"Okay," I replied, realizing I didn't want him to leave. I had thought I did, but when he walked out, I wasn't sure when I would see him again. *Bad train of thought, Rumor. Very bad.*

He turned and headed for the door. Didn't glance back once—and I would know. I watched him through the window, all the way to his truck, before looking back at my food.

Picking up a piece of bacon, I ate it slowly, wondering about sex with someone other than Hill. Women seemed to enjoy it. Did sex with someone who was good at it make it better? Was sex with King so good that it was worth all the pain involved?

TWENTY-THREE

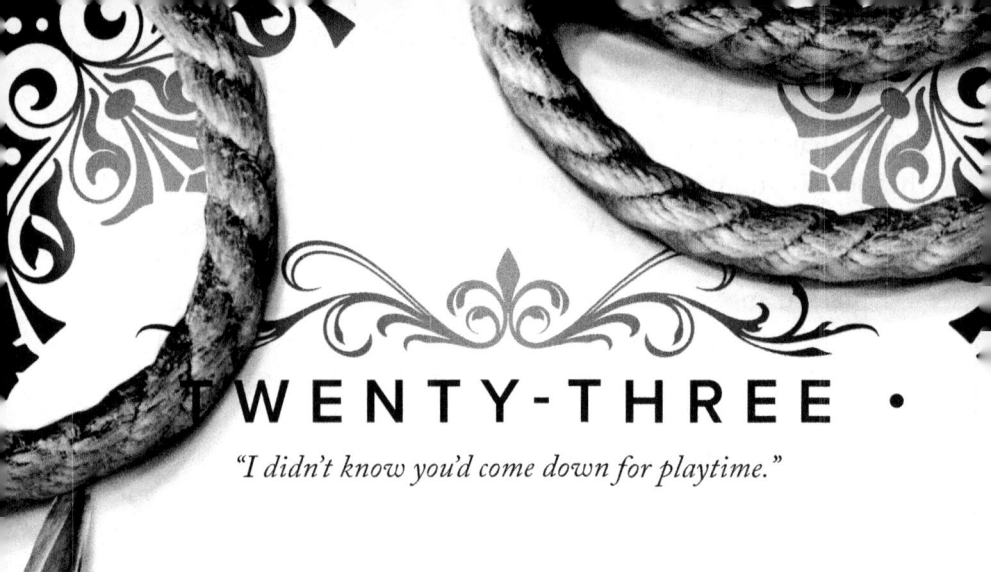

"I didn't know you'd come down for playtime."

KING

Churchill Millroe barely lifted his head to stare at me through his swollen and busted face as I entered the underground cell he had been kept in for the past eight days. This wasn't my first visit down to see him. I'd been the one to break his nose and all ten of his fingers—one by one—and pull out five of his teeth. The more brutal stuff had been Thatcher, but we'd all had a go at him. It was amazing how much torture the human body could withstand before finally giving up.

"Kill me," he begged—or at least, that was what I thought he'd said.

It was hard to decipher after I took out so many of his teeth. But Thatcher had sliced off the tip of his tongue, and that really hindered his speech.

He had stopped asking why, pleading for his life, his attempts at bribing, threatening—all the different phases a man went through while being strapped up and tortured. He cried silently most of the time now. I leaned a shoulder against the concrete column and crossed my arms over my chest as I studied him. This past week had been a living hell for him. It wasn't nearly long enough. That was the only reason he was still alive. I wasn't satisfied yet. I was wondering if I ever would be.

The more I got to know Rumor and realized how he'd abused her so deeply, the more I found myself being drawn back down here. To make him scream in pain. Hear him wail and beg. If he hadn't abused his wife, he'd probably be able to live. Sure, we would have taken his fingers or an ear. Maybe his balls. But once we had all our money, he'd have been set free. Living in fear for the rest of his life that we'd return, but still living.

"She's better. Smiling," I told him. "She's got the best damn laugh. I don't get to hear it often, but when I do, it's worth it."

I walked over to the pack of cigarettes that Thatcher had left and tapped one out of the package. I wasn't a smoker. Not really. I had one every once in a while when drinking, but I didn't need them.

I was lighting one up because back when Churchill could still speak and wasn't weeping all the time, he had shared his disgust with Thatcher's smoke in his face. We all made sure to smoke down here. Leaving the air thick with the stench when we left. His eyes were almost closed from the battering, but I knew he was watching me. I smirked, then took a pull before walking over to blow the smoke directly in his face. He no longer winced. I doubted he had much control of his expressions anymore.

"She stood at the top of the stairs, listening, when we came in your house," I told him, smiling at the memory. "Sweet thing heard what we said to you. She knew you were in trouble. I didn't let her see me watching her, of course. I didn't want to scare her. I figured she'd already been through enough that day, seeing as her pretty face was all beat up." I took the cigarette from between my teeth before I ended up biting off the tip.

"Then, she hid. I didn't check the closet in your bedroom because I knew that was where she had run to. I didn't want to find her. She was fucking terrified. Hell, we weren't real sure what to do with her. Would she call the cops when we left? Would she call 911?

We had no idea." I took a long pull and chuckled. "But, damn, I didn't expect to see her running out of that house with a suitcase and speeding away. Leaving you bleeding out on the floor. I was so goddamn amused that I laughed for the first hour I followed her. The farther away she got, the more I liked her. She was a fighter. She had gotten a chance to escape you, and she took it. Good girl," I said, praising her.

He made a sound, or maybe he was trying to talk. I couldn't tell. I didn't give a fuck either. I leaned back on the column again and took a few pulls, watching him there. Barely breathing. Gasping every few minutes. It calmed the fury inside me when I thought of all he'd done to Rumor.

"You had a prime piece of ass. She's completely out of your league," I told him. "Is that it? You knew she was too good for you? Could your pointless ego not handle it? Knowing men saw her and wanted her. Was it not enough that she'd married you?"

"Thhhubid bish," he spat out.

I straightened and took three long strides until I was inches from his face. "What did you just call her?" I asked, taking the cigarette and shoving the tip into his eye as he began to scream.

"Neither of those words apply to Rumor," I sneered.

"I didn't know you'd come down for playtime," Thatcher drawled behind me.

I left the cigarette sticking in his eye as I turned to look back at him. "Figured he'd be dead soon. I wanted to get my fill."

Thatcher walked over to the cigarettes. "Please, continue. Don't let me stop you. I'll watch."

I nodded toward the plyers. "Toss me those."

Thatcher picked them up. "I hope you tucked in our sweet little Rumor the other night. Sebastian should have warned her Minna's margaritas are three-fourths tequila."

I caught the plyers and grinned. "She was fine the next morning. I made sure of it before I left."

"Good to hear," he said before sticking the cigarette between his teeth.

When I turned back to Churchill, he was definitely looking at me, but with only one eye. The ash was jammed inside the other eye, and I could no longer see it. I wanted him to know she was enjoying life. Being taken care of properly. That while he was experiencing hell on earth before he burned in the real one, Rumor was starting anew.

"They're saying you drained your financial accounts and fled the country," I told him. "No one knows where, and there is even speculation that you killed your wife and hid. She can't be found either. Sweet Carmella Millroe's beatings were found on the video surveillance you'd kept in your home. How arrogant was that? You knew it was recording your abuse, and you didn't fear anyone would ever find it. But don't worry yourself. We made sure both our visits to your house were wiped clean before anyone else saw the tapes. It's even been said that your wife might have been the one who shot you and you killed her in revenge before fleeing. The nurse and cook who had been at your house when you escaped never saw who it was that tied them up. They can't be sure if it was you or not."

A tremor ran through his body, and I wasn't sure if it was from the pain or if it was from anger. He'd lost. He would die, and no one would know how or where. Rumor would get a new life. She could start over.

"Now, open wide," I demanded, jamming the plyers into his mouth and clamping down on one of the few molars left. "I wonder if you'll even bleed that much this time. You're so pale. Blood loss will do that to you."

Thatcher laughed from the stool he had taken a seat on across the room. "Finish with his teeth, and I'll cut off his dick and shove it in his mouth."

This time, when Churchill Millroe's body trembled, I knew it was from the fear.

TWENTY-FOUR

"This escape from reality was over."

RUMOR

Sitting on the front porch with my last unread book, I was lost in the story and didn't realize Maeme's golf cart was coming down the path. She was already parking it when I noticed I had company. I closed the book and stood up to greet her.

I'd not seen anyone since King had left two days ago. My plan was to finish the book, then text him to take me to Maeme's library to get more. I had almost done it yesterday, but I'd admitted to myself I didn't need to go yet. I was just thinking of an excuse to see him, and that wasn't healthy. I couldn't let my head go there. It was never happening.

She waved as she walked up the little stone-paved walkway. "Good morning," she called out. "Haven't seen you in a bit and wanted to come see how you were doing. Thought you might be getting a little stir-crazy around here."

A few weeks ago, I would have thought that was an impossibility. The idea of staying alone out in the woods like this had seemed like heaven. But it did get a little lonely. Left to my own thoughts with no distractions could be dark at times.

"I was going to text King and see if I could get a ride to your house to exchange some books later," I told her.

She put her hands on her hips and beamed brightly at me. "Well, good timing then. You can go get those books, and we will get you out of the house. Doc D is coming by later to see how you're healing up. Figured if he gave you the all clear, you might want King to take you to the stables. Teach you to ride."

The thought of King taking me to the stables instantly gave me an image of what King had been doing at the stables the last time I was there. Trying to think of anything but that since I was standing in front of his grandmother, I blurted, "Sebastian promised to do that."

Her eyebrows rose. "Did he now? Well, he always was a smart one. He's back in Vegas, but he'll be returning in a few days. Reckon your riding lesson can wait until then if you prefer he teach you."

Sebastian didn't rattle me the way King seemed to. I was comfortable with him. I wasn't sure I could focus enough on riding with King present, and I'd probably do something stupid and fall off a horse.

"I can wait until he returns," I replied.

Amusement flickered in her eyes, and I hoped she wasn't thinking I was interested in Sebastian as more than a friend. She was aware I would never do anything to put them in danger or get them mixed up in my messed-up life.

"Very well. Go on then and get the books. We can go on back to my house. I've got a warm lemon Bundt cake just sitting there, waiting on us. A glass of sweet tea and some cake in the sunroom will be nice. You can tell me all about your night over at the Shephards'."

I widened my eyes, surprised by the fact that she knew I'd been over there.

She chuckled at my expression. "Don't a thing happen in this family I don't know about. I got to keep this machine running smooth."

Her response was odd, and I thought about it as I went inside to grab my books. This was by far the strangest family I'd ever met. I guessed it made sense that they were all close, seeing as they were in business together and had been for generations. The way it all worked though, I felt like I was missing something. Even if I were, it wasn't like I should be told all the ins and outs. They were the ones helping me, not the other way around.

Maeme was already in the driver's seat of the golf cart when I returned. Holding the books to my chest, I hurried out to her, not wanting to make her wait any longer. I slid onto the seat, and she glanced up at me from her phone that she was texting on.

"That was King. Seems he has plans for you this evening. I'll bring you on back after Doc checks you out. You'll need time to get ready."

She reversed the cart, then turned it around without telling me more. Not happy with myself for the fact that my immediate reaction to King coming to get me had been…a slight flutter of…something. I straightened the books in my lap.

"Um, what are his plans?" I asked her nervously.

Maeme glanced over at me. "Got us some horses racing in Santa Anita. They've got the big screen at the stables playing it today, and King thought you'd enjoy coming over to watch it. But don't you worry. Everyone there is family. Your identity is safe."

I was torn between social anxiety and the desire to experience something new. Go to a party. Live outside of my own little world.

"That's nice of him," I finally said.

"He's got a good heart. I won't count that out, but he enjoys your company. Might be more him wanting to be around you than just a nice gesture."

Oh. I was about to smile, and I stopped myself. I didn't need to be happy about that. Besides, him enjoying my company was not anything more than that. I shouldn't even be considering anything else. It was ridiculous. For reasons I shouldn't have to keep reminding myself.

We were already parking in Maeme's backyard before I could think of anything to say about that. She was his grandmother and knew more than anyone that our relationship would only ever be friends. I didn't know how much longer I would be here, and she nor King had brought it up lately.

Following her into the house, I waited until she led me to the library to ask her about any update. I needed to start focusing on my future instead of getting excited about a party. When she stopped at the door to the library and looked at me, I knew I had to find out what was happening. Since the storm, all I could get my television to play was Netflix. I couldn't get the local channels anymore.

"Maeme," I began and gripped the books tighter to my chest, "I, uh…what is happening with my…Churchill?"

I couldn't call him my husband. I hated him. I feared him. I never wanted to see him again, yet if he found me, he would make me come back. He would make me pay for all he'd been through. For embarrassing him. It was a fate worse than prison.

She sighed. "Well, he went missing. Seems he drugged his nurse and cook. When they came to, they were tied up and blindfolded in closets. He took his car, and it hasn't been found. His bank accounts were wiped clean. The latest belief is, he fled the country for illegal activities he'd been involved in. Some believe he got mixed up with the Mafia. It isn't concrete yet. But…they also think he might have killed his wife and hidden her body. You see, he had surveillance videos in your home. They were hidden, and the authorities didn't find them until he went missing. Your abuse was on them, Rumor. But the men who came into your home were not. In fact, the only thing they found according to the news was the abuse."

I stood there, staring at her, not sure I had heard all that correctly. Video cameras? The Mafia? I shook my head. What in the world had Hill done? He hadn't fled the country. He wouldn't do that. He'd want revenge. He'd want to find me and make me pay. Fleeing would make him look guilty, and he never accepted blame for anything. It was always someone else's fault.

Was he…dead? Didn't the Mafia kill people? Had that been the Mafia who shot him, and then when they found out he wasn't dead, they came back to finish him off?

"I maybe should have said that a little less bluntly. You've gone pale," Maeme said, touching my arm. "I'm sorry. I thought it would come as a relief to you."

I shook my head. "I don't know. What if…what if it was the Mafia? What if they know I was in the house?" I felt the blood drain from my face, and I let out a panicked gasp. "Oh God. What if they are looking for me? I can't stay here. I have to go. They'll find me. They can do that, can't they? Don't they have connections? It's…it's a matter of time."

I backed up until my back was to the wall as realization spread through me. I was going to die. I wouldn't go to prison. I was going to be murdered.

"You've done not a thing wrong. The Mafia ain't coming for you. If they killed that bastard, he deserved it. They don't go killing people who don't need to be killed. And you were a victim. Now," she said, taking the books from my arms, "take a deep breath. I am going to set these books in the library, and we are going to get us some Bundt cake and sweet tea. We can talk about it. Whatever you need, but I promise you that you are safe."

I wanted to believe her, but she didn't know. She lived in a small town in Georgia. She owned a pecan orchard. She made Bundt cakes and cooked for a big family every Sunday morning. She knew nothing about the world that Churchill had gotten mixed up in. I couldn't stay here and bring that kind of danger to her doorstep. At least with the police, it was me they would come after. The Mafia could kill her, trying to get to me.

King. I had to tell King. He'd agree with me. He wouldn't want his grandmother harboring someone the Mafia was after. Finally, he'd take me somewhere and let me go into hiding, alone, which was what I should have done all along. Not living in this dream world where nothing bad happened and I had no responsibilities and read books all day. This escape from reality was over.

• TWENTY-FIVE

"If she wanted to look like a fucking snack, then so be it."

KING

Making sure Rumor didn't try and run had put a kink in my plans this afternoon. Moira, one of the newest in my line up of women, had been pissy about us not fucking. But she would get over it. That, or she could leave. I'd rather she sucked my dick before she did go, but right now, I had to get Rumor back to the stables and under all our surveillance.

Maeme had been worried she was going to try and leave the moment she was alone, but I'd been watching the cottage through the app on my phone since she'd been taken back to get ready, and she wasn't doing anything yet. Hopefully, she wouldn't. I had known it was time to tell her where things stood, but I'd been putting it off. Maeme should have let me do it. She was too fucking blunt.

I hadn't even put my truck in park when the front door opened, and Rumor stepped out onto the porch.

Motherfucker.

That was not what I'd expected. I had come here, prepared to see Rumor in dark jeans and a hoodie with her suitcase packed, demanding I take her to a bus stop again.

Rumor was wearing a pair of black shorts I hadn't seen on her before. They were shorter than anything she'd worn. Too fucking short. She needed more length. The sleeveless blouse she was wearing wasn't tight, but she had it tucked in, and it was showing cleavage. But it was the heels. A pair of red heels.

I opened my door and got out as she walked down the steps and headed in my direction. Moving around the front of the truck, I met her just before she reached the passenger side.

"Hey," I said when she stopped and looked up at me.

The uncertainty and fear on her pretty face bothered me. No, I fucking hated it. She was supposed to be happy. Enjoying life.

"Hey," she replied. "I, uh…I wasn't sure what to wear. I hope this is okay."

This was not okay. I didn't like the idea of the others looking. Besides the fact that she was off-limits to us all, I wanted her to go inside and put on some jeans and a baggy sweatshirt. I needed it for my sanity. But that would be ordering her around, and she'd had enough of that in her life. If she wanted to look like a fucking snack, then so be it. I'd just be the gatekeeper all night.

"You're perfect," I told her.

She blushed, and I wondered if the bastard had ever told her that. Probably in the beginning, but I doubted she'd heard it in a while. She deserved to hear it every fucking day. Several times. By a man who was good enough for her. One day, we'd be able to put her somewhere to start a new life. She'd have her chance at it. I'd stay out of sight, but I was coming to realize I wouldn't be able to not check on her. I wasn't going to just let her go. I had to know she was okay. She was safe. Even if she never knew I was there in the background, watching.

"Thank you," she replied softly.

I took her hand and helped her into the truck, trying like hell not to look at her ass and failing before I walked back around to get in the driver's side. Even if the boss hadn't made it clear that she was for us to keep safe until it was time to move her somewhere and give her a new identity, no fucking her, not even kissing her, I knew tonight was going to be difficult. I couldn't be the only one who was drawn to her. How could the others not be? At least Sebastian wasn't in town. I didn't want to deal with seeing them laughing together and her smiling at him. Talking about books and shit. The little fucker needed to stay in Vegas.

Once I was inside, I noticed her hands clasped tightly in her lap, as if she was nervous.

"You've met most of the guys, and you can stick by me. No need to worry about it."

She gave me a tight smile and nodded, but her hands didn't relax any.

I reached over and squeezed both small fists with my much larger palm. "I swear you have nothing to worry about. Stop with this before your nails break through your skin."

Her chest rose and fell with a deep breath, and she opened her fisted hands, placing her palms flat on her legs. "Okay. You're right. It's fine. Everything is fine."

It felt like she was telling herself that in hopes she would believe it. I backed up and turned the truck around, then headed back to the main road, letting her have a moment to calm down. Talking about what Maeme had told her today was going to happen before the night was over. She needed to be reassured, and I wanted to see her reaction to it all. If she was going to run, I would be able to tell. I could read her expressions well.

"You know about the Mafia?" she asked, glancing at me.

I nodded. "Yeah, I know, and you are safe. I swear it."

"You're not worried about Maeme's safety?" The frustration in her tone was cute.

I shook my head. "Nope."

"But she's your grandmother. I am living on her property, and they could very well be hunting me down right now. I don't know what Hill did, but…he did something bad. Really bad."

Yeah, he had. He had fucking sold buildings that we owned as if they belonged to him, thinking we wouldn't find out.

"You aren't him. They aren't looking for you."

She let out a weary sigh. "King, you can't know that."

I wanted to laugh. "Yeah, I can."

I looked at her before pulling out onto the main road. She was staring straight ahead, and her entire body was tense. I wished I could just tell her the goddamn truth. That we were the fucking Mafia and we had no desire to hurt her in any way. Maeme's aim was lethal. She'd taken out more than one man fifty yards away with a shot right between his eyes. Then, she'd walked away and told us to clean up the mess. But the boss had said we were to keep our place in all this from Rumor. He had no idea how hard that was getting to be.

"Just try to enjoy tonight. I'll teach you about racing. You might find you love it. If so, maybe one day, you can go to an actual race with me—us." I had to stop thinking of her as mine.

She nodded once. "I am going to try and not think about it."

I'd have to work extra hard to keep her mind off it.

TWENTY-SIX

"Rumor, do you trust me?"

RUMOR

King started to pull out onto the road when his eyes narrowed at something off to his right.

"GET DOWN!" he shouted as he reached over and pushed my head toward my lap. "ON THE FLOOR!"

My heart slammed against my chest, and I unbuckled quickly, then sank down to the floorboard, pulling my knees up to my chin. It was then that I heard the gunshot. I screamed, and my eyes swung up to King.

"Motherfucker," he hissed and reached behind him to pull a gun from the waistband of his jeans. "Don't move," he warned me, then rolled down his window and took a shot.

I heard more gunfire, but it seemed farther away.

King opened the door and got out, barely glancing at me. "Do not move," he repeated before slamming it shut and leaving me alone.

I sat there in horror. I'd imagined this. Feared this. And it was happening. They'd come for me. Someone was going to get hurt because of me.

Where was Maeme? Had they checked on her? Oh God, what if something had happened to her?

I needed to run. Get out. Take the danger away from them. They'd wanted to help me, and this was their reward.

What if King was shot? I'd let him just jump out of the truck into open gunfire. What had I been thinking? He couldn't die for me.

I moved then. I had to get up. He'd said not to, but I wasn't going to let him die. I didn't want anyone hurt. I couldn't live with myself if something happened to him or his family. Grabbing the door handle, I started to get out when King was there in front of me, blocking my way.

"I said not to move," he reminded me.

My eyes scanned him quickly for any sign of blood. He appeared to be fine.

"Maeme," I told him.

We needed to get to her. Check on her. Then, he needed to let me go. Far away from here.

"Maeme is just fine. Everything is okay. It's handled. Get back in the truck," he told me, placing his hands on my hips and pushing me back.

I shook my head. He wasn't going to tell me what to do. Not anymore. "I need to leave. This is my fault. I did this. I have to get away from here. I can't let something happen to you…or Maeme or anyone."

King grabbed my shoulders and stepped in between my legs. His eyes bored into mine as he moved in closer. "This isn't your fault. It has nothing to do with you. I swear. You aren't going anywhere, Rumor. You're staying here."

I stared at him, trying to decide if he was attempting to lie to me to make me feel better or if he truly thought that the gunshots weren't the Mafia coming for me. Why else would someone show up and start shooting at us? This wasn't some big city. We were in the country. I was the reason the guns were fired. They wanted me dead.

"Rumor, do you trust me?" he asked.

I blinked. Did I trust him? I wanted to. He'd saved me. He and his family had been more than generous to a complete stranger. Yes, I trusted him. I did. I had no reason not to. He'd proven himself trustworthy.

"Yes."

He looked relieved. "Then, please stay in this truck. I have to make a phone call, and"—he pointed down the road, where I saw another vehicle and several people—"I have to go talk to Thatcher."

My eyes stung. He was asking me to stay. I couldn't do that. Didn't he understand this? "I couldn't live with myself if something happened to you or…or anyone."

The corner of his lips quirked up. "It won't."

I threw my hands up in frustration. "We just got shot at!"

He leaned closer to me and grabbed my chin with his thumb and pointer finger. "It wasn't the Mafia. I swear to you. What just happened had nothing to do with you. It was someone trying to sneak onto family—" He paused and clenched his jaw. "The ranch. It happens. There is security, and it was already moving into place. We just showed up in the middle of it. All is taken care of. Now, please, sit back. Let me handle this."

It wasn't like I could run off alone without any of my things. I had no choice. I'd let him go talk to Thatcher and then make him take me back to the cottage. I had to leave, and I was out of time to figure out a plan. I didn't think there would ever be a successful one. That was impossible. I just had to go.

TWENTY-SEVEN

"I was just another evil in her life."

KING

Shoving one hand into my hair in frustration, I held the phone to my ear with the other. This hadn't been what Rumor needed to witness right now. She was convinced the Mafia was after her. I didn't know who the fucker was that Thatcher had shot and tied up to take underground, but I knew the bastard wasn't Mafia.

"King," Blaise Hughes came over the line.

"Boss. Thatch said you wanted to talk to me," I replied.

"Is she gonna bolt?" he asked me.

"Seems like it, but I'm going to watch her," I assured him.

"Do more than that. She needs to stay put for a while, and I have other shit to deal with. Fuck her. Use that charm shit and charm her."

My hand tightened on the phone. "Did you just say I was to fuck her?"

"Is there a problem? Thatcher seemed to think you were the one she'd want and that Sebastian would be the next choice. You rather I tell him to do it?"

Not what I'd expected to be told to do, and there was no way I was letting Sebastian do it. "I can do it, but is it necessary?"

"Are you questioning me?" he asked, his tone sounding as deadly as I knew he was.

"No, sir," I replied.

"Good. Now, handle it."

The call ended, and I stood there, staring back at the truck, making sure she wasn't going to open the door and bolt.

How the hell had it gone from *no one touch her* to me being ordered to fuck her?

"You don't look happy about it," Thatcher drawled, and I turned my head to see him standing a few feet behind me with a cigarette in his mouth and a smirk on his face.

"He wants me to fuck her. To get her to stay."

Thatcher chuckled. "Yeah, I know."

This wasn't funny. She had been abused. Emotionally and physically hurt. The thought of manipulating her with sex made my stomach knot up. She deserved more than that.

"It's fucking. Jesus Christ, what is your problem? You look like you were just ordered to put a gun to her pretty head and shoot."

I glared at him as he took a pull from his cigarette. "It's not fair to her. It's a lie."

He raised his eyebrows. "You don't want to fuck her? Because I could have sworn you've wanted to since day one. And everything we have told her has been a damn lie."

He was right. Still, it didn't make this easier. Sebastian would be the better match for her. He'd probably even be all in. Faithful and shit. Not lying. But, damn it, I couldn't let him touch her. I'd end up killing him.

"I'm just supposed to make her think we have something? A relationship?" I wasn't really asking him. I knew what Blaise wanted. I just couldn't seem to make it okay in my head.

"You are the charmer. It's what you do. Go do it. Stop making it hard."

I glanced back at the truck and knew I had to get back to her. She was scared and alone. She trusted me. Her eyes had widened as she admitted it. The fact that she trusted me had surprised her. Dammit, I didn't want to do this.

I would never be a real relationship for her. Or anyone. But especially someone like her. She was too sweet, fragile, broken for me. I wasn't the guy to heal her, help her get through the hell she'd lived. I was just another evil in her life.

"Go handle the bastard who was trying to get onto the property. I'll go do my job," I told him, not looking back as I started toward the truck.

"If you change your mind, I'm sure Sebastian will happily step in," he called out.

I didn't bother responding. He was trying to piss me off. If I were a good man, I'd do just that. Let Sebastian do this. But I wasn't good. I was selfish. I wouldn't be able to stand any of the others having her even if it was fake and temporary. This was going to be one of the things I shouldn't do, but did anyway. I had many of those in my life. This one would be different though. I might never forgive myself for it.

When I climbed into the truck, Rumor was sitting there, clasping her hands tightly in her lap. I didn't need to see her eyes to know she was terrified. She thought this was all on her, and Blaise was right. She was going to run or try to. I had to give her a reason to stay.

"Everything is fine. Wasn't the Mafia. Like I said," I told her as I closed the door.

She turned her head to me, and her eyes glistened with unshed tears. "Really?"

I nodded. "Swear."

"Should we check on Maeme?" she asked, her voice quavering.

I shook my head. "No, she's not home. She's gone to my dad's to stay with my little sister while my dad and stepmom go on a short trip."

Her eyes widened. "I forgot you had a sister."

I nodded. "Yeah. Birdie. She was in the kitchen at the family breakfast. You didn't get to meet her."

"You said she was five, right?"

I pulled out onto the road and drove the short distance to the ranch entrance. "Yep. Dad married Jupiter, her mom, seven years ago. She is wife number four and only two years older than me."

"Wow," she whispered.

Yeah, wow. My dad had shown me firsthand how relationships never worked. They always ended in tears, hate, and cost a lot of fucking money. I wanted nothing to do with that. Ever.

"We are still going to watch the race? Are the police not coming?" she asked warily.

I wasn't going to be able to explain this to her. Yet another lie to add to the many I had told her. I knew it was time that I turned my conscience off. I was attracted to her. That was not an issue. If I hadn't gotten to know her and…started to care about her, then I'd be able to do this without blinking an eye. But I cared. I wanted to protect her. Maybe one day, when this was over, she wouldn't hate me completely. Perhaps I could give her some memories that she wanted to keep.

"It's being handled," I said as I parked beside the other vehicles outside the stables. "The ranch has its own security team. They will deal with things. We are going to go inside and enjoy the evening."

TWENTY-EIGHT

*"You don't have to be jealous, sweets.
Your body has my complete attention."*

RUMOR

I understood that the life of the wealthy or uber-wealthy was different. That they handled things more discrete than most. Money was power, and the more you had of the first, the more you had of the second. It came hand in hand. I got all that.

However, I had not known that the billionaires of the world were unfazed by gunshots and criminals trying to get onto their property. King wasn't even shaken by what had happened. It was as if I hadn't been shoved onto the floor of his truck while he fired a gun at someone. This wasn't okay. Was it? I mean, shouldn't they have cops surrounding the place? They had shot at us. King had shot at someone. There should be…an investigation going on.

Yet here we were, in the large party room I'd been to before in the stables, while people yelled and cheered at the screen covering the wall as horses raced. King kept his hand on my lower back as he drank from the glass of whiskey in his other hand. He was smiling at the screen as if nothing had happened.

Not only was I trying to wrap my head around that, I was also struggling with the fact that there was an almost-naked brunette in Storm's lap and his hand was between her legs. She was rubbing against it like a dog in heat right in front of everyone. No one seemed to care or notice that either. I was afraid to look anywhere else. It seemed whenever I did, I saw something startling.

"King," a redhead, wearing a very tiny bikini, cooed as she came to curl up on his other side, the side I wasn't standing on, "you promised to go in the hot tub with me."

King glanced down at her, then back at the race. "Change of plans," he said simply.

Her hand slid around his waist, and I began to step away from him. I needed distance from whatever she was planning on doing, but King's hand moved from my back to my hip and clamped down on it, holding me still. I swung my gaze up to his face, and his jaw ticked, as if he were annoyed.

"Moira, go away." His tone was even, but the command in it wasn't missed on me or her.

She dropped her hand from his body and immediately walked back toward the door. I watched her trying to decide if she was his date tonight. Did the shooting that everyone was ignoring change his plans? He was afraid to leave my side now?

"I'm fine," I said bitterly. I didn't want to be in the way of his good time.

He stared down at me. "Okay. Good," he said in a slow drawl as he studied me.

Sighing, I shifted my eyes back to the door where Moira had exited. "Your date. You can go with her. I am fine watching the race."

His brows drew together, and then he turned to look back at the screen. "She's not my date. I don't date."

She thought she was something. He'd made a promise to her about the hot tub.

Unable to keep my mouth shut and let it go, I continued, "She was expecting you to go to the hot tub with her."

He dropped his gaze back to mine again. "Like I said, change of plans."

I was jealous. There. I admitted it. I was jealous of her and the blonde. I had no reason to be. Right now, I should be focused on the fact that the Mafia was after me or they could be. We had been shot at. A million other things. Not that King had women all over that he did things with. Like spanking and having sex in a tack room or getting into hot tubs with almost-naked girls.

"You can go. She looks like your type," I snapped and immediately wished I hadn't.

He turned toward me, and then his eyes darkened slightly, and I worried I'd said too much. "What do you know about my type?" he asked me.

Why had I said that? I wanted to go back to my cottage and read. Alone. Where I wouldn't say stupid things or know who King was with. It didn't matter anyway.

"Just that you like them sexy, beautiful with perfect bodies, barely clothed. She fits the checks."

The right corner of his mouth twitched, but he didn't smile. "That's what I like, huh?"

I swallowed hard, not liking the fact that we were still talking about this. "Yes, it would seem so."

His eyes slowly drifted down my body, stopping briefly at my chest, then traveling the rest of the way down. "In that case, you need to remove some clothing, and you'd fit the checks too."

Wait. What?

He reached out and ran the tip of his pointer finger over my collarbone, then barely dipped it into my cleavage. My breath got stuck in my throat, and I gasped, but I didn't move. Not an inch.

When his eyes came back to meet mine, he leaned down close to my ear. "You don't have to be jealous, sweets. Your body has my complete attention."

A shiver ran through me. One I couldn't define. Was it fear? Desire? Both? Was I even awake? This was not like King. He didn't talk to me this way. Or look at me this way.

"What? No comment this time?" he asked as his warm breath tickled just below my ear.

My knees felt slightly weak. I needed my head examined. That was it. The shooting had sent me into some sort of shock. I was fantasizing.

The sharp sting of his teeth biting down on my earlobe, then releasing it caused me to reach out and grab on to his arm for support. What was he doing to me?

"I bet you taste real fucking good, sweets," he whispered before running the tip of his nose along my neckline.

When he straightened back up, I was still standing there in a haze of confusion and need. Never in my life had I felt the things that he caused to stir up in my body. This had to be real. It felt more real than anything ever had in my life. I couldn't make this up. My imagination wasn't this creative.

I watched as he turned his focus back on the race. Forcing myself not to stare at him, I did the same. I didn't understand much of anything that was happening other than horses were being raced around a track. People were cheering. A few shouted curse words.

The warmth of King's body as he moved closer to my side made me tremble. His hand slid over my hip, and he leaned down. "The horse that just won was one of ours. Not here, but from our ranch in Ocala, Florida," he explained as his hand moved down over my butt. "A lot of bets were placed, so majority of the folk here won a good deal of money." His fingers brushed the skin just past the edge of my shorts.

I jerked, but said nothing, nor did I move when he slid his hand over until the tips of his fingers were underneath my shorts and edging between my legs. Breathing was getting more difficult.

"You want a drink?" he asked me, swiping a finger inside the crotch of my panties.

I grabbed his arm then and let out a small sound. The tingle that shot through me was unfamiliar and startling.

While I tried to suck in some air, King pulled his hand out from under my shorts and moved it back to my waist. "Let's go get you a drink. There's food too. You hungry?"

I stared up at him. Was he serious? My entire body felt flushed, and I was panting, yet he seemed as if he hadn't just had his hand inside my panties.

"What?" I asked when his eyes met mine.

He grinned and then stuck a finger inside his mouth and sucked. I stared at him, gaping. Was that the one he'd touched me with?

"That's even better than I imagined," he said in a husky tone, then tucked a lock of my hair behind my ear with his damp finger. "What do you want to drink?"

"Moira is fucking Wells in the hot tub," Thatcher announced as he walked into the room.

King didn't even glance his way. He nodded his head toward the bar, then pressed his palm to my back to lead me over to it so I could get a drink.

"I bet he's not spanking her ass the way she likes," Storm called out as he moved the girl in his lap to straddle him.

I jerked my eyes off them, wishing I hadn't looked over there again. She was topless now, and I wasn't sure if they were going to have sex right there in front of everyone. Surely not.

"Tell me what you want to drink, sweets," King said to me.

I shook my head. I didn't know. I wasn't sure I could drink. His hand covered mine, and he walked me around to the other side of the bar, then came up behind me, placing both his hands on either side of me, caging me in.

"They've all been drinking. Three of our horses won today. Everyone is celebrating," he said as he bent down and pressed a kiss to my bare shoulder. "They're gonna fuck, sweets. It's what they do. They will do it so everyone can see. Tell me what you want to drink, and I'll take you upstairs so you don't have to watch."

Was he going to leave me there? Then what? Come back down here and join the orgy or whatever this was about to become?

"Vodka soda," I whispered, deciding I needed something stronger if I was going to survive this.

He dropped his arms and moved away from my back. I immediately missed his warmth, but I didn't want to think about that too deeply. I had too many other thoughts going through my head. Like the fact that he'd touched me and sucked his finger.

I placed a hand on my cheek, and it was warm. I was warm. Everything was warm.

"Here you go, sweets," he said, placing a drink in my hand.

My fingers wrapped around the cold glass, and I was tempted to press it against my flushed face. Just to cool off.

King's hand was on my back again. "Time to leave unless you want to watch the show."

I started walking as he nudged me on. My eyes locked with Thatcher's, and he smirked, then closed his eyes and stretched his neck. It was then that I realized a woman was on her knees in front of him. Holy crap. I jerked my gaze back to the door and kept it focused on the exit. Getting out of here.

When we were out of the sex den, I stopped walking. "I want to go back to the cottage. I don't want to be left alone upstairs." Why had he brought me to this? Clearly, he'd known this was what would happen.

"I'm not leaving you alone upstairs," King replied and turned me the opposite way from where we had entered.

I continued on, but I wanted clarification. "Are you not coming back down here…for the celebrating?"

"No."

We reached a set of stairs, and I turned around fully to stare up at him. "Why don't you just take me back to the house and leave me?"

His gaze ran over my face as if he was trying to memorize it. "Because you had a shock tonight and I'm not leaving you alone. You'll be scared. You won't get any rest."

This was all very true. Being alone at the house probably was going to be hard to do now. After all I'd found out and the gunfire.

I nodded.

"Can we go upstairs now?" he asked me with a crooked grin on his gorgeous face.

I sighed and headed up the stairs. This was all getting more confusing and messed up, the longer I stayed. My life no longer made sense. Nothing did. I was developing feelings for a man, and I had no business doing that. I had no future. Not really. At least not anymore.

At the top of the stairs, I stopped, and King pointed toward the door to the right. "That's my room."

"Your room?" I asked, glancing back at him.

He nodded. "I live here most of the time."

He lived in a barn? Or stables? Granted, they were nicer than most homes in the neighborhood I had lived in with Hill, but still, why would he live here?

King stepped around me and opened the door, then waved a hand for me to go inside. Curious to see where it was King lived most of the time, whatever that meant, I walked into the room. It was much bigger than I had anticipated.

The king-size bed sat against the far wall with black sheets and a charcoal-gray quilt. To the right was a gray leather sofa that sat caddy-corner and a coffee table that had paperwork spread out on it, like he had been working on something. I realized it was facing the flat screen on the wall in front of the bed.

Underneath the television was a wide dresser in flat black, and then on the left side of the room was an open door to the en suite. There were no pictures on the walls or any other kind of decor. There were no windows, but oddly enough, it didn't feel closed in. It was clean, tidy even.

King stepped inside behind me, and I heard the click of the door as it closed, and then his body stood too close. The warmth from it made me want to turn around and snuggle closer. Inhale his woodsy cinnamon scent. I wasn't going to do that though. Didn't mean I couldn't fantasize about it.

"You going to stand here all night or go get comfortable on the sofa? We can watch a movie," he said so close to my ear that his breath tickled my skin.

I tensed as his hand touched my waist. Now that we were up here, I wasn't sure what to expect. Not after what he had done downstairs.

"What are you…we…what are—" I stumbled over my words, not sure how to ask this.

"Go sit down, Rumor," he replied as he squeezed my side.

Since I wasn't the best at forming complete sentences currently, I did as he'd asked—or perhaps told me to do would be more accurate. I went to the sofa, not looking back at him and wondering if he was going to follow. My gaze dropped to the paperwork spread out on the table just as he leaned over and began to pick it up, placing it in a pile before taking it away. I turned and watched as he opened a drawer on his dresser and placed the papers inside. Before he could look back at me, I took a seat on the sofa with my glass clasped firmly with both hands.

When his eyes met mine again, he flashed me the smile he had, the one that was so charming that it was unfair. It flustered me. I couldn't stop thinking about how he had touched me. His finger inside his mouth. It all seemed so…dirty. Yet here I was, achy between my legs from the thought of it.

Hill hadn't been my first sexual experience. I'd lost my virginity to the senior quarterback on the football team in high school when I was a sophomore. Our relationship was short-lived once his mother found out. Elliot was the mayor's son. His family was wealthy and well respected. His father had plans for loftier political positions—which he had accomplished, seeing as he was now the governor. Elliot dating a girl living in the foster system had horrified his mother, and he'd broken up with me, apologizing that he couldn't hinder his father's future and that a lot was expected of him.

Then, there had been two others between Elliot and Hill. Neither was around long. One wasn't…one wasn't a relationship at all. He had taken me by force, and in doing so, I had been blamed and kicked out of my last foster home.

Shaking those thoughts away, not wanting to remember them, I got my focus back on King. He was different. None of the others had made me feel…like he did.

The thrill, tingle, whatever it was that he'd caused, was new to me.

"What did I do to cause that pretty face to frown?" King asked as he sat down beside me, close enough that our bodies were touching.

I shook my head nervously. "Nothing. I was just thinking… not…not about you. I mean, about things. But not you." I stopped. He had me so flustered that I needed to just quit trying to converse. I sounded like an idiot.

"Rumor." The way he said my name made me shiver.

I turned to look at him. It was hard not to get lost in those blue eyes of his. The way he looked at me, as if he saw nothing else. When he locked in on me, I wanted things I could not have. Ever. With anyone.

"Relax. It's just me. You look ready to bolt from the room," he said, reaching out and running the pad of his thumb over my chin. "Was it so bad? Having my finger slip inside you?"

Oh, good Lord. I opened my mouth, then closed it. How did I respond to that? My face was warm again as I stared up at him, wishing I knew what to say.

With the tip of his thumb, he traced my lips slowly, studying them. "Your lip is all healed up. I never want to see this mouth hurt again. I'd have to kill someone." He grinned as his eyes lifted to mine. "Don't get me wrong. I like the idea of them swollen, but not from abuse."

I swallowed hard. There wasn't a place on my body I wasn't being affected by this man. He was barely touching me, and I was panting. Did he realize the effect he had on me? Yes, I was sure he did. He wasn't blind to his ability to mesmerize a female. I would bet he'd been doing it most of his life.

"When was the last time someone made you feel good?" he asked, still caressing my face.

I blinked, but said nothing.

"Did the stupid fucker you married take care of you? Did he ever take his time and bring you pleasure?"

Again no words. I was doing good to breathe.

"So fucking sweet," he murmured as his fingers slid into my unruly curls. "You taste like honey. Did you know that? I've yet to take a drink of my whiskey because I don't want to wash the taste of your pussy from my mouth."

My eyes widened as I sucked in a breath.

He smirked and leaned closer to me. "You're trembling, sweets."

Yes, I was trembling. What did he expect? No man had ever talked to me like this. Especially one who looked like him. He made it hard to concentrate and keep my head on straight.

"Don't be scared of me," he pleaded. "I would never do anything to you that didn't feel good."

I'd heard the screams of pain from the woman he'd been having sex with in the tack room. I tensed at that memory, and it helped snap me out of this haze he had pulled me into. I shook my head and backed up, putting some distance between us. I was possibly still married if Hill was alive. I was running from the police or the Mafia—I no longer knew for sure. I shouldn't be doing this... whatever it was.

Yes, I was attracted to King. What woman in her right mind wouldn't be? He was gorgeous, sexy, charming, and he'd been there to help me when I had no one. He had continued to be there for me. It was impossible not to feel things for him. But having sex with him wasn't an option. It would be stupid. Really, really stupid.

"I...I disagree," I choked out in a whisper. "I don't like being... hit or...or spanked. Whatever it is you do."

A serious expression came over his face. "I'd never hurt you, Rumor."

Stop it! Stop with the look and the eyes! I tried to tear my gaze off him, but he made it impossible.

"You like to hit women who want to be tied up and spanked."

A deep chuckle came from him that made my entire body feel it, as if it had vibrated throughout me. There was a large part of me that wanted to rub up against him like a cat. I would fight that, of course. It was just getting more difficult.

"I enjoy rough sex, yes. But, sweets, I would never do that to you. I know why you wouldn't want that, and even if you did, I don't think I could," he said, running the back of his hand over my right cheek. "But I want to open those pretty legs and put my mouth on your pussy. I want to hear you scream my name as you orgasm and I taste every sweet drop."

I sucked in air as I stared up at him. Holy crap, had he just said that?

He moved in closer to me and leaned in to press a kiss against my cheek, then my neck. "You smell amazing," he whispered against my skin.

I should be pushing him off me now. Moving him back. Telling him no. But my hands disagreed as they ran up his arms to squeeze his biceps. I didn't want him to move. My eyes fluttered closed as he trailed kisses down further to my collarbone.

"Come here," he said in a husky tone as he grabbed my thigh and pulled it over his lap until I was straddling him.

Both of his hands moved up and underneath my blouse. I dropped my gaze to see his fingers tugging the cups of my bra down beneath the fabric. Okay, I was doing this. We were doing this. I shouldn't. A smart woman would stop him. I had too much uncertainty in my future.

But…but maybe that was why I should stop thinking. Let this happen. I wasn't promised tomorrow. No one was, but my odds were much worse than the norm. If this was my one chance to enjoy sex the way King's touch promised I would, then shouldn't I have that?

Just once in my life, I wanted to know what it felt like for someone to take my breath away.

TWENTY-NINE

"Such a fucking good girl."

KING

If I wasn't already positive that there was a room waiting on me in hell, then I knew that, tonight, I was about to make that reservation solid. Everything about this was wrong, but, fuck, I'd never wanted anyone this much. Each little sharp intake of breath Rumor took went straight to my cock. Seducing someone as fragile and uncertain as her shouldn't be such a goddamn turn-on.

But, fuck me, it was. And if I didn't get my face between her legs soon, I was going to lose it. I hadn't been lying to her when I said she tasted like honey. Damn, her pussy was sweet. I wanted more of it. I wanted to lap at her cunt while she moaned and begged me not to stop. I wanted a lot of things with this woman, and one night wasn't going to be enough to do all of them. I had to be easy with her. Slow.

Cupping her face with my hand, I brushed a soft kiss against her lips. The need to suck that fat upper lip was strong, but I had time. First she deserved gentle. This needed to be all about her. Her entire body was strung so tight that I was afraid she was going to try and bolt at any moment.

I ran the tip of my tongue over her lips, and she opened them, gasping in the process. Taking advantage of it, I slid inside. I wasn't much into kissing. It had always seemed like a pointless thing meant for foreplay that bored me. But this wasn't that. Not even close.

A soft moan came from her throat, and she rocked her hips, pressing her pussy against my dick as her hands gripped my shoulders. The way her tongue flicked against mine almost shyly was causing triggers to go off inside me I'd never experienced before. I wanted to wrap her in my arms and hold her here. Like this. Not let her go. Maybe get her naked and my dick buried inside of her, but I didn't want to stop kissing her.

When she moved against me again, she broke the kiss and let out a small cry. Her eyes closed, and long lashes brushed her high cheekbones.

I'd never believed in angels until now. Fuck. She had me thinking poetic shit. I had to get this back on track. This wasn't me. This was dangerous.

Taking the hem of her shirt, I tugged it up and over her head. She raised her arms, letting me pull it completely off. Both of her big, full tits were already free of the cups of her bra. I took a nipple into my mouth and sucked hard while unclasping the back of it and taking it off her body. Taking a moment, I let myself appreciate the view. Her smooth skin was flawless. I knew if I studied it closer, near her ribs, I would see scars, but that didn't mar its perfection. It reminded me how fucking strong she was.

"Stand up," I told her, and she blinked with a slightly confused look on her pretty face.

Just when I thought she was going to end this, she stood up obediently. I didn't give her time to think about what we were doing. I had to keep her in this. With me. Wanting me.

I stood up and ran my hands from her shoulders to her fingertips before lowering myself and unbuttoning her shorts, then sliding them down her long legs, followed by the black satin panties she was wearing.

Once I had her naked, I stood back up and saw the pink flush on her face and chest.

"You're perfect," I told her, somehow knowing she needed to hear it.

The insecure glint in her green eyes eased, but I could tell she wasn't sure she believed me.

"Rumor," I said firmly as I placed my hands on her small waist, "you are beautiful."

She pulled her bottom lip between her teeth and bit down on it as a small smile tugged at the corner of her lips. I wanted to laugh at how fucking cute it was.

I nodded my head toward the bed. "Go lie down on your back," I told her.

She glanced at the bed, then back at me, but she didn't move.

I stepped closer to her and pressed a kiss to her lips. "If you don't lie on my bed, I'm going to pick you up and toss your sexy ass on it."

She sucked in a breath, then blinked up at me before turning and walking to my bed. This time, it was me biting my lip to keep from grinning. My eyes dropped to her ass, and I had to adjust my already-throbbing dick pressing against the zipper in my jeans. She had two dimples right above her ass. It was as fucking sweet as she was. The urge to drop to my knees and kiss and lick those two indentions was strong. I would do it. But not tonight.

When she sat down and slid back onto my bed, I stood there, taking it in. Memorizing the picture she made. Searing the image to my brain for when this was done. When I wouldn't see it again. The thought of my limited time didn't sit well. I didn't like it.

"That's good," I told her as I unzipped my jeans and shoved them down, stepping out of them before I walked over to stand between her legs.

Grabbing her knees, I opened her thighs, ignoring her strangled cry. The wet folds of her pink pussy made me slightly crazed.

Not bothering to give her any more direction, I put her legs over my shoulders and pressed my mouth against her needy cunt. The moment my tongue ran along her folds, her body bucked beneath me as she cried out my name. Loving the sound of it, I continued tasting her. I flicked her clit with my tongue, and her hands grabbed the back of my head.

"OH GOD!"

I gave special attention to that swollen pulse, swirling my tongue around it, then sucking on it.

"KING! Don't...don't stop, please," she panted as her nails bit into my skull.

"This is a perfect little pussy, sweets," I told her, then began to slowly lap at her in a rhythm that I knew would drive her crazy.

She began panting and begging. The uncertainty I'd seen in her eyes was gone now. I had brought her to the brink, and I knew she would do anything to get more. Wanting to push her further and let her know what being in control felt like, I stood over her, then climbed on the bed to lie on my back.

The desperate gaze in her eyes as she watched me was exactly where she needed to be for this.

"Straddle my face, Rumor," I urged her.

The way her green eyes widened, I was almost afraid I'd lost her. She'd back away now. I had been sure I had her so close to an orgasm that she wouldn't withdraw on me.

"Come on, sweets," I said, holding out my hand to her. "I want your pussy on my face. Come use my mouth the way you want. You control this."

She moved then, and I smiled as she rolled over, then got on her knees before adjusting herself over me.

When she looked down at me, I grabbed her juicy ass and squeezed, then pushed her further up. "Come on."

She reached forward and grabbed the headboard as she spread her legs wider and settled her open cunt over my face. I inhaled deeply and soaked in her arousal. With my hands on her hips, I pulled her down until my mouth was latched back on her needy pussy. It didn't take much from me before she began rocking her hips to get more pleasure.

"Rub it on my face," I told her, then placed a gentle slap on her ass.

She jerked and froze, but only a moment before she dropped even lower and began to work herself over my mouth. Fuck, this was hot. I didn't let women take control, and I sure as hell didn't let them ride my face like this, but knowing my sweet little Rumor was doing it had me reaching to free my cock from my boxer briefs and fisting it.

"King," she moaned, and the hand I still had on her plump ass squeezed.

"That's it, baby. Fuck my face," I encouraged.

When her thighs began to tremble, I let go of myself and held onto her as she rode through the orgasm.

"Oh!!! OH GOD!" she screamed and slapped her spasming pussy against my face wildly.

I savored every moment of it, giving her everything she needed until she slowed, then stilled.

Giving her time to think about what she had just done wasn't on the agenda. I flipped her over onto her back and climbed over her, nudging her legs open wider as I finished getting off my boxers. She was still panting as she stared at my impressive erection. I nodded toward the table beside the bed that she was closest to now.

"Open it. Get a condom."

She didn't move right away, and I was real damn close to sinking into her raw before she could decide this was a bad idea. But she finally turned enough to open the drawer and pull out a condom. It was well stocked, and she paused, holding it, as if the fact that I'd fucked a lot of women in this room was just dawning on her. Not where I wanted her head right now. Especially since it was rare I did anything with a woman in the bed. I normally had them tied up in the tack room.

Reaching over, I took it from her hand and kept my eyes locked on hers as I tore it open with my teeth and began to roll it down over me. She swallowed hard, and it was as if I could hear her thoughts; she was so damn expressive.

I placed a hand on either side of her head and lowered my face to hover over hers. "I've never let a woman fuck my face. You were a first."

The softness and flash of relief in her eyes was all I needed. I held her gaze as I began to sink inside her tight entrance. Hissing through my teeth as I was sucked into her wet heat.

"AH!" Her eyes closed as her mouth opened once I was fully inside.

"Fuck, that's a tight pussy," I groaned, dropping my head to the curve of her neck and trying not to lose it and fuck her like an animal.

"It's…a lot," she breathed.

I grinned, but didn't let her see it. "Does it hurt?"

She shook her head. "No. It's…just big."

My cock jerked inside her at hearing the praise from her sweet mouth. I had to be gentle. She needed gentle. This wasn't about me wanting to fuck her into the damn wall and then doing it again and again. I was giving her what she deserved. Not what I suddenly wanted so bad that I could barely contain my need.

Slowly, I began to slide out and in, hoping I could keep this up. When she ran her hands over my arms and she moaned my name, I began to move a little harder and faster. Not much, but more.

"Can you…" she breathed, and I looked down at her. That was a mistake. Seeing her face, letting those eyes meet mine. I was trying to keep it together and not fuck like I wanted to. "Can you do it harder?"

Jesus H. Christ.

The control I thought I'd had snapped. I forgot all my good intentions. Taking her left thigh, I pulled it up higher and held myself over her as I began to thrust into her deeper, taking more. Watching her tits bounce as I took what I wanted.

"This what you want?" I growled.

"Yes!"

I slid my hand under her head and covered her mouth with mine. Sucking her tongue into my mouth the way I was sinking inside her. She began to meet me, lifting her hips from the bed. Sexy sounds came from her mouth, filling mine.

"Good girl," I praised her, kissing the corner of her mouth.

With her lips parted, she gazed up at me. Lost in her own pleasure.

I slammed into her hard. "Such a fucking good girl."

"Oh! KING!" she cried out just as her eyes fluttered closed and her body shook beneath me.

Her tight walls clamped down on my dick and squeezed me so tight that I let out a roar.

"FUUUCK!!!" I shouted as I filled the condom, still driving inside her. Over and over. I didn't want to stop. I wanted her tight cunt to keep milking me.

Shuddering one last time, I pulled out of her and rolled onto my side, taking her with me. Closing my eyes, I didn't look at her as she curled up against my side. I needed a minute. I was torn. Part of me wanted to do it again. The other part...well, it was dealing with guilt. Not an emotion I felt often. If ever.

At least not since Rumor had walked into my life.

I'd been ordered to fuck her. Make her stay. Use sex as a tool. And it had taken me what...three hours to do it? I was a selfish motherfucker. I'd been given the green light on what I'd been wanting since I'd laid eyes on her picture almost a month ago, and I had taken it. And I was going to take it again.

"King."

Her soft voice snapped me out of my inner turmoil, and I opened my eyes to look at her.

She was watching me closely. I had to reassure her. Take that worry out of her eyes. I was lying to her and manipulating her. The least I could do was make sure she knew how incredible she was. Her insecurities ran deep.

"Yeah, sweets?" I replied, picking up her hand and kissing her fingers.

Her body instantly relaxed. That was all it took. Something that simple, and she was okay.

"That was…" She stopped and dropped her gaze from mine.

"That was amazing," I finished for her.

Her eyes shot back up to mine.

Unable not to smile at her expressive face, I asked, "Wasn't it?"

She nodded. "Yes, it…was."

I rolled over to face her and continued pressing my lips to each of her fingers. "Are you trying to make me insecure, sweets?" I teased.

The blush on her cheeks was adorable. "No. It was…I never…I didn't know it could be like that."

Fuck. The guilt was back. Dammit. I had to get control over that pesky emotion. This was a job. I had to keep myself from making it more.

"You've been fucking the wrong men," I told her, then kissed her hand one more time before letting it go. I had to get some distance. Get my head straight. I sat up and discarded the condom before glancing back at her. "I'll go get a shower, then run you a bubble bath," I told her, then winked before leaving her there, curled up on my bed, naked and tempting as hell.

I was so screwed.

• THIRTY •

"You in a hurry to get away from me, sweets?"

RUMOR

I wasn't sure how long I should lie in this bed alone. There were no windows, so the room was pitch-black, except for the clock beside the bed that said it was 9:32 in the morning. Sitting up, I held the covers up to my neck since I was naked underneath. I'd opened my eyes sixteen minutes ago, and I was still debating if I should go get dressed and leave. I knew the way back to the cottage.

Closing my eyes, I tried not to think about what I had done last night. At least not right now. I would think about it later. When I was gone. Not while I was still naked in King's room. I wanted to remember it. I would remember it often. Just not at the moment. This was not the place.

Especially since he had left me here without a word. Granted, it was late, and it was a Saturday. Maybe he had gone to Maeme's for breakfast. Wouldn't he have woken me up to go there?

Dropping the blankets, I tossed them aside and slid over to get out of the bed. Staying here in the dark was silly. I should go. What we had done was just sex. We'd had a weird night. It was over.

My reality was back. Although my reality was going to suck even more than it had already. Now that I'd experienced a night in King's arms and in his bed, knowing what it was like to orgasm while having sex and not just once, being held and treated as if I was special…yeah, that had ruined me. Life would be easier if I'd never known what that was like.

I felt my way to the en suite and flicked on the lights, then squinted against the brightness in the luxurious white bathroom. My eyes went to the massive tub with its fancy jets. I'd taken a bath in there last night. When I had gotten out, King had wrapped me in a fluffy towel, then carried me to bed and held me until I fell asleep. Yes, I was in fact ruined.

Trying to not think about King, I took a white robe from the hook by the door and slipped it on. I still wasn't sure where my clothes were. After I had it tied on at the waist, I used the bathroom, worked my fingers through my curls the best I could without my conditioning spray and comb, then put some toothpaste on my finger and did the best I could with my teeth.

The sound of the bedroom door opening caused me to freeze and stare at myself in the mirror, trying to decide what to do. It was King. It had to be King. But…did I thank him? Ask for a ride to the house? Apologize for sleeping late?

Before I could think of what to do, his large form filled the doorway. My gaze swung to his, and the smile on his chiseled face instantly eased my anxiety that had been about to spin out of control.

"I brought breakfast," he said, then nodded his head back toward the bedroom. "Come eat."

"I didn't mean to sleep so late," I said.

He shrugged. "You were tired. I had worn you out. Maeme sent you waffles to recover. She never makes them on Saturdays. You're special."

My eyes flew open wide, and I covered my mouth in horror. Had he told her what we had done? Oh God, what did Maeme think of me?

The deep chuckle that came from him had me gaping at him. Why was he laughing?

"Relax, sweets. She doesn't know. I was teasing you."

I narrowed my eyes as I dropped my hand from my face. "That wasn't funny," I accused.

He took a step toward me and tilted his head. "Yeah, it was." The twinkle in his blue eyes made it hard to stay mad at him. "Come eat with me." He held out his hand.

"You didn't eat already?" I asked.

"I wanted to eat with you," he replied.

Giving in, I slipped my hand into his and watched as his fingers closed over mine before walking toward him.

"Are you naked under that robe?" he asked me as I reached his side.

I glanced down at it, then back at him. "I didn't know where my clothes were."

His eyes dropped to the gaping neckline. "I know what I want for dessert."

I tensed up as he pulled me into the bedroom and toward the sofa, where a large, covered tray sat on the coffee table in front of it.

"I need to go downstairs and get drinks. You want coffee? Juice?" he asked.

"Coffee," I replied, "but I can go get it."

He shook his head. "You're not going downstairs like that. I'll get it. Cream and sugar?"

I didn't bother asking about Splenda and almond milk, so I nodded. "Yes. Thank you."

He took the cover off the tray, revealing two plates sitting there, full of Maeme's biscuits, bacon, cheese grits, and tomato gravy. On the third plate was four of her thick, fluffy waffles stacked on it.

"Go ahead and get started. I'll be right back," he told me before turning and heading for the door.

I watched him go, wondering if any man alive had ever looked that good in jeans. He wore them so well. I'd had sex with him.

That gorgeous man…I'd straddled his face. I still couldn't believe I had done it, but *oh wow*. That experience had been life-altering. Taking a deep breath, I tried to stop thinking about it. I didn't want him returning to me looking hot and bothered. He was acting so normal. As if the fact that we had slept together was no big deal. He knew the Mafia had possibly killed Hill and could be after me. He knew I was being hunted, but he was acting as if that wasn't a fact. Like what we had done was okay.

But then he was a man. He was King. He had sex a lot. I'd seen the lifetime supply of condoms beside his bed. My mood soured as I stared at the bed. How many women had he done those things to in that bed? Or did he tie them up and spank them first? Did he use a belt? A whip? Those things that Christian Grey used? I shook my head. I had to stop this.

I heard his footsteps outside the door, and I reached to pick up a slice of bacon and took a bite before he walked back inside. I was actively chewing when his gaze met mine. God, he had the best eyes.

"Hungry?" he asked as he made his way over to me with two coffee cups in his hands.

I nodded, although that wasn't true. Not anymore at least.

He set a cup in front of me, then went to take the spot beside me. "We should enjoy this. Tomorrow might be a good Sunday breakfast to miss. Jupiter, my stepmom, is going to be there. She's annoying as fuck."

I glanced over at him. "What did you tell Maeme about my staying here?"

He took a waffle and put it on his plate. "That you slept in the bed and I slept on the sofa."

Maeme wasn't a stupid woman. What if she knew the truth? Would she ask me to leave?

"I should probably get dressed and walk back to the house once I'm done," I told him.

He took a bite of the waffle and chewed while looking at me. I tried not to watch the way his jaw worked or the way the muscles in his neck stood out. I had sat on that face. Ugh! I wasn't going to think about that anymore. I jerked my gaze off his and stared down at the food.

"You in a hurry to get away from me, sweets?"

I reached for my fork and shook my head. "No. It's not that. I know you have things to do, and I need to get out of the way." I jabbed at the scrambled eggs nervously.

"I was hoping you'd go for a ride with me. You can ride on Malta. She's old and slow."

I stopped attacking the eggs and looked back at him. "She's a horse."

He nodded, smirking at me.

"You want to take me horseback riding?"

He stuck a forkful of cheese grits in his mouth and nodded again.

Okay. He didn't want me to leave. He wanted to spend time with me. Why? I didn't understand this. What were we doing?

"I have to leave soon," I told him.

He swallowed. "Not technically. You can sleep in my bed as long as you want."

I shook my head. "I mean, leave. As in leave the cottage. Figure out where I am going to start over. We"—I waved a finger between the two of us—"shouldn't be doing this…what we did."

"We shouldn't be fucking?" he asked.

I nodded.

He licked his lips, and I found myself watching it as if it were porn. "Why can't we fuck, sweets? You enjoyed yourself, didn't you? You liked having my mouth on your pussy? The way you came on my cock said you were having a real good time."

Why did he have to talk like that? I was hot again. I needed some air. A fan. A freezer to perhaps stick my head inside.

"It's not…" I began and took a deep breath. "I didn't say I didn't like it. You know I did. But…it confuses things. Makes it complicated."

King reached over and wrapped one of my curls around his finger. "It doesn't have to. I can make you feel good. We can enjoy the hell out of it. No need to make it complicated. When it's time for you to go, I'll make sure you have everything you need. Sex isn't a bad thing. It's fun, sweets. It's two people bringing each other pleasure."

Why was it that when he explained it, things seemed normal? In my head, it wasn't so simple, but he made it sound like it was easy. Could it be? Was this just my inexperience with men and relationships?

"We're friends, aren't we?" he asked.

I nodded. He was possibly my only friend. There was Maeme, but I didn't really talk to her about things the way I did King. I trusted her, but not as much as I did him.

"Stop overthinking it. This is just another step in our friendship."

I stared at him. I might not know a lot, but friends didn't do what we had done. I'd read books. That got messed up real fast.

"I don't know."

His hand went to my leg, and he slid it up my thigh before pulling my left leg toward him, causing the robe to open up. "So, if I get on my knees and start eating that pussy, you're gonna tell me no?"

I tried to pull the robe back over my exposed vagina, but he grabbed my wrist and stopped me.

"No. I like looking at it. I like smelling it. I fucking love tasting it."

This was unfair. I had to get some kind of grip on the way he controlled me so easily with his words.

"You will get bored with me!" I blurted the fear I hadn't been able to admit to myself.

I was never going to let him tie me up and hit me. He wanted that, and I just couldn't do it.

The way his turquoise eyes turned to an ice blue as he stood up, still holding my arm, and pulled me up with him caused a slight twinge of panic, laced with excitement. I should be pushing him away. Not standing here, waiting on him to tell me what we were doing.

"Take off the robe and go put your hands on the edge of the bed with your ass up," he ordered.

"Wh-what?" I stammered.

He took the tie around my waist and tugged it free, dropping it to the floor. "Don't make me tell you again, Rumor."

I should run. Scream for help. Get away.

But I didn't want to.

This was King. I trusted King. I wanted King. The way I was tingling between my legs meant my body was in complete accord on doing what he said. When I shrugged my shoulders, the robe slid down them, and I dropped my arms so that it would fall off my body.

King's jaw tensed. "Good girl," he whispered huskily.

I'd never been praised before. Never. Not until last night. Maybe it was twisted and because I was broken inside, but hearing him tell me I was a good girl made me want to do whatever he asked. Just to hear him tell me I had done something right. That I hadn't messed up. That I hadn't disappointed him. That I was enough.

Turning, I walked over to the bed and took a long, steady breath before I bent over and placed my hands on the edge of it. Feeling completely exposed to King and not feeling embarrassment at all.

"Fuck," he swore.

I looked back over my shoulder to see him pulling his shirt off and then making quick work of his jeans. His eyes were locked on my ass. Wanting to be good for him, I opened my legs a little wider so he could see between them. The way his eyes lit up and his nostrils flared made me ache. He was looking at me like that. *Me.*

With four long strides, he was behind me, leaning over and opening the condom supply drawer. I wasn't going to think about the other women now. He was with me at the moment. Not someone else. This was just us. I was the one he was praising.

I listened to the sound of the wrapper opening, and I sucked in a breath, anticipating what was coming next. His hand slipping between my legs wasn't it. I shivered from his gentle touch.

"I'll get checked, make sure I'm clean, and then I want to fill this pussy up. Let you stand over me as I watch my cum leak out of you."

I let out a moan, unable to help myself. The way he said the dirtiest things and made my entire body tremble with need should be embarrassing. But it wasn't. I wanted it. All of it.

"Will you let me do that?" he asked, still touching me. "Can I fuck you raw?"

I gulped and nodded. "I'm on birth control."

"I know," he said huskily as he ran his finger up inside of me, then eased it out slowly before sliding it up my bottom. I tensed, and he chuckled. "I love your ass." His hand slapped it, but not hard enough for it to even sting. "Fuck, it bounces pretty."

He was going to make me get off from his words alone. I fisted the covers and closed my eyes as my body trembled. He slapped it again and groaned.

"Such a good girl," he said in a husky tone. "Letting me spank your sweet ass."

His hand hit me again, and I found myself pressing back against him. Each time he touched me, my body hummed with a promise of release.

"You want more?" His voice took on a deeper timbre as he caressed where he had just popped. "You like having me spank you, sweets? Does it make your pussy feel good?"

"Yes!" I panted, so close to something. I just needed more. A little more.

When his hand connected with my bottom this time, it was harder, and I cried out, shoving back against him as a sharp ache throbbed between my legs. That was different. I wanted more of it.

"Please," I moaned, desperate for it. Whatever it was building inside me.

"I don't want to hurt you," he cooed, running his hand over my bottom, then sliding it between my legs. "Dripping wet. You're close, aren't you?" he asked with excitement in his tone.

I nodded frantically. "Yes. Please, King. Please," I begged, pressing back and wiggling.

"Jesus," he whispered.

Then, his hand landed harder on my butt. The smack echoed in the room, and I jerked as his name tore from my lips. It felt like an explosion went off inside of me, and a wet gush ran down my legs, startling me as I continued to shake and let out moans and cries mixed together.

"Fuckin' hell!" King growled, then slammed inside of me, sending me spiraling further into this blissful realm he'd sent me to.

"Hottest damn pussy," he grunted as he began to drive into me. "FUCK, RUMOR!"

I clawed at the sheets and met his thrusts, pleading with each wonderful stretch and bite of pain. Beautiful pain. I'd never believed those two words went together, but in this moment, I understood. I'd do anything to feel this with him.

"I want my cum inside you," he said hoarsely. His fingers dug into my hips as he slammed me back against him. "Fuck, that's it. Fuck me hard like the good girl you are."

Those two words. I was sent shooting off into another orgasm. My knees buckled, and I no longer recognized my own voice as King's name tore from my chest.

"GAAAAH!" he roared as his body jerked behind me.

I collapsed onto the bed as I struggled to catch my breath. He held my hips up as he continued to pump into me several more times before he stilled. I listened to his ragged breathing as he stayed inside of me. We remained like that for several moments before he slid free. He let out a long sigh as he ran his hand down the inside of my legs.

The wet gush. My eyes flew open as I remembered it now. I'd been so far gone that I didn't care. But now…what was that?

"Easy, sweets," he said gently. "I'm not gonna fuck you again. Yet. I just want to taste it."

Taste it? I turned my head and looked back at him, not sure if my legs could hold me just yet without the bed's support. He was licking his fingers when his eyes met mine, and he grinned.

"We're gonna have to do that again when my face is down there."

"What?" I croaked.

"You're gonna squirt on my face. I didn't know you could do that. You were holding back on me."

I moved then, flipping over to sit on the bed. "What do you mean?"

He stood there with his finger still in his mouth as he studied me. I watched as he let it pop free of his lips.

"Was that the first time you squirted?" he asked me with a pleased look in his eyes.

I shook my head. "I don't know. What do you mean, squirted?"

A slow grin spread across his face, and he bit his bottom lip, then groaned. "Fuck."

I waited for him to say more, but he reached for the robe and picked it up, then wrapped it around me before dropping down to his haunches so that we were eye level.

"Your cunt ejaculated. It's not common, and most females find out they do it when they orgasm during sex the first time."

My eyes went wide. "Ejaculated…like…like a man?" I asked, horrified.

King chuckled and ran his hand inside my legs. "No, sweets. Nothing about that was like a man. It was fucking hot. The fact that you did it from me spanking you…" He stopped and shook his head. "We gotta stop talking about it. I'm gonna want to put you over my knee."

I opened my mouth and closed it. Had he just said that?

King stood back up. "I need to feed you," he said. "Then bathe you. If I have to smell sex on you all day, I won't be able to keep my hands off you."

This was not how I had expected our conversation to go.

Nothing about this would lead to something good. It would be bad. Especially for me when I had to walk away. Leave.

This was going to be one of the things in life I shouldn't have done, but I was going to do it anyway.

THIRTY-ONE

"She's got a magic pussy."

KING

"Who's here?" Rumor asked me when I pulled the truck up beside my dad's matte-black Range Rover outside Maeme's house.

"My father," I replied, glancing over at her. "He wanted to talk to me about some business before we go for a ride."

And Maeme wanted to set eyes on Rumor and make sure I hadn't done anything to upset her. She wasn't happy about Blaise's orders, but he was the boss.

Rumor fidgeted with the hem of her shorts nervously.

I reached over and covered her hands with one of mine. "What's wrong?"

She glanced up at me. "I…I feel like they will know."

They knew all right. They all fucking knew. I hated it. I hated that I had to lie to her. That was all I hated. The rest was…well, I wasn't so upset with Blaise anymore. There were some things a man could get over. Especially when he'd had the best sex of his life and he got to do it again. And again.

"They know you were scared last night. Do you really think that they are gonna believe I got between those pretty legs of yours when you'd been traumatized?"

She stared at me and thought about it. The relief in her green eyes had me wanting to grab her face and kiss those soft lips. I wasn't going to do it because I had to keep some lines drawn. I didn't want her hurt. I would do whatever I could to protect her. I didn't want her to get emotionally attached to me. I just wasn't sure how I was supposed to pull that off. Kissing when we weren't fucking was definitely a bad thing. That I knew.

"Let's go," I said, opening my door and getting the hell out of this truck and the temptation to get a taste of her mouth again.

By the time I reached her side, she had opened the door and was starting to get down. I'd blurred some lines now, and I figured picking her up to get her out was okay. It wasn't kissing. It would be fine. Besides, the smile that touched her lips when I did it made me feel like I'd won some prize. Which I had. Her hot little body.

I let her go and closed the door. "Let's go. Maeme is worried about you after last night. She's ready to see you and check to make sure you're okay." That was half the truth. Not a complete lie.

She nodded, and I headed for the house as she fell into step beside me. This was easier when we were locked up in my room at the stables. The lies, deceit, and manipulation weren't there. It was just us. Facing my father and Maeme was just going to remind me how this was not something I got to keep.

Keep? Where the hell had that come from? I hadn't meant keep. Not keep. Just…have longer.

The door to the house swung open, and Birdie came running out with her long black hair flying wildly behind her. She had my eyes. They were Salazar blue, as Maeme called it. In fact, she looked very little like Jupiter. The Salazar DNA was strong.

"KING!" she squealed just before hurling her tiny body into my arms.

I had stopped and bent down to catch her, prepared for it. As I swung her in a circle, she laughed happily before I slowed, then placed her back on her own two feet.

"Hey, my Birdie girl," I said and ruffled her hair. "This is my friend Rumor."

I turned to Rumor then and saw a soft smile on her face as she looked at Birdie. "Rumor, this is Birdie. My little sister I told you about."

Rumor held out her hand to Birdie. "It's very nice to meet you," she said.

Birdie scanned her up and down, then studied her hand before sticking her smaller one into it. "You are really pretty," Birdie said, staring up at her.

Rumor squatted down so she was eye level with Birdie. "I was just thinking about how beautiful you are. You look like a little girl version of your brother."

Birdie beamed at her. "That's cause Salazar NDA is superior."

"That's DNA," I corrected her, chuckling.

Rumor nodded. "I can see that."

Birdie smiled, pleased by her response. "I like your hair. Mine won't curl, but yours is like my favorite American Girl doll, Evette."

"That's high praise," I told Rumor, who tilted her head back and smiled up at me before standing back up.

"I can't brush her hair though, or it will ruin her curls. I did it once, and Mommy had to take it to get it fixed at the American Girl store. Can you brush your hair?" Birdie asked, frowning. "I hate brushing my hair."

"I can't use a brush," Rumor told her. "I have to use a special spray or just some water and a comb."

"Can I show you to my Maeme?" Birdie asked, completely forgetting my presence, which never happened. I'd hung the moon, where my little sister was concerned.

"She's met Maeme," I told Birdie. "But she is here to visit her, so why don't we go inside?"

Birdie reached up and took Rumor's hand again. "Come on. I know where she is," she told her and began to lead Rumor to the house.

I followed them inside, listening to Birdie tell Rumor about her American Girl doll collection, wondering if I should rescue her or if she was enjoying herself.

"There you are!" Maeme called out, walking from the kitchen, drying her hands on her apron. "I see you met Birdie."

"I have indeed had the pleasure," Rumor informed her.

Maeme glanced at me, but only barely. It was enough for me to know that my father, Stellan, and Thatcher were in the basement, waiting on me.

"I need to go find Dad," I said, and Rumor turned to look back at me. "I'll leave you with these two."

"Come now and help Birdie and me decorate the cupcakes that just finished cooling," Maeme said to her, waving the two of them toward the kitchen.

I left them there and headed for the back staircase. Last night's incident had been more than I let on with Rumor. The man they had underground right now, being watched by Storm and Wells, had finally talked after Thatcher got ahold of him. I didn't have all the details, and I knew I needed them. Especially since it was connected to Rumor.

Stepping into the sitting area in the basement, I found my father on the far-right sofa with one ankle propped on a knee as he leaned back, staring at me. I glanced over at Stellan, who was smoking a cigar on the middle sofa and looking at his phone. Thatcher was already drinking as he leaned against the bar.

"Took you long enough," Dad said, annoyed.

I shrugged. "I'm here."

"She's a good fuck, isn't she?" Thatcher asked me with a smirk.

I shot him a warning glare and took the sofa across from my father.

"Seems we weren't the only people Churchill Millroe tried to fuck over. He sold some other real estate that wasn't his to sell and took the profit. Since his disappearance, those wronged are finding out that they no longer own things that they didn't sell. Their signatures were forged. Most of them will handle it the legal way, although they will never find him.

"But it seems two grocery stores owned by the Insantos, used for laundering their drug money since that's their MO, were sold by Millroe to a luxury food chain company in England. They want to open some of their stores in the US and have bought three buildings in the Southeast, as well as three on the West Coast and two in the Midwest. Two of the ones in the Southeast, however, belonged to the Insantos. They tracked Rumor here, but we don't know how. The man is claiming he doesn't know. He was sent here to see if the informant was lying or not. He said they don't want her dead. They want her alive because they believe she has information." Stellan stopped talking then and stared at me hard as I let all this sink in.

If Millroe wasn't already dead, I'd go put a gun in his mouth and blow his motherfucking brains out for this.

"We make sure the Insantos know she is clueless, and we keep her here," I stated before either he or my father could tell me the plan. No other plan was going to work for me.

My father dropped his propped-up foot to the ground and leaned forward, looking hard at me. "It's the Insantos. They are out three million, and you think we can just tell them she knows nothing and they'll walk away? They are looking for her husband. We killed him. They think she will lead them to him."

I stood back up, needing to move. "Well, we tell them we killed his sorry ass and she knows nothing."

"She's got a magic pussy," Thatcher drawled. "Shoulda let me do it."

"Thatcher!" Stellan shouted as I clenched my fists at my sides.

"This has nothing to do with her pussy," I told him, wanting to put my fist through his smug face. "She's innocent. She was beaten by that bastard, and all she wants is to be free. Live a normal, SAFE life. That's what I want her to have."

"Away from here? You gonna let her give her cunt to someone else?" Thatcher asked, then took a drink from his glass.

"That's enough!" my dad said, standing up. "We are waiting on Blaise to make the call. He will decide what we do. You know that. But for now, she needs to stay with you. In the stables. It's safer than the cottage. Now that they are looking for her, she has to be kept out of sight."

"Fine. She stays in my room. I'll keep her safe. Out of sight," I replied, feeling a small ounce of relief.

"With your dick shoved in her many holes," Thatcher said.

"I'm this fucking close," I warned him.

He swirled his glass. "To what?"

"BOYS!" Stellan said, holding out a hand to both of us. "Enough."

I turned my attention back to Stellan. "I was going to take her riding today."

He shook his head. "Not today. We are adding more security. Keep her inside the stables. Bring her into the house. Use the theater, the pool. Sebastian said she loves books. Take her to the library. Whatever. Just not out in the open."

"Fine," I replied, ready to get out of here and back to Rumor.

I didn't like this. I didn't want to sit and wait on Blaise to make a call on our next move. He didn't know her. She was just a woman he wanted us to do right by since we had killed her abusive husband. She was more than that. She wasn't expendable. We were her family. She had no one else.

"Fuck her, son, but don't get attached," my father warned me.

"Too late," Thatcher drawled over his glass.

I turned and left the room before I took a swing at him and ended up with his knife at my throat. Crazy fucker pushed me too far sometimes. This was one of those times.

Taking the stairs two at a time, I got back to the main floor and followed the sound of Birdie's giggling coming from the kitchen.

I had to help Rumor. Save her. I wasn't going to let anyone put her in front of the fucking Insantos gang. We'd never had a run-in with them, and as far as I knew their leader, Falcon Socorro, wasn't a pleasant man. They would get nowhere near her. Last night had been as close as it was going to ever get. They could all go fuck themselves.

When I walked into the kitchen, my chest eased slightly at the sight of Birdie standing on a stool, bent over a cupcake with a squeeze tube of icing, while Rumor slowly turned it for her. Pink icing was on her nose, and Birdie held up the tube in her hands to squirt some on her cheek this time. Rumor threw her head back and laughed. I stilled, watching her.

I'd never heard her laugh like that before. It was…it was…no. I shook my head. I wasn't getting sappy and shit. She had a great laugh. One she needed to do more often. I wondered how long it had been since she'd laughed that way.

She turned her head then, and her green eyes locked on mine. The sparkle in them was almost painful. She was happy. The constant uncertainty and shade of fear that never seemed to leave her was gone. I wanted her like this all the time. She deserved it. If anyone deserved it, she did. I just didn't know how the fuck I was going to give that to her.

She was being lied to every day by people she was starting to trust. Me. Maeme. Even Sebastian. I hated it.

"Hey." Her smile began to fade as she studied me, and I quickly saved it by smiling. The one I had perfected in childhood.

"You look good in pink," I told her.

She laughed again, but not as carefree as before. There was tension in her shoulders. She was worried. I'd unintentionally put it there. I kept fucking up with her.

"We made Barbie cupcakes!" Birdie announced happily. "Eat one."

I walked over to see the dozen cupcakes that were covered in pink icing with a white *B* in the center. "It's not very manly. Not sure I can eat that," I teased her.

Birdie placed a hand on her hip. "Don't be stupid."

"Birdie!" Maeme scolded as she walked into the room. "I have told you that ladies do not say *stupid*."

Birdie lifted her shoulders in a shrug. "And I told you that I am not a lady yet, Maeme."

I cut my eyes over to see Rumor pressing her lips together to keep from laughing. I wished she would. I wanted to hear it again.

THIRTY-TWO

"You have a dirty mouth."

RUMOR

King stood at the door of the cottage as if he was guarding it.

"Do I just get a few things? How long do I need to stay at the stables?" I asked him, still not sure I believed his reason.

He seemed tense, and the way he kept scanning the area, as if he was ready for someone to jump out with a gun and start shooting, was making me nervous.

"Put all your things in the suitcase," he said, taking one more look out over the property before closing the door and locking it. He turned to me then and nodded his head toward the bedroom. "I'll help you. Come on."

I pointed at the fridge. "What about the food? It'll go bad."

"I'll send someone to get it. You just worry about your things."

He made his way toward me and smiled. It wasn't his real smile. He was on edge and trying to cover it up.

"Maybe it's time you take me to a bus stop," I suggested.

He froze and stepped closer to me. "No. Pack your things, sweets. You're going to the stables. My room. Not a fucking bus station."

"This *is* about me. You're lying. The shooter was after me. Hill has someone looking for me, doesn't he? I'm bringing this all to your door. To Maeme's door." As I said the words, I saw the truth in his eyes. I was right. They were hiding me. Trying to protect me. I shook my head. "NO! I am leaving. I will not have you or Maeme shot because of me. I don't want this. I won't stay here!" Panic was rising in my chest as I said the words. Fear for the people who had helped me. Fear that I might not live another day.

I had to run. There was no other answer. My time was up.

He reached out and wrapped his fingers around my arm. "You aren't leaving. We are safe. You will be safe. Here. With me," King said through clenched teeth.

I tried to pull my arm free of his grip. "I can't stay here!"

King's much larger body backed me up until my back hit the wall. "You will do as I say, Rumor. You're gonna pack your things and get in my truck. We're going to the stables."

Tears filled my eyes. "I don't want to be here."

He grabbed my jaw. "Yes, you do."

"Just let me go," I sobbed as a tear rolled down my right cheek, then my left.

King's nostrils flared as he stared down at me. "I'm not letting you go. I'm keeping you safe. I swear to God, the only ones who will get hurt are the ones trying to get to you. Trust me, sweets. You gotta trust me."

I laid my head back against the wall and closed my eyes. I felt so helpless. This was a disaster that I had created. I should have never run. I should have stayed.

"I did this," I whispered.

"The fuck you did," he said angrily. "That bastard you were married to did it."

I opened my eyes and stared up at him. "Were? I'm not divorced."

His jaw flexed, and there was something there in his eyes. He knew something. Did he know where Hill was? Was Hill dead? Had I missed that on the news?

"Is he dead?" I whispered, almost afraid to hope. Ashamed to hope.

King nodded his head once, and I let out a sob as my knees buckled. He was gone. Dead. He'd never find me. I'd never have to see him again. I was the target of the Mafia right now, it seemed, but Hill was no longer a nightmare I had to face.

"Rumor," King said, almost like a warning.

I wiped at my face. "He's dead." Just saying the words gave me the strength to live. I could survive this. Whoever it was after me. I had survived Hill.

"Yeah, he is. Why the fuck are you crying?"

I let out a long sigh. "Because I'm a bad person. I'm glad. Relieved."

King ran a knuckle over my cheek to catch a tear. "So, these are happy tears?"

"Yeah," I admitted.

"Thank fuck," he muttered, then lowered his mouth until it covered mine.

There were moments in life when you made a decision. Accepted who you were. What you had become. This was one of those times. I wasn't good. Living with Hill had twisted me inside. I hadn't realized it until now.

Running my hands up King's arms, I held on to his biceps and went up onto my toes to press closer to him. Take more of what he was giving.

My feet left the floor as he lifted me up until I wrapped my legs around his waist. Then, we were walking. Through the house. His lips never left mine. The minty taste of his mouth continued to take more and give at the same time. I buried my hands in his hair as I moaned, aching for what I knew he could make me feel.

When we reached the bedroom, his lips left mine as he laid me down onto the bed, then jerked my shorts down, along with my panties. My breaths came in short, quick, anxious gasps as he tossed them down, then unzipped his jeans. His eyes felt hot as he stared down at me hungrily. As if I was all he wanted. It was a powerful feeling.

"Fuck," he swore, pausing from getting his jeans out of the way. "No condom," he said, letting out a heavy breath as his eyes met mine.

There were two choices that could be made here. One was responsible, and the other was the inevitable.

"When were you tested last?" I asked, already knowing I didn't care. I should, but with King standing there over me, I couldn't bring myself to.

"A month ago. I've not…I always use a condom," he replied, then ran a hand through his hair with a frustrated scowl.

"Okay," I replied hesitantly.

He stared at me, as if waiting for me to say more. "You trust me? With this?"

"Yes, and everything else," I admitted.

The pained look that crossed his face wasn't what I'd expected. What had I said wrong? When he didn't move, I started to sit up, but he cursed and shoved his boxer briefs down with his jeans and climbed over me, forcing me back onto the bed again.

"I need this, sweets," he said huskily before thrusting inside of me, then stilled once he was as deep as he could go.

The sting from the way he stretched me had become something I craved. Lifting my hips, I urged him on. I was ready for more. His jaw was clenched tight as he held himself over me. I stared up at him and things stirred inside my chest that I knew were dangerous. What we were doing wasn't going to end well. I was already feeling it. The heartbreak of when I would leave. When this would be over.

King pulled out slowly, then rocked back into me. He hissed through his teeth as he closed his eyes. "Fuuuck, that's incredible."

I wanted to reach up and caress his beautiful face, but that would make this…more. I was afraid it would scare him off. That we wouldn't get to do this again. Instead, I moved under him, pressing for more. His eyes opened, and the dark, fierce gleam in them caused an excited shiver to run over me.

He stood up, then grabbed my hips, pulling me with him. He began to drive into me. I watched as the muscles on his arms flexed with each movement. The veins on his neck stood out while he stared down at where our bodies met.

"So fucking wet, hot," he growled as he began to pump faster, his breathing heavy.

I lifted my legs up and over his hip bones and arched my back off the mattress as the delicious tingle began to build. "AHHH!"

"So goddamn beautiful," he said with a grunt and sank into me with more force than before. "I love this fucking pussy."

The array of emotions already stirring inside me, mixed with the way he played my body, like an instrument he controlled, sent me crying out just before the wave of release hit me. My body shook as the wet gush came from deep inside me. Words fell from my lips, but I wasn't sure what they were. I was being tossed into a spiral again of supreme blissfulness.

"FUCK! FUCK! That's it! Coat my cock with that sweet juice. FUUUCK!" He ended with a shout as his body shook, then jerked. His fingers clutched my hips, tightly holding me against him. "GAH!"

I could feel it. His release filling me. Each hot jet, deep inside. I tried to get closer even if it wasn't possible. He trembled slightly, and his grip on me eased as he opened his eyes and stared down at me. The slow smile that curled his lips was one I wanted to burn into my brain. Never to forget. It was hedonistic, sated, and I'd put it there.

"I want to see it." His voice was hoarse from the shouting.

"See it?" I asked, still trying to catch my breath.

He pulled out of me, then took my ankles and bent my knees, placing my feet flat on the bed. Holding my legs wide open, he stood there and stared at my completely exposed vagina. I opened my mouth to ask him what he was doing when his gaze darkened.

"Damn, that's pretty."

I covered my face with both hands, embarrassed. "Are you done?" I asked.

"Just let me watch a little more trickle out, sweets."

Sucking in a sharp breath, I realized what he was doing. He'd said he wanted to see it, but that had been in the moment. I hadn't really thought…oh my God.

"King…" I trailed off, not sure what to say.

"Yeah, sweets?" His tone was soft.

Just the sound of it made me feel warm and tingly all over again. My eyes flew back open, and I moved my hands from my face when I felt his finger slide over my opening. His complete focus was between my legs. The fascination in his gaze silenced anything I was about to say.

"Just let me play," he whispered, not looking up at me while he ran his finger inside of me, then all around my sensitive flesh. "Damn, that's nice."

Snapping out of whatever this was, I closed my legs with his arm still between them. His eyes swung up to my face with a confused look. As if I had taken something away from him and he didn't understand why.

"Stop it," I told him.

A crooked grin touched his face. "But I was enjoying myself."

I reached up and pushed his hand out of my legs. "I saw that, but I was the one lying there, exposed."

"You're not cleaning it up," he said. "I want my cum in your panties."

I laughed then as he took my hands and pulled me up to stand in front of him. "You have a dirty mouth," I told him.

"And you like my dirty mouth. Especially between your legs."

Before I could respond, King's phone started ringing. He let out a heavy sigh and reached down to get his jeans and take it out.

"Yeah," he said into the phone, putting it to his ear, then pointing at my panties on the floor and nodding for me to get them.

"We're finishing up now," he said, watching me as I put my panties back on.

"I know," he all but growled into the phone, then ended the call.

"We have to make this quick," he told me as he went to get my shorts. "Get dressed, sweets."

THIRTY-THREE

"He's got some feral shit in his eyes."

KING

"If you want to go back to your place, she can move into the house," Sebastian said from the sofa in the lounge room in the stables.

He'd been back from Vegas for two hours, and he was already pissing me off.

"Yeah, King. You want to go home? I'm sure Rumor would love the guest room across from Sebastian's," Thatcher added as he poured himself another drink.

"Rumor and I will be staying upstairs," I bit out.

Thatcher was trying to be an ass, but I knew Sebastian was serious. He meant well, but it still made me livid. She wasn't available.

"So, you're doing it then?" Sebastian asked me.

I glared at him, wondering why I had come down here. Oh yeah, because I'd told Rumor to take a bubble bath, and if I'd stayed up there, I'd have ended up fucking her again. It was starting to become harder and harder to keep my hands and dick off her. Fucking her raw earlier had been the most phenomenal mistake I had ever made in my life. I was going to want that. A lot. More than she could handle. Seeing my cum dripping out of her had fucked me up.

"Look at him, brother. Yes, he's doing it," Thatcher said, pointing his glass at me. "He's got some feral shit in his eyes."

"Stop," I warned him. "This is off-limits."

Sebastian frowned. "Are you…are you feeling things for her?"

Why was off-limits such a hard concept for these two? I didn't know what I was feeling. I wanted to sink my dick in her over and over. I wanted to see her pussy full of my cum. I wanted to hear her make those noises she did when she was getting off. I cared about her. I didn't want her hurt. But feelings like Sebastian was talking about? No. I didn't feel that kind of thing. That kind of thing wasn't something that was long-term. Sure, I believed people fell in love, but I also knew that time always stole that away. It never lasted.

I cared about Rumor enough not to ever put her through that. One day, she would find out I'd lied to her from the beginning, and she'd never forgive me. Anything more than fucking her would only lead her down a road of heartbreak. She'd had enough of that. I wanted her happy.

"I want her safe. That's it. There are no feelings beyond that," I told him.

"Except a hard dick," Thatcher said.

The door swung open, and for a moment, my chest tightened as fear gripped me that it was Rumor. That she had heard me. Heard us. The sight of Storm and Wells had never been the massive relief that it was now. I let out a breath as they walked into the room with guests. Ruby, Fall, Moira, and Sedona. Fuck. I didn't need this shit right now.

"I brought friends," Wells announced, holding out his arms as if he were the freaking Lord and Savior come to save our souls.

"Not the time to be bringing people here," I snapped angrily.

He held up his hands. "What? You're the only one who gets to fuck? Don't think so."

Ruby made her way over to Thatcher. She was one of his favorites, if he even had those. She seemed to thrive from his cruelty.

It was twisted. Fall had fucked us all, but she went straight to Sebastian, cooing over him being back. I ignored the others. Thatcher's gaze locked on mine, and he raised one of his eyebrows. I knew that look. There was more going on here than just fucking.

I needed another drink. Turning, I went back to the bar and found the bottle of Maker's Mark and poured two shots into my glass. I'd give Rumor another thirty minutes, and then I was going back up there.

"If you want to share, I'm game," Storm said. "I like watching you chain them up and whip them."

I turned to glare at him, lifting my drink to my mouth, only for my eyes to lock on Rumor standing in the doorway. Fucking hell. Her eyes flashed with shit I didn't want to put a name to. It would mess this up.

"Hey, sweets," I called out to her. "You done with your bath already?" I started toward her, not sure what I was going to need to do to make her stop looking…hurt. I didn't want her hurt.

"I, uh…" she stammered, her eyes scanning the room nervously. "I should have stayed up there."

"And deprive me of that pretty face?" I said as I reached her and took her hand, pulling her inside. I didn't want her down here, but I also didn't want her thinking she was a prisoner in my room.

"Hey, Rumor," Sebastian called out to her.

She smiled shyly and lifted her hand in a small wave.

"I still owe you a visit to the library up at the house. I'm home for a few weeks. Just tell me when you want to go, and I'm here."

Like fuck he was. He needed to back up. I'd take her to the damn library.

"Thanks," she said, looking anywhere but at me.

"Same girl twice in a week," Moira said tartly. "So unlike you, King."

"Easy, don't wake the bear," Storm told her, placing a hand on her back.

"I like the bear," Moira replied.

Ignoring her, I slid my hand over Rumor's hip and pulled her closer to me. "You want a drink?" I asked her. "Hungry?"

She was tense. I didn't like it. I had gotten used to her leaning into me. Cuddling close. Not this reaction. When she tilted her head back to look up at me, I saw the accusations in her eyes. That wasn't fair. Yes, we had fucked three times in less than twenty-four hours, and I'd taken her without protection, but there were no promises between us. No commitment. So, what if she had heard what Storm said about Moira? She didn't have to get uptight about it.

"I think I'll take a water and go back upstairs," she said softly.

Dammit. I didn't want her going up there alone.

"Okay. If that's what you want," I replied, finding myself annoyed, but not sure who at. Me or her. Or this entire situation.

I wanted to see what it was that Storm planned on doing with the four women they'd brought here. I had a feeling I already knew the answer though.

I left her to go get a bottle of water from the fridge, then took it back to her, still debating what my next move was. Did I go with her? Did I stay down here? If I went up there, I was almost positive I'd fuck her. If I stayed down here, I would be worrying about her.

"Thanks," she said, giving me a tight smile, then turned and headed for the door.

"Don't leave," Sebastian called out.

She gave him a real smile when she glanced back. "Long day," she replied, then continued to the exit.

I stood there, watching her until the door closed behind her.

"You really gonna let her go? What if she runs?" Storm asked.

"Security is everywhere," I replied.

"She's had a lot to deal with today. If you don't go after her, I will," Sebastian told me, moving Fall off his lap as he stood up.

"Sit," I snarled.

His brows drew together. "You're not my fucking boss."

No. I wasn't. But right now, he needed to step down.

"We both know I will have you on your ass in seconds."

"I would have done this right," he snapped and started for the door.

I moved then. Fast. My decision was made, thanks to Sebastian and his fucking annoying ways. "If you walk out that door, I'm going to break your goddamn face."

He stopped and turned, glowering at me. "Are you going?" he asked.

"Yes!" I shouted, stalking past him and jerking the door open, ready to get the fuck away from all of them.

The last thing I heard before I slammed the door was Thatcher's cackle of laughter.

THIRTY-FOUR

"It was deeper than blood. Stronger than a bond of family."

RUMOR

I was overreacting. I had acted jealous. Did I have that right? *No.* I knew that. We had been friends this time yesterday. Having sex didn't make us more. We were adults. King had sex with a lot of women. Seemed they all did.

I pulled my feet up onto the sofa and crossed my legs, staring at the television even though I hadn't turned it on. I shouldn't have had sex without a condom. That was stupid. Stupid. Stupid. I should probably get tested again.

The door opened, and King came inside. His gaze swung over the room until it landed on me. He closed the door behind him, and I watched as his shoulders seemed to drop with a sigh. He'd come to check on me. Great. Not only had I acted jealous, but I'd made him feel as if he'd done something wrong. I was really bad at this.

"What are you doing up here?" I asked, wanting to get this over with.

I tried to ignore his distractingly sexy saunter as he made his way over to me. He was a chick magnet, and I had been one of his chicks. Who could blame me? The man oozed sex appeal.

"You seemed upset and left me. I was going to come up after your bath anyway," he said as he took the seat beside me. "You good?"

"I'm fine. You can go back to your friends. I was just about to find a movie to watch."

He leaned forward and picked up the remote control from the coffee table. "Sounds good. What do you want to watch?"

I turned my head to look at him. "You don't have to stay up here. I'm fine. Just tired."

He ignored me, turning on the television and leaning back. "It's been a busy day. We need some comedy."

"King," I said, making him look at me.

His eyes met mine this time. "Yes?"

I could do this. Be a big girl. Act like a grown-ass woman. "I am okay. You do not have to babysit me. I acted weird downstairs. I'm sorry about that. It won't happen again." That was as good as it was going to get. I couldn't lay it out there better than that.

"Not here to babysit you, sweets. Came up here to hang out with you. I prefer your company. Do you want food? I'm getting fucking hungry. I can call up to the main house and get Minna to send us something down here."

He was back to the food thing. How frustrating. I was giving him an out, and he wasn't taking it.

"I don't think that because we had sex that we are…are…anything more than friends. I also know we aren't in some commitment, and you…we can have sex with other people."

He stopped scanning through Netflix and swung his gaze back to me. "You have someone else you're thinking of fucking, sweets?"

I shook my head. "No. But that isn't the point I was trying to make."

"So, your point is that you acted a little territorial down there, and you didn't mean to. You won't do it again. We are friends who fuck. Really well. Olympic-worthy fucking."

Olympic-worthy? That was a good thing. Right? Yes, I was sure it was.

"Yes, I think that was my point," I agreed.

He stretched his arm out behind me on the back of the sofa and turned his body slightly toward me. "We are friends. And if you fuck someone else, I'll kill him."

A surprised laugh burst from me as I stared at him. Was he serious?

"You look shocked, sweets," he drawled.

I nodded my head several times. "That's not exactly fair."

He narrowed his eyes. "What?"

He was serious. He didn't see how one-sided this was even if I had no plans on having sex with one of his friends or family or whatever.

"You can have sex with...those women down there, but I am only supposed to have sex with you?"

He reached over and ran a knuckle over my lips, then down my neck. "Sweets, if we're fucking, I don't need to fuck anyone else. You're keeping me real damn sated. Am I not doing the same for you?"

I shifted and dropped my focus to my lap. "Yes, you are."

"Good. Then, that's settled. We are friends who fuck. A lot. We don't need to fuck anyone else while we have this setup."

I nodded, glancing back at him.

His hand clamped over my shoulder and pulled me against him. "Finally. Now, pick a movie, and I'll call for food. Then, we can fuck again. I want to eat your pussy in the shower."

Was there a woman who would turn that down?

We didn't skip Sunday breakfast the next morning and it was more intimidating this time than it had been the first time. Even though I didn't think King had told anyone we were having sex, I just felt like they all might think we were. Since we were sleeping in the same room. That, and I felt as if it was written all over my face when they looked at me. King didn't sit beside me, which I wasn't sure if I should take personally or be thankful. It made us look less...uh...affectionate maybe?

"Why can't I sit in here beside Rumor?" Birdie asked, standing at the head of the table beside Maeme with her hands on her hips.

Her eyes, so much like King's, locked on me, and she grinned brightly. "You want me to sit by you, don't you, Rumor?"

Feeling trapped, I glanced at Maeme, hoping she'd come to my rescue. I would in fact love for Birdie to sit by me, but I also didn't want to overstep. I was indebted to everyone in this room for helping me and putting themselves in danger by doing it.

"Annette isn't here yet," Maeme replied. "Take her seat, and she can take your usual spot. Now, give me a bite of sugar, missy."

Bridie squealed and kissed Maeme on the cheek before running over to pull out the chair beside me.

"You never demanded to sit by me before. I'm wounded," King said from farther down the table.

I glimpsed at him but looked away quickly, afraid I would blush. My panties were currently wet with his cum. No one knew that, but we did, and looking at him made my cheeks warm.

"You don't like to talk about American Girl dolls," Birdie informed him.

"Ah, well, in that case, I'll let it slide," King replied.

"I brought three of them with me," Birdie informed me. "I can show you after we eat."

"That sounds—"

"She's going to the library with me to get some books," Sebastian said, cutting me off.

I lifted my gaze from Birdie to look over at Sebastian. He winked at me. I didn't mind going to see Birdie's dolls first. I was about to say that, but King spoke first.

"I'm taking her."

"To my library?" Sebastian challenged.

"It's my library," Stellan Shephard said from the other end of the table. "King will take her."

My eyes cut from Stellan to King, who was watching me. When our gazes met, he flashed me a smug smile that made me want to scold him and kiss him at the same time. I didn't want to be rude to Sebastian, but I preferred to be with King. All parts of my body were in agreement.

"King, you'll let her see my dolls first? Right? I brought Evette. She has the same hair!"

King's eyes dropped to his sister. "Yes, of course. But I'll need a hug in return."

Birdie grinned and clapped her hands together. "Deal!" Then, she turned her head and looked at me. "I'm a master manipu-la-lay-tator—or whatever that word is. Momma said so."

I pressed my lips together, not wanting to laugh at her, and nodded in agreement. She was in fact very good at it. She knew how to work this crowd like a charm.

Barrett and Annette Kingston arrived, followed by Roland and Luella Jones. Different conversations broke out all around the room, and I listened as Birdie told me about her new bunk beds for her dolls and a diner she was wanting for her birthday. While she went on to describe it, I took quick glimpses at King as he spoke to his father and Stellan. Thatcher wasn't here today, but Storm was, and he seemed deeply involved in the conversation too.

When King's eyes cut toward me and he caught me looking his way, I quickly jerked mine back to Birdie. She was explaining the ins and outs of proper hair care for her dolls. I had no idea it was so in depth, but it seemed there was a lot to know about these dolls of hers.

"Rumor," Annette said, drawing my focus off Birdie to look up at her sitting on the other side of the little girl.

"Yes?"

"I brought you a few bags of clothing. Things that Lela left at the house and never wears. Maeme mentioned you might like some more things to wear. I'll have King go get them from the car before you leave."

Oh. Wow. How nice of her.

"Thank you," I replied. "I really appreciate it."

She gave me a pleased smile. "You're welcome. Someone needs to use them. I'm happy that you can."

I hoped Lela was okay with this, but she wasn't here today. I didn't have a way to ask her. I'd mention it to King. He'd know what to do about that.

"She needs some riding boots," Maeme announced.

"She's not riding anytime soon," Stellan said.

Maeme frowned at him.

"Not for the time being, Maeme," he told her pointedly.

I thought she was going to argue, but she simply nodded her head and took another bite of her food. Maybe Maeme didn't boss them all around after all. It seemed like Stellan was the one in control right now. Was it because I was staying on his property with King?

"I have a horse for each of my American Girls. And stables!" Birdie told me excitedly, bringing my attention back to her.

"I would be disappointed if you didn't," I replied honestly.

She stuck a piece of sausage in her mouth and grinned as she chewed it.

A strange sense settled over me as I scanned the people in the room. There was something here…something I didn't know. A connection that went beyond owning businesses together. It was deeper than blood. Stronger than a bond of family. There was a hierarchy. Even if they didn't make it clear, I could suddenly see it. I just didn't understand it. What was it that I was missing? What made them what they were?

THIRTY-FIVE

*"As if I were his marionette doll,
I did exactly what he wanted."*

RUMOR

After King took me to the Shephards' library, he brought me back to his room and left me with my new books. He had some work to handle. I never got details on what it was he was doing, but was it my business? Not really. But I wanted to know. I wanted to know all the things about him. Not to mention, the more I was left in the dark, the more my imagination went into overdrive.

The three large shopping bags of Lela's clothes that Annette had given me sat on the bed. King had assured me Lela wouldn't mind and would be glad they were going to someone who could use them. Apparently, she had three full walk-in closets at home, and she didn't even live there most of the time. Needing something to do since reading wasn't distracting me, I began to unpack the bags.

Jeans, shorts, tops, dresses, skirts—all designer, and most still had tags on them. This was more than generous. Why wouldn't they have taken the clothes back to the store if she wasn't going to wear them? It seemed wasteful…but then they had given them to me. They wanted someone to use them.

Slipping off the sundress I had worn to breakfast, I laid it on the bed, and I began to try on things. I didn't want to keep something if it didn't fit, although most appeared to be my size. Once I had on a pair of pink shorts and a ruffled white tank top, I went to the bathroom to look in the full-length mirror.

I turned several times, admiring how nice it looked. Hill had bought me clothing that he thought was appropriate for me, but never anything this expensive. The tag on the top said it was over seven hundred dollars. I felt guilty about taking the tags off. It was more than I needed. I wasn't sure the rest of my life wouldn't be me hiding out. Where was I gonna wear clothes that cost this much?

When I walked back into the bedroom, my mood sank as reality managed to seep back in. I took off the shorts and top and folded them neatly on the bed before taking out a short, colorful skirt that also had a tag on it. I tried not to look as I set it down and reached in to find a top to go with it.

The door behind me opened, and I covered my bare breasts before I spun around to see King stepping inside. His eyes slowly traveled down my body.

"I was coming to get something," he said, closing the door behind him without taking his eyes off me. "But looks like I'll be a little longer than I anticipated."

He stalked toward me and grabbed my wrists, pulling them away from my body. "Don't cover your tits."

I realized I was panting as he grabbed the hem of his shirt and tugged it over his head and dropped it to the ground. His hands went to the zipper of his jeans. "Turn around and put your hands on the dresser. I don't have much time, but after this view, I need to fuck you if I'm gonna get anything else done."

I'd told myself I wasn't going to have sex with him again today. We had to stop doing so much of it. I was finding it hard to not feel things when I looked at him, and I was blaming it on all the sex. He was a man, and I had thought I'd never let another touch me again after Hill. But King had changed a lot. He had taught me that I could trust again. That not all men were cruel.

I went over to the dresser and placed my palms on the cool surface. I could hear the rustle of King's jeans as he discarded them. Closing my eyes, I inhaled deeply when his hands grabbed my hips, and I felt him come up behind me.

"It's gonna be a quick fuck, sweets. Stick that ass out for me."

As if I were his marionette doll, I did exactly what he wanted. Except with King, I knew I was getting something from this too. Pleasure came with this. The kind that made the bad in my life fade away. It didn't haunt me when I was thinking about him. When he was inside of me. When he was reminding me how good it felt to live.

I felt his hand between my legs, and I opened them wider.

"Still wet and sticky from this morning's fuck. Good girl," he murmured, then slammed into me so hard that I fell forward onto the dresser. The edge of the wood biting into my lower stomach. "HOLY FUCK, that's good. So damn slippery with my cum inside you."

I held on to the dresser to keep from being shoved into it any further and pushed back to meet his rhythm. He was right; having his earlier release inside me made it insanely hot. I moaned his name as he drove in harder.

He wrapped my hair around his hand and pulled my head back toward him with a hard tug. "Take that dick, sweets. Take it like the good girl you are. Walking around with me leaking out of you all day. Fuuuck, that makes me crazy. I want to watch you play with it when it oozes out of you. See those pretty little fingers covered in it."

I was close already. So very close. I bucked wildly, wanting to get there. Knowing how amazing it would feel. Craving it. The electric feel of it intensifying. Drawing deep inside me. I clawed at the wood, crying out as my body started to convulse.

"SUCH. A. GOOD. GIRL," he shouted with each grunt.

Those words. It was a trigger. The best kind for me. I screamed out as the euphoria of my orgasm claimed me.

"FUCK, BABY! FUCK!" he roared as he jerked against me twice, then stilled.

I could feel him twitching inside of me as his body shuddered.

I laid my cheek down on the smooth surface and let out a contented sigh. I was positive my legs wouldn't hold me up just yet. I gasped as he pulled free of me, and then his hand covered where he had exited.

"Put your legs together," he ordered.

I managed to do it, but I was moving slow. Once I had them closed, he moved his hand away.

"Leave it in there. Don't shower until I get back."

I nodded and stayed like I was trying to recover while I listened to him get dressed behind me. He let out a breathy laugh, and I turned my head to look over at him. His gaze was on me, and the smile that touched his lips was…gentle. Soft. Almost as if…as if I were special. More than whatever this was that we were doing.

He pulled his shirt back over his head and then came back over to me and scooped me up. "Come on, sweets," he said, carrying me over to the bed. He laid me down, then reached for the throw and covered me up. "I'll be back later."

I nodded, and he turned and headed for the door. It wasn't until he left that I realized he'd never gotten whatever it was he had come for. My eyes closed, however, before I could think much more about it.

THIRTY-SIX

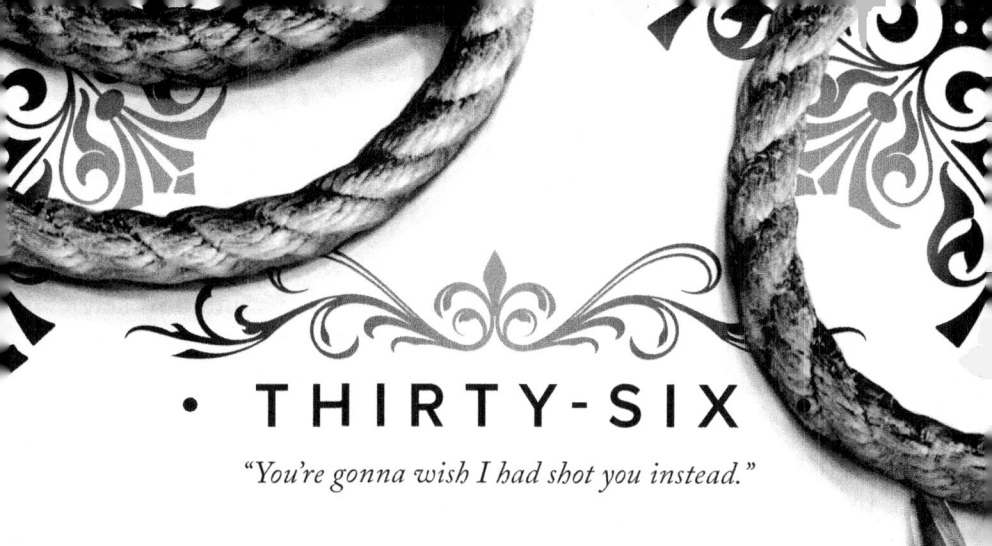

"You're gonna wish I had shot you instead."

KING

I'd left Rumor curled up, asleep in my bed, before the sun came up. Last night, I had been too fucking tense to sleep. I woke her up twice. Once with my head between her legs and another time with my cock inside her. She'd been adorable. All sleepy but instantly ready to fuck. She was becoming an addiction. It was a cruel circle. The longer I kept her with me, the more I was craving her. To stop this, she needed to be moved, but the thought of that made me feel unhinged.

It had been five days since the Insantos had sent someone to find Rumor. The bastard we had underground was still alive. Blaise was coming here today. He wanted to speak to the prisoner himself. Which meant this might be the gang member's last day on earth and a real war was going to begin.

The stress of what Blaise's decision was going to be on what we were going to do with Rumor was making me feel caged in. Like I couldn't breathe deep. I didn't like not having control. She was in my bed. He'd had me keep her safe. Told me to fuck her. Make her want to stay. Now, I had to wait and let him make the next call on her safety.

What if he took her? There was talk he was going to have her moved to Ocala. She'd be safer there. Thinking about it was making me crazy. She trusted me. It was me that she wanted to stay with. I would keep her safe. She would be scared if he made her leave. She wouldn't know anyone. There was no Maeme there.

There was no *me* there.

But she was never meant to be mine. No one was.

The door to the lounge room opened, and I looked up from the cup of coffee in my hand to see Thatcher walking in, followed by Storm and Sedona. They hadn't brought her here to fuck. I knew without them saying it why she was here, even before I noticed Storm's Glock pressed against her back.

Setting my cup down, I stood up from the sofa and looked at her. She wasn't the one I'd expected. The airheaded blonde thing had thrown me off. I wouldn't have guessed she could pull anything off like this or that she had the balls to try.

"I can explain," she said, staring at me with tearful eyes and terror on her face.

"Not sure he cares, but we need to know before I let him kill you," Thatcher replied, pulling out a cigarette from his pocket and lighting it up.

"You put trackers on them?" I said to Thatcher.

He nodded and let out smoke through his nose. "Yeah. This one left here and went straight to the Insantos' compound. It's always the stupid ones."

"I didn't know who they were. Who Falcon was. He came into the club and tossed a lot of money my way. I was in too deep with him before I knew it. They're dangerous," she blubbered as tears rolled down her face.

Thatcher let out a dark, maniacal laugh. "They're dangerous," he repeated, then laughed again.

She had done it. She was who had led them to Rumor.

Stalking toward her, I tried to get control of the fury rolling through me. Rumor had been shot at because of me. I'd brought Sedona here, and Rumor was now in danger because of it.

Storm dropped his gun from her and stepped back, grinning. "You're gonna wish I had shot you instead," he drawled just before I got to her.

She started to back up frantically, shaking her head and pleading with me to believe her. When she hit the wall, I was there. My hand wrapped around her throat.

"What did you tell them?" I asked her, flexing my fingers that ached to dig in. Make her pay for what she'd done.

"He asked me to look for her. Showed me a picture," she rasped as I tightened my hold on her neck.

"Might want to get all the info before you kill her," Thatcher called out from across the room.

"I can't…" she gasped, trying to breathe.

I eased my grip just enough so she could talk. Thatcher was right. We needed all the information she could give us.

"Uh, Rumor, you need to go back upstairs, yeah," Sebastian said behind me, causing me to swing my head around to see her standing there.

Fucking hell.

THIRTY-SEVEN

"He had managed to reach my soul and wrap it around his finger."

RUMOR

I heard Sebastian's voice, but I was frozen. Unable to look away from King. My chest hurt in ways I'd never experienced. It was hard to breathe. It didn't matter that we were friends. Because it was more than that to me now. How could it not be? King had been…was…everything to me. He'd been my savior, then my friend, now my lover. How was I not supposed to feel more?

Seeing him with her. Again. Knowing what he liked to do with her and other women like her tore through me like a knife. The pain was almost unbearable. The truth sank in like a brick in my stomach…I'd let myself fall in love with this man. A man who would never be more than what we were. He would always want women like her. Need them.

King's blue eyes were almost black as he stared at me. I'd caught him in a moment of his twisted sexual passion. I could see the way his pupils had almost taken over the color I had come to adore. I was so stupid. Last night, I had let myself believe he wanted me like I did him.

"Go back to the room, Rumor," he demanded.

Really? That was what he was going to say? He had just been inside of me four hours ago, screwing me like he couldn't get deep enough.

"Rumor! GO!" he shouted this time.

I couldn't breathe. His words were equivalent to a boulder being slammed into my chest. I backed up slowly, not looking to see who else was in the room. I knew Sebastian was there, but I didn't want to see his face. See the pity there. I was crumbling, and I needed to do it alone. Find a way to pull myself back together.

Turning, I ran. Back upstairs, just like I had been told to do. I always seemed to find myself in this position. Doing what a man ordered me to do. Falling for a man who hurt me. I should have never gotten in his truck that day. I should have gone back to the house and faced whatever was to come with Hill. The videos would have come out. He'd have been arrested. Or killed. I wouldn't have to live in hiding.

But the Mafia…they might have killed me.

Shoving open the bedroom door, I went inside and slammed it behind me. My breathing coming in erratically. Each intake more difficult than the last. I looked to the closet, where my empty suitcase was stored. My clothes were all hanging inside now. The ones I had come with and the ones that had been given to me. I wouldn't take those with me. I wasn't taking anything from here with me. Just what I had come with.

Wrapping my arms around my middle, I sank down onto the edge of the bed. How was I going to leave him? I didn't hate him. I wasn't sure I ever could. I had let myself fall for him. That wasn't his fault. It was mine. I was broken inside, and he'd come into my world, being everything I had never had. Giving me things I hadn't known I needed. A family. A place where I was wanted. Someone I could trust. A place to feel safe.

But what was I to him? Was I only seeing this through my eyes? Had I just seen what I wanted to? Believed what I wanted to?

The door to the room swung open, and King stalked inside. His eyes leveled on me.

"That was not what you think." His voice sounded hoarse, as if he'd been shouting.

I stared at him. The man who had so quickly and effortlessly become everything to me. Who still was.

"It doesn't matter what I think," I replied.

His nostrils flared, and he took another step in my direction. "Yeah, it fucking does. Don't go there in your head, Rumor. I fucked you on that bed just a few hours ago. So, yeah, it does matter. You matter. What you feel matters to me."

It was that easy for him. He said those words, and all the heartache eased. The misery I had found myself drowning in stopped. Air filled my lungs without stinging. This was worse than I'd thought. He had control over me and not just physically. He had managed to reach my soul and wrap it around his finger.

"What you saw," he said, pointing toward the door, "was me trying not to kill a woman."

I stilled. What had he just said?

"She is the reason they found you here. She'd told them. She was the rat."

My mouth went slack. Was he serious?

"Why?" I asked, my voice barely above a whisper.

He shook his head. "Because she's a fucking bitch. She'll pay for it. I swear to you, she will."

I stood up. "What do you mean? You'll call the police? If you call them, they'll take me. Won't they? I'll be a suspect in Hill's murder. They will no longer think I'm dead."

I began to tremble. This was all unraveling. I'd put them in the middle of it all. Just like I had feared. What if they were arrested too? Because of me.

King was in front of me instantly. His hands on my arms gripping me tightly. "No cops. No one will know you're here and alive. I swore to you I'd keep you safe, and I will."

"How? You can't promise that!" I felt myself growing hysterical. There was no answer to this that ended well. I couldn't think of a way to fix it. I was tired of thinking about it.

"We take care of our own. No cops. She will be dealt with here. You will remain safe. I have to leave you and go make some decisions, but I'll be back. Maeme will bring you some breakfast. Just stay in here. This room. Don't leave. Don't go downstairs. Not until I return. Promise me."

I stared up at him. His blue eyes were back, and the pleading in them for me to do as he asked trumped everything else I was thinking. Even if staying here wasn't what I should do, it was what I would do. For him.

"Okay," I replied.

He let out a relieved sigh and pressed a kiss to my lips. It was hard and demanding, but ended much too quickly.

"I'll be back," he whispered before leaving one more brief touch on my mouth.

Then, he turned and left me standing there. Staring after him. Afraid of the future, but knowing I had someone. Even if that someone wasn't telling me everything.

THIRTY-EIGHT

"I had to calm the fuck down."

KING

I recognized his voice before I reached the underground cellar, where Blaise Hughes stood with Stellan, my father, and Thatcher. The prisoner was hanging from the ceiling with his wrists bound in a metal latch. He wasn't near death, but he was pale, and there was some blood from where Thatcher had lost his temper while getting him to talk.

Blaise cut his eyes from Stellan to me. Although I was bigger than the boss of the family, he still wielded power that intimidated men much larger than me. Like his main enforcer, for example, Huck Kingston. Huck was the son of Barrett's second cousin, Creed Kingston, who had died, along with Huck's mom years ago. The man was huge. Even by my standards.

"You get her calmed down?" Thatcher asked, sounding amused.

I ignored him. I wasn't going to take his bait in front of Blaise. When I said nothing, Blaise narrowed his eyes.

"Well, did you?"

Thatcher and his big fucking mouth.

"Yes, sir, she's fine. In my room."

Blaise continued to study me. "She's developed feelings for you."

You didn't lie to the boss. Even if it was something you wanted to lie to yourself about.

"Yes, I believe so."

"You're thorough," he replied and shifted his attention back to Stellan. "If he has nothing more to tell us, then there is no reason to keep him alive."

"I have more to tell you!" the man cried out behind us.

Blaise turned around to face him. He tilted his head to the side as he studied the prisoner. "Do you know what I do to those who lie to me?"

"What do you want to know?" The man sounded close to breaking into a fit of tears.

"Who is involved. Exactly what they are after—and don't tell me the woman. I want names. Locations."

The man let out a panicked laugh. "They'll kill me."

"So will I," Blaise replied. "I can promise your death by their hands will result in less agony."

The man whimpered, but said nothing.

"I don't have time to dirty my clothes. My son has a soccer game this evening. Thatcher, make it brutal," Blaise said, turning back to us. His gaze swung to me. "As for the woman, I think it's time I take her to Ocala. She'll be safer there. If we have to shut down the Insantos, then we need everyone focused. She is clearly under your skin."

I shook my head. "She needs me. She's safe here."

"KING!" my father shouted.

I knew speaking back to the boss wasn't smart, but he couldn't take her from me. She'd be scared.

Blaise didn't seem angry, but that meant nothing. The man could put a bullet in my head and walk away without a single glance or trace of remorse. I waited to see if I had stepped out of line too far. I was no help to Rumor if I was dead.

"I'll let her make that decision. It's her life. If she wants to stay with you, then so be it," he said, then glanced over at Stellan and my father. "Have her brought to your office without King."

"Yes, sir," my father replied.

She would choose to stay with me. Unless they told her things. About us. Who we were. She'd ask questions. She would want to know who Blaise was and why we would send her with him. If he told her even a sliver of the truth…she'd know I had lied to her.

As Blaise walked past me toward the exit, my father and Stellan followed behind him. I didn't look at either of them. Instead, I stood there as a frantic energy began to pulse through my veins. I had to get control. Find a release. Focus. I had to calm the fuck down.

• THIRTY-NINE •

"I had read The Godfather. *This was nothing like that."*

RUMOR

Sebastian waved a hand for me to go inside the room. He had come to get me from the stables and said there was someone that they wanted me to meet with. I asked where King was, but he said he was currently held up elsewhere. All I had been told was, this was about my safety and King wanted me to go.

I stepped into the room and instantly recognized Stellan and Ronan. This was an office, and since it was Stellan's house, I assumed it was his. But the man behind the massive, ornate desk was not Ronan. It was a younger man. Closer to King's age than his father's. He was also gorgeous. Where King was dark, this man was light. Blond hair, green eyes, with features that seemed to have been handpicked to create the perfect face. I still preferred King's.

I scanned the rest of the room and found a man in the far-right corner that caused me to pause mid-step. He was massive. The scowl on his face didn't help matters. He was downright terrifying. His arms were crossed over his wide chest, and I found myself afraid to move.

"Huck," the man behind the desk said, and the scary man eyes swung over to him.

"It's okay," Sebastian said beside me, causing me to jump. I had forgotten he was there. "That's Storm's cousin. He's family."

He looked nothing like Storm, but I nodded anyway and tore my eyes from him to look back at the man behind the desk. He was watching me as if he wasn't sure what to do with me. I wasn't sure what to make of him either.

Why was he here, and why did I get the feeling that he was in charge? Who was he?

"Have a seat, Rumor," the blond man told me. Although he didn't sound angry or demanding, there was something about the way he spoke that made me feel as if I had to do what he said. He expected it.

I took a seat across from the desk in a leather high-back chair. Stellan and Ronan stood on either side of the desk, as if they were awaiting orders themselves. This was all very odd. I was starting to wish I had waited for King to return first. He would explain all this. Sebastian had told me nothing about the strangers in the room. Had they hired security? Was that what this was? If so, then the beast in the corner made me feel very freaking safe.

No, wait. The beast was a cousin. But maybe the cousin worked for a security team.

"I'm sure you have questions, and I'm going to give you the answers you need. Along with an option," the man said.

I looked at him, relieved to hear he was going to explain things.

"My name is Blaise Hughes," he told me. "You've been here under the protection of the Shephards and Salazars due to my order."

His order?

"I've been told that you're afraid the Mafia, who broke into your home and shot your husband, will come for you now that they've killed Churchill."

I nodded once. Hearing him say the Mafia had killed Hill sank in deeper. I hadn't known for sure how he had been killed. Yet he knew. Had King known the details and not told me? Was that his way of protecting me?

"That is the first thing we need to clear up. You are not a target for the Mafia. They will not kill you. They don't want to kill you. The day when they broke into your home, they knew you were there and left you alone. Churchill Millroe was our only target."

Our. I stiffened and replayed his words in my head. Had he meant to say *our*? Had I heard him incorrectly?

"You've been protected by the Southern Mafia," he said, waving a hand, as if showcasing the room. "Churchill Millroe stole from us. From me. No one steals from me and lives," he said, then stood up. "When you fled your home that day, King had been outside waiting to see what you would do. From you battered face he realized you'd been abused by your husband. So much so that you didn't want to help him. Instead you chose to run. Take your chance to escape. I have a wife, Rumor. One I worship. She was mistreated by the only family she had once too. I don't like men who use their strength to hurt the weak and innocent. Not to mention, if Madeline, my wife, found out I had left a woman in your situation and didn't help her, she'd put a pistol to my head." He smirked then, as if that was funny to him.

There were so many things running through my head at the same time that it was hard to focus on any one thing. And as much as I should be in shock right now, it all made sense. Everything this man was saying made complete sense. The things that didn't add up, they fit. Except…Maeme. That didn't fit.

"Churchill was stealing from several people, it seemed. He wasn't a smart man. The Insantos gang is a powerful underworld drug trafficking empire. We stay out of each other's way. Always have. Until now. They believe you can lead them to Churchill and their money. We've not shared that we tortured and killed him. As for their money, I am working out something that might end this without a war."

Blaise walked around the desk and stood in front of it, crossing his arms over his chest. "You've been under the protection of the

Georgia branch of the family. I live in Ocala, Florida, and control this branch, as well as the other Southern Mafia branches. I'm the boss. Everyone answers to me. Even King. That being said, I don't want to take your control from you. That's been done enough in your life. I'm going to let you decide now that you know who we are and how you got here. You can stay here. Move back into Maeme's cottage and live there as long as you'd like. She's taken with you. Claimed you as one of hers. Kudos to that, I might add. She's a tough one to win over. Or you can go with me. You'll be out of the line of fire. I can give you a job, help you get settled in your own place once this is done, and you can start a new life. Like I said, the choice is yours."

I had read *The Godfather*. This was nothing like that. This man was young, and he was a boss? I shook my head, trying to make sense of all this. Why was I thinking about a stupid fictional book? This was my life. This was real. I had to focus.

King had lied to me.

From the very beginning, he had been lying.

I pressed a hand to my chest. The gnawing horror that everything with him had been a lie was worse than the deceit.

I knew he didn't love me, but I had thought…he felt something. He cared.

He wasn't my savior. He never had been. I had been a job to him. Something this beautiful, intimidating blond man had told him to do.

And Maeme…she was in on this? She had known? But then Blaise had said she had wanted me. She wasn't acting. Could I stay for her? With King so close? Was what we had over now that I knew? Was he just going to go back to the women he beat and fucked?

"I've given you a lot to digest," Blaise said. "Sebastian will take you back to the stables, and you can take your time. I need to leave here in an hour—my son has a soccer game this evening. If you haven't made up your mind by then, the plane can be sent for you at any time. Just let…whoever you want to know that you would like to come to Ocala."

He hadn't said King. Was that his way of telling me my time with King was done? Why hadn't King come for this? He had known what I was about to hear, and he had sent Sebastian to bring me. What was he doing that was so important that he didn't care that I was going to learn he had been lying to me all this time?

Because he didn't care. I had been a job. That was it. I'd been a job for him. Nothing more. If I had meant anything to him, he'd be by my side right now. Asking me to stay with him. Telling me that he had developed feelings for me.

"I'll go," I said, the words surprising myself as I heard them fall from my mouth.

But I couldn't stay here. Not now. I'd miss Maeme. I'd miss Birdie. My heart wouldn't recover for a long time, and seeing King would rebreak it over and over. I had to go. There was no other choice.

Blaise nodded and dropped his hands to his sides. "Very well. Go get your things packed up. You'll be picked up in forty-five minutes out in front of the stables. We have to head to the airstrip." He shifted his gaze to Sebastian. "Go with her."

Sebastian stood. "Yes, sir."

I glanced up at him, and I saw the pity in his eyes. The concern for me. He was truly worried about my feelings. I could see it there. Maybe someone other than Maeme had cared for me more than just being a job.

"Let's go," he said gently.

I followed behind him and kept my head down, not wanting to make eye contact with any of the others. They would all see too much. I'd been broken many times before, but never had someone wielded the power to crush my soul. Until King.

• FORTY •

"How much abuse could a heart take before it stopped?"

RUMOR

I heard the screams well before we reached the hallway. A sick knot formed in my stomach, and I felt bile rise up in my throat. I couldn't keep walking. Not that way. Not in that direction.

"Fuck," Sebastian muttered under his breath, hearing the female cries of pleasure and pain that were coming from the tack room.

I shook my head, backing up as a wall of bricks sat heavily on my chest. Just when I'd thought I couldn't be hurt anymore, when I'd believed the agony couldn't get any worse, I was slapped in the face with yet another truth.

"I can't," I rasped. It hurt to speak. My throat was constricted.

"I'm sorry, Rumor. I'm so fucking sorry," Sebastian said as his hand closed over mine. "We'll go another way. Come with me."

Unable to do anything else, I let him lead me back out the door and around the buildings until we reached a door on the far side of the main structure. How much abuse could a heart take before it stopped? Shattered? Was that possible?

I much preferred broken ribs. Those I could heal from. Those I understood. This…I was afraid this had ruined me. Completely.

How could I ever recover? I couldn't even hate him. I wanted to. I wanted to hate him for all he'd done. For making me love him. For letting me believe he cared. But I couldn't. I knew what hate was. I had hated Hill. I had wished he were dead. If King were dead, I wouldn't be able to survive it. Even after all this.

Sebastian kept my hand in his as he led me up a set of stairs I hadn't been on before, then down the hallway I was familiar with to King's bedroom.

He opened the door, then turned to me. "Do you want my help, or do you want to be alone?"

"Alone," I replied. I needed one last moment to grieve what I'd never truly had before I left it forever.

He squeezed my hand before letting it go. "I understand. I'll be downstairs if you need me."

I only nodded. I didn't want to say more. It was too difficult. Stepping inside, I left the door open. Not wanting to be closed in here. I stood for a moment and took in the bed, the dresser, the sofa, all the memories that I'd thought were special and I now knew they were a lie. All of it.

Wincing, I took in a deep breath as I walked over and opened the closet to get out my suitcase. I would survive this. I would. I had to. Life was about survival. I'd learned that at an early age. I was surviving yet again. I was beginning to accept that there would never be a day that I wasn't just surviving. Getting through. There wasn't going to be happiness in my future. I'd been born with a curse on my head. That had to be it. I hadn't been given any real breaks in this life. The moments that I had believed were my breaks in the past were always facades. Cruel, manipulative lies that I'd wanted to be real so badly that I walked right into them.

Never again.

Laying my suitcase on the bed, I went to get my clothes. The ones that were mine alone. I didn't want to take any memories with me from here. Not bothering to fold them, I shoved everything inside, then went to the bathroom to get my few toiletries and makeup bag. This was reminiscent of the many times I had packed up and had to leave a home as a child. Except I had a suitcase now. Back then, I had always been given a trash bag and told to put my stuff in it.

Just as I was placing my last item in the suitcase, heavy footsteps caught my attention, and I spun around to see King stalking into the room with a wild expression in his eyes. He was shirtless, and his body was damp with sweat. From having rough sex in the tack room.

A wave of nausea rolled over me as my chest twisted inside. I turned away from him, unable to see him, especially like that. Knowing he'd been busy fucking another woman while I was told that he had been lying to me. I'd been a job for him. Not his friend. Not…not anything.

"You're not leaving!" he said in a fierce tone. Then, he was behind me, grabbing my arm and spinning me around.

Stunned, I glared up at him. Was he kidding me right now? He had destroyed me, and now, he was here to cause a scene. Act as if he cared where I went. He pulled me to him, and I shivered, not wanting to touch his body. The sweat he had from being with another woman.

"DON'T TOUCH ME!" I shouted, pushing at his chest and trying to back away from him.

"Rumor," he said gently, as if he was trying to calm me. He couldn't calm me. Not now. Not after all this. "Baby, listen to me."

"BABY?!" I spit at him. "YOU DO NOT get to call me that." I let out a sob as the emotion inside of me began to unravel.

"He told you," he said as if he hadn't realized I had been at a meeting, being clued in on his deceit.

"Yes, he did. While you were…were in the tack room." I couldn't say more. I was going to be sick, thinking about it. "Please go away. Let me finish."

"Rumor, listen to me. What you heard in the tack room wasn't what you think." His tone was pleading. Almost desperate.

I found myself caving, wanting to turn back to him. Listen. What was wrong with me? Why was I so weak?

"Were you whipping a female?" I bit out, staring at my open suitcase.

"Yes. But it isn't—"

"Were you punishing her, or was she enjoying it?" I would not let him lie to me.

When he didn't answer right away, I knew. I closed the suitcase, fighting back the tears. I wasn't going to let him know how devastated I was.

"She was enjoying it. But I didn't fuck her. Storm was in there. He fucked her. I just needed…I had to…I was strung tight, and I needed a release. She was willing, and…DAMMIT! I shouldn't have done it, but I had to do something. I had to clear my head. Burn off some of the shit clawing at me."

He hadn't fucked her.

GOD! Why did I feel relief? There was so much more wrong here. Like the fact that he got off on doing it. His lies. His lies. I had to remember his lies!

He grabbed my upper arms and pulled me back against his chest. "Is he making you leave me? I'll stop it. I will. I need you to let me explain."

I wouldn't melt. I wouldn't give in to him. I didn't trust him anymore. That was gone. Without trust, what did we have?

"He gave me a choice. I chose to leave. I'm not your job anymore."

His hands tightened on me. "You were not my job, Rumor."

"YES, I was. Stop lying to me. Please just stop. I've had all of it I can handle. You followed me, King. FOLLOWED ME from my house that day. You were at the service station to get me. It has been a lie since the moment I met you. And…and I let myself believe you. Think there was more."

I closed my eyes and tried to break free from his hold, but I couldn't. He wasn't easing up.

"I followed you. My job was to get you here. But it became more than that. I got to know you. We became friends. We became more."

Every word out of his mouth was bittersweet. I wanted them to be true, yet they had come from a man I could never trust again. Too little, too late.

"Stay with me. Don't go. Don't leave me," he pleaded close to my ear. "I'm sorry, sweets. I am so fucking sorry."

And here I'd thought, my destruction couldn't get any worse.

"I can't," I told him, even as the words felt as if I had just ripped out my own heart.

"Don't say that. You can. He gave you a choice. Choose me. It's not a job, baby. It was in the beginning, but it hasn't been for a while. It changed. I changed. You changed me."

No, no, no, no. I wouldn't listen to this. I had to save myself this time. I had to put myself first. Protect what was left of my heart—if there was anything left at all. He wasn't my future. He never was going to be. He was in the Mafia. They all were. I didn't belong in this world. I wanted to be free.

"Let go of me," I said, jerking away from his hold, and thankfully, he let me this time. I stumbled forward slightly but caught myself and bent over to zip up the suitcase.

"I won't let you leave me." He said the words as if he meant them.

"You don't get to decide that."

The voice wasn't mine. I straightened and looked at the door, where Blaise Hughes stood. The energy in the room changed, and it felt suddenly dangerous. I looked at King, who took a step between me and the door. What was he doing? That man was the boss. His boss. Mafia bosses killed people. I'd read the books. I knew that much.

"She's had a lot dropped on her. I should have been there. She needs time," King told his boss.

"Are you correcting me, King?" There was a deadly threat in Blaise's voice.

Panic gripped me, and I moved quickly, getting around King to stand in front of him. His hands shot out to grab me, and I looked back at him.

"STOP!" I warned him.

He was not going to get shot by the Mafia boss over this. I turned back to Blaise.

"I am coming. Just, please, don't make him say anything more he will be punished for," I asked him.

I prayed there was a soul somewhere inside this man. He had a kid whose soccer game he wanted to get back to. He'd said he worshipped his wife. He had a heart. I had to make sure he used it.

Blaise looked from me to King. "Get her things, Huck," he said, stepping aside as the massive man entered.

I moved back, basically plastering myself in front of King. I was afraid he'd do something stupid, and I didn't think the Huck dude had a heart or emotion. He was a killer, and I'd be damned if he killed King.

Huck stalked past us and grabbed the handle on my suitcase, then looked at me. "Is this it?" he asked in a deep voice that made me tremble and press further into King.

"Yes," I whispered.

"You've got a shopping trip in your future," he muttered as he walked back to the door.

That was an odd thing to hear someone like him say. Did he think I needed more things?

"Don't go," King begged me quietly as his hand brushed against my side.

Blaise Hughes's eyes were on both of us, but he said nothing. I was afraid to move until Huck was out of the room and away from King.

"We need to go," Blaise said, breaking the silence.

King's hand twitched against me as if he was struggling not to grab me. I was a very stupid woman. Possibly the stupidest female to ever walk the earth. I took in a deep breath and met Blaise's hard expression with a determined one of my own.

"I've changed my mind," I told him.

The corner of his mouth twitched so slightly that I wasn't sure if I had imagined it or not.

"Is that so?" he drawled as if he wasn't surprised in the least.

I nodded. "Yes. I'm going to stay here."

King fisted my shirt with his hand, and his arm flexed as he held me firmly to him, as if he thought Blaise would come rip me away.

"Like I said, your choice," he said. "Huck, leave the suitcase."

Huck dropped the suitcase on the floor, and Blaise gave King one last look before turning and walking out of the room. The beast followed him. I stood there, not moving until their footsteps were gone.

"Fuck," King sighed and grabbed my waist to turn me around.

I held up a hand to stop whatever he was going to do next.

"I said I was staying. I didn't mean here, in this room. I have conditions, and I have lines that I'm going to draw, and you're going to respect them."

I wasn't sure what those lines were yet. I just knew I had to find a way to heal the damage he had caused before I could accept even a friendship with him. He wanted me here, but I didn't trust the reasons why.

"Anything you want, sweets," he replied, reaching up to cup my face.

He was going to make this so freaking hard.

King and Rumor's story continues in *SLAY KING*, coming April 14, 2024.

Preorder Now
https://a.co/d/9XBzJcp

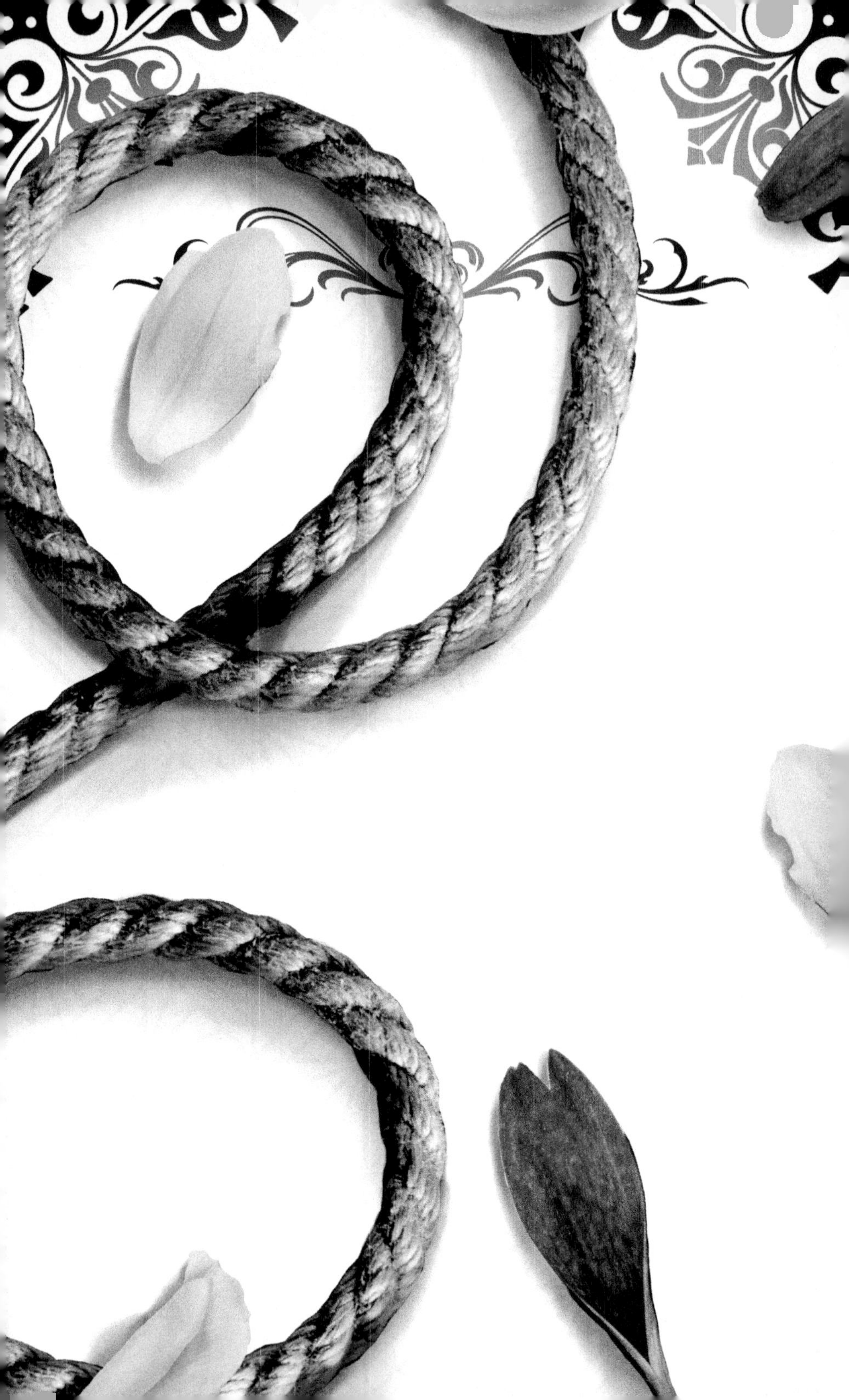

• ONE •

"Someone had to be honest with me. Might as well be me."

RUMOR

When one made rules, drew boundaries, protected themselves from situations that could cause damage, it must be something they stood firm on. That they demanded others to respect. Showing weakness made those rules and boundaries seem like a suggestion instead of guidelines.

King Salazar made it very difficult to remember why I had set the rules. He had been the cause of them, yet every time he tried to push too far, I found myself unable to stop it.

Craving a man wasn't smart. Ever.

Especially a man who had lied to you and manipulated you. Yet that was where I stood at the moment. Wanting what I shouldn't have. Wishing it were something it would never be.

I sat on the bed in the cottage that was located on the back of Maeme's property and listened to the silence around me. I'd been back in this house and out of King's bed for a week now. Every night, King showed up with dinner. He talked to me while we ate. Acted as if we were old friends. Then, when I went to bed, he slept on the sofa. He refused to let me stay here at night alone. He didn't believe it was safe yet.

I didn't know who or what to believe.

What I did know was that I was a widow, and I wasn't sad about it. My husband had been hell-bent on eventually beating me to death. King had made it possible for me to escape that life. Something I struggled to hold against him. If he and the others hadn't come after Hill, then I'd still be there, being beaten.

I also knew that I was willingly living under the protection of the Southern Mafia family. The sweet grandmother who had brought me in, given me a roof over my head, a sanctuary, was also part of the Mafia, just like King, her grandson.

Lastly, I was aware that there was a gang who wanted me for information on my dead husband. Which I did not have. Hill had never told me anything about his life. I knew nothing of his work or illegal activities.

So, I was here. This was the only safe place for me. Living in a storybook cottage with no bills. I'd stopped feeling guilty for being here. I no longer thought I was taking advantage of a nice lady's hospitality. They'd come and gotten me. Brought me here. It shed new light on the situation.

The door to the cottage opened, and I heard the screen slam shut. Standing up quickly, I stood there, frozen, listening. The only person who walked in without knocking was King, and he'd been gone when I woke up this morning. His pillow and blanket in a neat, folded pile on the end of the sofa.

"It's me," his familiar voice called out.

Sighing in relief, I made my way to the door that led into the living room just as he walked into it from the kitchen. My eyes locked on him, and the way my stomach fluttered at the sight of him frustrated me to no end. I didn't want to feel these things for him. I needed to protect my heart. But I couldn't seem to manage it.

The sexy smile that spread across his face didn't help matters. My chest joined my stomach with its fluttery mess of feelings.

"Morning, sweets," he drawled. "Sleep good?"

Yes, and no. Once I'd finally gotten to sleep and stopped fantasizing about him, then, yes, I slept well. It'd just taken me two hours for that to happen. Knowing he was asleep on my sofa, wearing a pair of boxer briefs, had messed with my head.

I simply nodded.

"Good," he replied, closing the space between us. He reached out and wrapped one of my curls around his fingers. "Damn, I like the way you look when you get up in the morning."

Hello, area between my legs. It was now wide awake, along with my stomach and chest. On high alert that the traitorous, lying man in front of me was close. Touching me. Making me want things.

"What are you doing back?" I asked, wishing I hadn't sounded breathless.

He didn't respond right away. Instead, he continued to play with my hair. I should move away. I had rules, and this was breaking one of those rules.

"I came to get you. Take you to breakfast at Maeme's," he replied finally.

Do not react. Do not melt.

"We had Sunday breakfast there three days ago," I replied.

It had also been difficult. Seeing all these people, this family, and knowing the truth about them. Finding a way to associate the Mafia with these people I had come to care for wasn't easy.

Having morals and realizing that your loyalty could shake the ground on which you had thought you stood firm wasn't an easy pill to swallow. It was a reevaluation of yourself. Who you were. What you had become. What made you who you were. Your core.

"This isn't a family event," he said as my curl slid from his fingers.

"Then, what is it?"

He slipped a finger under my chin. "It's Maeme wanting to check on you."

She worried about me more than anyone ever had. One of those things that nagged at me. I had known many people in my life. I had been placed in different homes. Had to trust strangers. Never had I trusted any of them the same way I did Maeme. With her, I truly felt that she cared. She wanted me safe.

It seemed unfair. Why couldn't I overlook the bad with King? Trust him like I did her. They were the same essentially. They were a part of this dark underworld thing. She'd lied to me just like he had.

The difference was the fact that I hadn't slept with her. I hadn't fallen in love with her. It made a monumental difference. One I could not control. One I wish I had power over.

"She doesn't have to feed me for that," I replied.

King took another strand of hair between his fingers and chuckled. "I'll let you tell her that."

He knew I would never do such a thing. I said nothing in return as I stood there.

"Come on, sweets. You know you want to go spend hours in the library."

That was true. Maeme's library was full of books I wanted to get lost in.

"So, you're not staying?" I asked him. Unsure what I wanted the answer to be.

"No, I'm not. I've got somewhere to be," he replied. "But I'll be back tonight. I'll bring tacos."

He'd be back. Just hearing him say it made my mood improve.

"I need to get dressed," I said, moving back away from him. "I won't be long."

The last thing I saw before I spun around to rush back into the bedroom was the amused gleam in his eyes. He knew I was weak. His coming every night was him trying to break me down. Win my forgiveness or trust. And I wanted him there. Another one of my problems, but at least I was willing to admit it. I wasn't lying to myself. Someone had to be honest with me. Might as well be me.

If he was here, then he wasn't with another woman. I wasn't positive that he wasn't with someone else during the day though. But did I really have the right to ask? Maybe before I had drawn the line in our relationship and brought it back to pre-friendship, but now? No, I didn't.

My mood instantly sank again as I put on a pair of shorts, a blouse, and my sandals.

King was a very sexual man. He had his kinks, and he was used to women throwing themselves at him. Just because he was coming here to babysit me at night didn't mean he wasn't tying up some female in the tack room and doing those things to her before he screwed her.

"Give me a grocery list, and I'll go grab what you want today," King called from the other room.

I glanced at myself in the mirror. I'd forgotten what it was like to go without makeup. When I'd been married to Hill, I'd had to cover up the bruises so often, and he'd believed I was being lazy if I didn't put it on every day. I brushed my fingers over my cheekbone. The smooth, unmarked skin reminded me what all I had been given here.

They had lied to me. But they had also saved me. The reflection staring back at me wasn't the same trusting, wide-eyed girl I had been before marrying Hill. There was a darkness in my eyes that time had placed there. Betrayal had stolen so much from me. A large part of who I was had been snatched away.

Not by the people who had given me somewhere safe to stay, but by the man I had married. All Hill had ever done to me was take from me. Hurt me. Steal any cause for happiness.

King had lied to me, but he'd never hurt me. Being around him made me happy even if I didn't want it to. Letting myself love him had been a mistake, but it was already done. I just didn't know where we went from here or how.

"Rumor?" he said as he walked into the room.

My gaze swung from the mirror to him standing just inside the doorframe.

"You good?"

The grocery list. I'd forgotten he'd said that.

I smiled and nodded. "I'm fine," I replied, then turned to pick up my purse.

"Damn, you sure are filling out a pair of shorts real nice. I like your ass with that bubble to it."

I narrowed my eyes and glared at him. "Are you saying my butt is getting fat?"

King walked over to me, and I took one step back, not sure I trusted myself to get close to him again and not bury my nose in his shirt.

"I'm saying, I like you eating properly. Your body has always been sexy as fuck, sweets. But with the new curves, it's damn near poetic."

"Poetic?" I asked.

His hand slid over my hip. "The kind of dips and swells that inspire the greatest of poetry." Then, he squeezed the undeniable extra plump that had been added to my bottom, thanks to Maeme's cooking. "I'd kill whoever you asked me to if I could watch this sweet ass bounce while I was spanking it."

Oh, good Lord. I took a deep, steadying breath. *Stay focused.*

We needed to go to Maeme's. He had things to do. Later, while alone, I'd live out that little fantasy in my head while getting some relief.

"We should go," I blurted out.

"I'd kiss it real nice," King said in a husky whisper, pulling me up against him. "But I'd bite it first. Make you scream out. Then, I'd lick it."

I closed my eyes and sucked in a deep gulp of oxygen. "Stop!" I demanded in a strangled voice.

King let out a low groan before dropping his hand and stepping back. He looked at me through hooded lids, and the hunger flashing in his blue eyes made me tremble.

With a lift of his hands, he moved farther away from me. "I'll wait outside in the truck," he said in a raspy voice before leaving me there alone. With my own racing heart and ache between my legs.

• ABOUT ABBI •

Abbi Glines is a #1 New York Times, USA Today, Wall Street Journal, and International bestselling author of the Rosemary Beach, Sea Breeze, Smoke Series, Vincent Boys, Boys South of the Mason Dixon, and The Field Party Series. She is also author to the Sweet Trilogy and the Black Souls Trilogy. She believes in ghosts and has a habit of asking people if their house is haunted before she goes in it. Her house was built in 1820 and she finally has her own haunted house but they're friendly spirits. She drinks afternoon tea because she wants to be British but alas she was born in Alabama although she now lives in New England (which makes her feel a little closer to the British). When asked how many books she has written she has to stop and count on her fingers and even then she still forgets a few. When she's not locked away writing, she is entertaining her first grade daughter, she is reading (if everyone in her house including the ghosts will leave her alone long enough), shopping online (major Amazon Prime addiction), and planning her next Disney World vacation (and now that her oldest daughter Annabelle works at Disney she has an excuse to frequent it often).

You can connect with Abbi online in several different ways. She uses social media to procrastinate.

Facebook: AbbiGlinesAuthor
Twitter: abbiglines
Instagram: abbiglines
Snapchat: abbiglines
TikTok: abbiglines

Printed in Great Britain
by Amazon